# CORNERS CHURCH

## WHERE TWO DIRT ROADS MEET

### DONNA POOLE

Copyright © 2020 by Donna Poole

All rights reserved worldwide.

No part of this book may be reproduced in any form or by any electronic or mechanical means, including information storage and retrieval systems, without written permission from the author, except for the use of brief quotations in a book review.

Original cover art painted by Megan Poole

Edited by Kimberlee Kiefer

Cover design by SelfPubbookCovers.com/RLSather

ISBN: 9798654497116

# FOREWORD

Mark Twain said, "The reports of my death are greatly exaggerated."

Some say the country church is dead or dying, but the author of this book says that report is greatly exaggerated. Not only is it alive and well, in a unique way it fosters faith, family, and community. It's like a mom-and-pop store on the corner where the cashier asks about your mother-in-law's sick brother's neighbor. In a word, the country church is home.

The following chapters will draw you into the life of a country church. Please, don't ask the author what's fact and what's fiction. She has lived in these pages so long she no longer knows or cares. She only hopes this book will do for you what her favorite books do for her, wipe the fog from your vision and add a shine to your soul. Life's about to become very country. Get ready to laugh, cry, and have fun!

> "I hope that someday when I am gone, someone, somewhere, picks my soul up off these pages and thinks, 'I would have loved her.'"
>
> — NICOLE LYONS

## Dedication

I dedicate this book with forever love to my dear husband, John, and to my amazing children and their spouses: Angie and Kim, John and Katie, Danny and Mindy, and Kimmee and Drew.
I also dedicate it the dynamic dozen, my delightful grandchildren: Megan, Macy, Reece, Ruby, Kaleb, Kinzie, Levi, Lincoln, Oliver, Griffin, Iris, and Theodore, and to any who may join their tribe. You're forever in my heart and prayers. Grow up, and do right, or I'll come back and haunt you.
Thank you, Ruth Kyser, veteran Christian novelist for encouraging me and answering 1,001 questions, and Mary Lickly Hill for sharing a historical paper compiled by Ralph M. Lickley.[1] Thank you, Colleen Rufenacht, for sharing facts about Reverend Milton Wright.
I especially want to thank my wonderful church family and the neighbors of our own church. Past and present, young and old—you all have my heart. Most of you won't find yourselves on these pages, so breathe a sigh of relief, and thank me later.
Thank you, my beloved friends. Your prayers have made me who I am today, so you share the blame. May God keep you all strong in life's storms and help you say with George Matheson, "Show me that my tears have made my rainbow."
To everyone who knows me: If you think you see a shadow of

*yourself in a character in this book, and you don't like what you see, maybe you should have behaved better?*

*And to my readers, thanks for giving me a chance.*

*Thank you, my dear granddaughter, Megan Poole, for the beautiful church painting depicted on the cover of this book.*

*Last but not least, thank you, editor extraordinaire, Kimberlee Kiefer, for your hard work and patience. You went far beyond editing; you co-wrote much of this book.*

# 1
## DON'T BE LONG

The hospice nurse says there hasn't been much change today, perhaps a bit more mottling, so Darlene sends the children and grandchildren home.

"Get some sleep. The nurse says it could be several more days." She isn't interested in sleeping herself; she wants to sit close to him.

The nurse sees Jim and Darlene holding hands and thinks of her troubled marriage. *Maybe they're the lucky ones.*

She checks Jim's vitals, looks sympathetically at the old lady, and whispers, "I'll be back to check on him at seven in the morning."

"Tomorrow? Tomorrow is Sunday."

"That's okay. Call me at home tonight if you need me." She scribbles her number on a scrap of paper and presses it into Darlene's hand.

Jim wakes a little later and asks, "Is this 1985?"

Darlene doesn't want to tell him 1985 had been long ago.

Jim says, "I think this will be the night I go Home to heaven."

The hospital bed fills the center of their living room. The nurse has cranked the head of the bed high, but Jim still struggles to breathe. Darlene's tears drip over their clasped hands; those old, gnarled hands don't tell the truth about how young their love still is.

"Don't cry, babe; don't cry." He gasps for breath between words.

"Should I call the nurse and ask her to come back? Should I call the kids?"

Jim shakes his head. "Just us, please."

That seems right to her. They've done everything together all these years. He'd die the same way he'd lived, with courage, with grace, and with her holding his hand.

Darlene tries to make him smile. "Don't you dare die first. You know what I've warned you about." She'd threatened him if he'd had the bad manners to die first, she'd take dancing lessons and go to a movie the very next day.

He'd sighed, her old dinosaur, one of the last of a dying breed of old preachers who thought Christians should abstain from drinking, dancing, and movie-going. He'd attended Bible college in a day when the divinity students had chanted, only half-jokingly, "We don't smoke; we don't chew, and we don't go with girls who do."

A smile tugs at a corner of his mouth. "Still a dinosaur," he whispers.

"Yes, you are, but you're my dinosaur."

He dozes, and she sits quietly next to him, loving every line on his face. He opens his eyes partway. "Come to bed soon. Don't be long."

"I won't."

He doesn't realize he's in a hospital bed, the same one she'd used many years before after brain aneurysm surgery. Just last week she'd found out she has another aneurysm, but she hasn't told him. She can't bear to add to his burden, not now.

Jim moves restlessly, and she asks if he needs more pain medication. He shakes his head. "Tell me more of our story. You always were the keeper of our story."

"And you were always the hero of our story."

He frowns and points upward.

"Yes, I know, honey. God is the hero of our story. At least He was when we let Him be."

For months, as Jim's kidney and heart failure have worsened, Darlene has been telling him stories about their lives together and about his years as pastor of Corners Church.

Her mind wanders: "moderate cognitive dysfunction," the neurologist calls it, so her recitation of their story is like an old box full of photos, jumbled and out of order. She knows she's forgotten a lot and perhaps confused fact with fiction. She leaves out some sad parts, stories they'd never been able to share, even with their closest friends. Jim and Darlene had refused to betray confidences.

Darlene relates the story in third person, as if she's talking about someone else. In a way, the story is about someone else—two young, happy people who have little resemblance to the old couple they are now. Most of the stories she tells happened during the first twenty years at Corners Church. Those years are clearer in her memory than the more recent ones.

He sleeps, but she continues talking. Sometimes she laughs; sometimes she cries. It's a long story, mostly a good one, and it's nearing the final chapter.

## 2
## ME? A PASTOR'S WIFE?

When Jim first told Darlene he felt God had called him to be a pastor, she was horrified.

"Wait! Me? A pastor's wife? God hasn't said a word about it. He hasn't called me; I know that for sure."

Not feeling called would bother her for many years. Not only hadn't Darlene felt *the call* to be a pastor's wife; she'd thought she could do anything else better: fly a single-engine plane solo across the Atlantic, become a whaler, or open a dogsled business in Alaska.

In Darlene's mind a pastor's wife was sweet, angelic Mrs. Kole, who sat in the first pew and looked reverently at her husband during every word of his lengthy sermon. Darlene was certain Mrs. Kole hadn't told or laughed at a joke in her life. Darlene loved to laugh, a laugh that sometimes dissolved into a snort that made people look strangely at her.

Mrs. Kole was a serene, lovely woman, who refused to say an unkind word about anyone, even when people gave her good reason. Her refusal to gossip was legendary. Three women in the church once hatched a plot to make her say something bad about someone.

They surrounded Mrs. Kole at the church door where she stood next to her husband, saying gracious goodbyes to the congregation.

"So, Mrs. Kole, what do you think of the devil?"

Mrs. Kole's gentle, ever-present smile faded, and a tiny frown line appeared between her kind, blue eyes. The three women had all they could do not to jab each other in the ribs with glee. Here it came!

"Well. . . ." Mrs. Kole paused, troubled. Then her face brightened. "The devil certainly is good at what he does, isn't he?"

The women gave up on Mrs. Kole the way the Pharisees and Sadducees did when they threw their hands in the air and stopped trying to stump Jesus with questions.

"No wonder she's so quiet all the time," they grumbled to each other. "What do people talk about if they don't talk about other people?"

When Darlene mentioned to her mother-in-law she couldn't be as perfect as Mrs. Kole, Mom Peters assured her Mrs. Kole hadn't always been so perfect; although, she had given her husband her undivided attention, hanging onto every word of his sermon, oblivious to all else.

That focused attention once kept Mrs. Kole from noticing their daughter, two-year-old Judi, stand on the pew next to her and remove every piece of clothing except her ruffled white socks and her tiny black patent leather shoes. Though no one in those days giggled in church, and if someone did, a lightning bolt zapped through a stained glass window and struck the offender where he or she sat, there was a noticeable stirring in the pews.

Pastor Kole stopped pounding the pulpit long enough to notice his daughter. He looked at his wife and jerked his head toward Judi. Mrs. Kole smiled sweetly at him. He scowled and jerked his head a few more times. Finally, she noticed Judi, standing on the pew, not at all concerned about her parents' reputation. When you're only two, you figure the clergy can take care of itself.

If the clergy wanted to wear clothes, let them; Judi wasn't clergy.

Mortified, Mrs. Kole pulled Judi off the pew and dressed her.

After Mom Peters recounted this story, Darlene asked, "Did anyone say anything to Mrs. Kole about it?"

"Oh, no!" Her mother-in-law laughed. "No one mentioned it to her. It wasn't done, you know."

Darlene thought it may have been easier to have been a pastor's wife in the 1930s than in the 1970s. She was sure if her two-year-old did that, someone, everyone, would say something.

Darlene didn't think she'd ever make a good pastor's wife. So many women were better suited to the job. Maybe Jim should have married one of them. What was God thinking?

Darlene had heard some pious testimonies given by pastors' wives. In martyr-like tones they'd said they could withstand the battle only because God had called them to be pastors' wives, even before they'd met their husbands. Because of this, they hadn't considered marrying anyone but a pastor. Darlene didn't question their testimonies, but she hadn't felt anything like what they'd described. That bothered her.

Darlene had married Jim because she loved him, and she hadn't cared if he became a pastor, a factory worker, or a garbage man. She might have objected to mob hitman.

Well, called or not, being a pastor's wife was about to become her job. She had definite opinions on most things—okay, on everything—but hopefully God would put His hand over her mouth at the appropriate times because, unlike Mrs. Kole, she wasn't all that quiet.

## 3
## OUTSIDE AND AROUND BACK

It was a warm Sunday in May 1974 when Jim first preached at Corners Church in rural Hillsdale County, Michigan. The church was looking for a pastor. Darlene was more nervous than Jim was when they pulled into the dirt parking lot next to the tiny, white frame building. They were early, and as they waited for people to arrive, they looked around. They saw open fields or farmhouses in every direction. Dust flew every time the rare truck or tractor went down the gravel road.

As Jim looked at the old church building, white paint peeling from its sides, he remembered what Professor Nick Machiavelli from Bible college had told the divinity students: "If your first church is small, don't despise the day of small things, but don't stay there either. Think of it as the first rung on a ladder, and aim always to climb to a place of greater usefulness. Climb higher!"

Jim and the other divinity students almost worshipped Professor Machiavelli who had rugged good looks, prematurely gray hair, and an authoritative voice. A child prodigy, the professor had started college young. Though he had his doctorate, he was only a few years older than his students. Jim felt there was something almost apostolic about him and kept an entire notebook he'd titled "Machiavelli's Maxims." He'd memorized most of the sayings. But, something about the "climb higher" advice made Jim feel uneasy, and he didn't know why.

Jim mentioned his feelings to Darlene as they sat in the parking lot, but she had other worries. She was expecting their second baby and couldn't seem to stay awake. She hoped she didn't fall asleep in Jim's sermon. Also, April, their daughter, wasn't quite two, and Darlene was concerned about how she was going to act during a long day filled with strangers. She looked back at their toddler who had blessedly fallen asleep on the long drive. Maybe the nap would help her behave.

Darlene grinned, remembering a story she'd read about a pastor's wife whose husband was preaching at a church he hoped would hire him. Unlike Darlene, this woman was a fantastic piano player, and she thought it might help her husband's chances of being called as pastor if she volunteered to play the offertory. She felt apprehensive as she left her three-year-old in the back pew and went up to play her special number.

"Be good until Mommy comes back," she whispered. He looked at her and nodded, his brown eyes bright, his yellow curls making him look like the angel he wasn't.

She was into the most impressive part of her offertory when she heard her little boy shout, "Ride 'em, cowboy!"

Horrified, she glanced back to see him straddling the pew, pretending to ride a horse. She abruptly ended the offertory before the ushers had even half-finished collecting the offering.

She hurried back to her pew, and when her son saw her

coming, he hollered, "Giddyup, Old Paint. Faster! Bad guy coming!"

Darlene wondered if their angel would behave while Jim preached. She doubted it.

First impressions matter, and Darlene worried about what the congregation would think of her as a potential pastor's wife. With her straight hair that hung past her waist, her long skirt, and no paint or polish, she thought she looked more like an ad for a hippie clothing company than a pastor's wife. She knew she couldn't measure up to the previous pastor's wife, but maybe the congregation would like her a little.

Darlene reached over and smoothed Jim's hair back. He only sat that stiff and straight when he was nervous. She didn't think it would boost his confidence to tell him he looked more like he was sixteen than twenty-five. His light brown hair insisted on falling on his forehead, and his serious brown eyes looked like a little boy's expecting a scolding.

A few cars pulled into the parking lot, and Jim, Darlene, and April went into the church. The tiny building was charming with its stained glass windows, native lumber wainscoting, and bare hardwood floors. Including the three of them, there were fifteen people in the congregation.

Darlene sat quietly, listening to Jim preach, until April whispered, "Potty, potty!"

"Can you wait?"

April shook her head vigorously. Darlene looked around. *Where in this tiny building could there possibly be a bathroom?*

She tapped an older woman in front of her on the shoulder. "Where's the bathroom?" she whispered. Darlene sat back in the pew, confused by the answer. Maybe she hadn't heard correctly.

"You have to wait," Darlene told April.

"No! Potty! Potty!" April was getting louder.

Darlene touched the older lady on the shoulder again. "Where did you say the bathroom was?"

This time the answer was louder, and there was no mistaking when she said, "Outside and around back."

The heavy, wooden church door creaked as Darlene tugged it open. Outside and around back she went. She stood there a minute and laughed. The bathroom was an outhouse.

As Darlene and April exited the outhouse, she wondered how they would wash their hands. There was no running water. She felt frustrated for a minute, but as she looked out over the fields, she felt a deep peace. If Jim was sure he wanted to be a preacher, then she hoped God would call them to this church. She already loved the simplicity of this place.

Darlene loved simplicity. So many large churches complicated things and handled church more like a corporation than a ministry. Darlene agreed with her friend Julie who said, "Churches didn't get complicated until they got electric lights to show off their stained glass windows."

As they went back inside the church, Darlene considered what to do about hand washing. Then she remembered the wet washcloth she'd tucked into the diaper bag. It would have to do. She washed her hands and April's and hoped that would be the last trip she'd ever have to make to the outhouse. It wasn't.

DARLENE TOUCHES Jim's face as he lies in the hospital bed and chuckles, recounting to him how strange it was that children at church didn't need to use the outhouse in the winter, but as soon as it got warm, they all had to go at least once during every service. The flicker of a smile lets her know he's still listening.

## 4
## THE CANDIDATE

The church liked Jim and invited him to preach again. After that service, Jim and Darlene stood at the door that was propped opened to let in the sweet spring air and shook hands with the congregation.

Sam Fairchild, the church trustee who always seemed to be smiling, grabbed a thick rope dangling from a hole in the ceiling. As he pulled it, Darlene heard the beautiful sound of the old church bell ringing out over the fields. Something caught in her throat.

*Is this the place for us? Oh, please, Lord, let them like us. Let this be the place for us.*

During the wonderful potluck after the service, Darlene wondered how so few ladies could fix so much wonderful food. After the potluck, Jim and Darlene met with the board. Looking around, Darlene realized the board included everyone except the few children and the one lady appointed to watch them.

The elderly Reverend Hane, who was retiring from Corners Church, led the meeting. The list of questions the board asked Jim seemed long to Darlene, but he answered them all with his usual quiet grace and sense of humor. The board chuckled more than once. After they finished their questions, they asked Jim if he had any.

Darlene's mind drifted. *How is April doing with that lady who's watching her? Is she behaving? Is she scared?* Darlene suddenly realized everyone was looking at her.

"They want to know if you have questions," Jim said.

"Um, no, I can't think of any."

That was innocence for you. A few years later, she would have been able to compile a rather long list.

A week passed, and the phone rang.

"The vote was unanimous," a deacon said. "Can you start preaching the first Sunday in July?"

And so, they moved to "the Corners" as the locals called the area, on July 3, 1974, and Jim preached his first sermon as pastor on July 7.

Later, they learned why the church had chosen them over the other candidates. It wasn't their youth, personality, talents, or enthusiasm.

"You were the only ones who didn't ask how much you'd get paid," a deacon told them. "We figured that showed what spiritual people you are."

Spiritual? The truth was, they'd forgotten to ask.

## 5

## A DISCOVERY

Darlene hummed as she fixed Sunday dinner after their third Sunday at Corners Church. It had been a good morning. With her growing pregnancy, she felt tired after teaching Sunday school and children's church while corralling April, but she didn't mind hard work, and she loved teaching children. Besides, she couldn't wait until Jim came out of his study for dinner. Did she ever have news to share!

They joined hands at the table. Jim prayed, "Thank you, Lord, for these blessings you have provided. We rejoice in your goodness to us. We thank you for the blessing of a visitor at church this morning, and—"

"And for food. Amen!" April interrupted.

Darlene grinned. She was hungry too. A couple from church had needed to talk to them after the morning service, and it was now 3:00 p.m. Darlene was amazed April wasn't having a meltdown.

"And we thank you for the food. In Jesus' name. Amen," Jim concluded.

Darlene let him take a few bites before she broke the news.

"Do you want to hear the good news first or the bad news?" She knew he'd say the bad news, to get it over with, so she kept going before he could say anything. "I'll tell you the good news. You know how worried I've been that I couldn't measure up to the previous pastor's wife?"

He nodded.

"Well, I shouldn't have worried. The poor lady had an emotional problem and couldn't be around people. Even the noise of her husband typing his sermons bothered her so much he had to type in the garage. In the ten years he pastored Corner's Church she only came once!"

"And the bad news?" Jim looked worried.

"Don't make anyone at church mad."

"I hadn't planned to."

"Seriously, don't make even one person angry."

"Why do you keep saying that?"

"Because," Darlene gleefully reported, "they're all related, everyone except Mary Beth!"

"No!" He sighed. "Funny no one mentioned that to us before. I guess they thought it wasn't important."

They looked at each other and chuckled. "I won't upset anyone," Jim promised. It was a promise he wouldn't keep.

## 6
## CLEANING, CANNING, AND A FISHY TALE

For the first three months, the young family lived in a tiny house that belonged to a deacon. The house the church had rented for them to use as a parsonage wasn't yet livable.

Cleaning the rented parsonage and getting it ready to live in was a challenge. Every day, while Jim studied, Darlene loaded the playpen, toys, and toddler into the car and drove from the place they were staying to the little tenant house that would become their home for the next twenty-one-years.

On the first day of cleaning, the job looked like Goliath, and Darlene felt like a pregnant David. The thought of a pregnant David made her laugh and gave her a little more energy to tackle the job. Dead bugs with feet up filled every drawer. Thick, black cobwebs stretched from the top of the archway to the floor, leaving barely enough room to squeeze through on one side. The rooms smelled old and musty. Well, it was a challenge, and Darlene loved challenges. In a way she felt as if she was living someone else's life, something she'd read in a book.

Darlene took a deep breath and sang in her usual style,

loudly and off-key. "Young McDarlene had a farmhouse. E-I-E-I-O! With a cockroach here and a cockroach there, here a bug, there a bug, everywhere a bug-bug—"

"Hello!"

Darlene jumped. She'd been singing so loudly she hadn't heard anyone come in. She would soon learn that knocking on doors at the Corners was optional. She whirled around, face red. A short, sweet-looking lady stood there. Her cheeks were pink, and her white hair curled on her forehead.

"I hope I didn't startle you. You must be Darlene Peters? I'm Mabel Hall. My husband and I live next door, and we rented this house to the church to use for a parsonage."

Darlene knew from Mabel's first smile she would love her. Mabel told Darlene she and her husband, Kenyon, had lived in the little house before they'd moved to the big house next door. "We'd hoped our son and his wife would live here," Mabel said sadly, "but she was a city girl, and we couldn't make her happy here."

An old, stained calendar hung on the wall. Someone had turned the page to August 1961. That's when Mabel's son, the young farmer who'd lived there, had given in and had moved his unhappy, city-girl wife back to the city. Trying to keep her happy, Mabel and Kenyon had installed indoor plumbing, but it hadn't done the trick.

Darlene felt immensely thankful for that city girl. *Thank you, city girl, wherever you are,* she thought, *for my running water and a toilet that isn't outside and around back.*

Mabel left after a nice long chat, and Darlene put up a new calendar. July 1974. *There. It symbolized a fresh start.*

The little house needed a fresh start. After the young farmer and his city girl wife had left, someone had used it for a chicken coop. Then a tenant farmer had lived there for years. The Corners' gossip said he and his wife had never thrown out a piece of garbage. They had lived downstairs and had thrown all the garbage upstairs and in the backyard. Before Darlene began cleaning, Mr. Hall had hauled six truckloads of garbage out of the house and yard.

Next, a sweet young couple had lived in the house and worked on it for a few months, but they hadn't had time to do much. They'd painted the bathroom a brilliant yellow and had wallpapered one wall in a bedroom with red, white, and blue stripes.

Day after day, that long, hot summer, Darlene worked on the house. The more energy she put into it, the more she liked the house. The poet Edgar A. Guest said, "It takes a heap o' livin' in a house t' make it home." Here, it took a heap o' cleaning.

Darlene did more than clean the first few months of her new life as a pastor's wife. She learned a life-skill every country woman knew in those days, putting up food for the coming winter. She'd heard the church ladies talk about how many quarts and pints of produce they'd canned. She had a hunch that to be respected in the community, she'd have to learn this skill. Because they'd moved to Michigan in July, they had no garden that year, but that didn't save Darlene from her fate.

"Do you have any cans?" Betty Fairchild and Janet Sanders, two church ladies, asked one August Sunday.

"Cans of what?"

The two women looked at each other and back at her. "That's okay. We'll bring you some."

The next morning Betty and Janet arrived at the house with a blue and white speckled canner, mason jars, rings, lids, a how to book on canning called the *Ball Blue Book*, and a bushel of tomatoes. They explained how to can tomatoes and offered to stay and help.

"Thank you, but I can do it. The lids will seal with a snap then?"

Betty and Janet nodded. "If you're sure you don't need us, we'll head home and work on our own canning. But we'll stop by later and see how you're doing."

This canning was hard work. It was stifling hot in the tiny house. After reading the book twice, Darlene felt confident enough to begin. She dipped the tomatoes into boiling water for one minute, and like the book said, the peels slid right off. She stuffed the tomatoes into the jars, splashing her glasses and maternity shirt, and realizing she needed an apron. Seven quarts in the water bath made her feel proud; although, she felt apprehensive when she saw how many tomatoes still sat in the bushel basket.

Hours later, Betty and Janet stopped by to see how Darlene was doing.

"Terrible!" she exclaimed. "The book said the tomatoes would be ready in thirty minutes. I've had them in there for four hours and those lids still haven't sealed."

They tried to hide their smiles. "Oh, honey!" one of them said. "Remember, we told you the lids will seal *after* you take the jars out of the canner and let them cool on the counter?"

No, she hadn't remembered.

By summer's end, however, Darlene was an experienced canner, and she learned the hard way that when someone asked, "Could you use a few beans?" they were likely to give you four large paper grocery bags full.

Once, a young man dropped off four bushels of corn. "Mom says you need to do this corn up right away. It's past prime."

In years to come, Darlene would freeze and can 1,200 quarts a year. She learned to love putting up food for the winter. It felt gratifying to look at rainbow colored rows of beans, corn, tomatoes, squash, vegetable soup, spaghetti sauce, peaches, pears, grape juice, and applesauce.

She had a huge garden every summer and asked Jim if they could plant their own fruit trees.

"I don't think so, honey. We probably won't stay here that long," Jim said. He wasn't sure how long he wanted to stay on the first rung of the ladder at the small country church.

"Honey," Darlene says to Jim, stroking his wrinkled cheek as he dozes in the hospital bed, "do you remember when I first learned to can and Betty and Janet came back to check on me, and I had cooked the tomatoes for four hours?"

His eyes twinkle through the morphine-induced fog.

"I asked them later how they'd kept from laughing. They said they didn't want to hurt my feelings, so they didn't laugh until they got out of the driveway. Then they laughed for the next twenty minutes! We had wonderful people, didn't we?"

He nods and drifts back to sleep.

Darlene never said no when offered food, except for the one time she did. One spring, a neighbor called. "My husband loves to catch smelt. I'll bring you some."

She hung up before Darlene could explain she and Jim hated fish, and Darlene didn't have the heart to tell her later when she arrived at the door with two five gallon pails of smelt and another pail in the car.

"Some people cook them like this," the neighbor said, "but if you want to clean them, snip their heads off, and gut them."

Darlene tried her best not to gag as she snipped and gutted.

Jim came into the kitchen and saw Darlene gagging, snipping, and gutting. "What are you doing? And what's that smell?" He looked closer. "I'm not eating that."

"We have to eat them," Darlene objected. "What if she asks how we liked them? We can't hurt her feelings."

"She won't ask. I'll pray she won't." He grabbed the cleaned and not cleaned smelt and headed out the door.

"Where are you going?"

"To have a fishy funeral."

Darlene learned smelt is a saltwater species except for one freshwater kind in Green Lake, Maine. Someone stocked Crystal Lake, Michigan with freshwater smelt in 1912. They didn't stay where they belonged and escaped into Lake Michigan. Fishermen first caught them there in 1923. Apparently, it's more fun to catch them than it is to clean and eat them.

"Learn to say no," Charles Spurgeon once said. "It will be of more use to you than to be able to read Latin."

The next year when the same neighbor offered smelt, Darlene politely refused.

The surprised neighbor said, "I should think a preacher's family would be grateful for any food they got!"

*Maybe,* Darlene thought, *they should be, but in this case, they were not.*

## 7
## MOVING IN

Darlene could hardly contain her excitement when moving day arrived in late September. Jim, Darlene, and April moved into the little six-room, red-shingled tenant house that would be their home for the next twenty-one years. Two of the rooms were over one-hundred years old. Open fields framed the house to the south, west, and east. To the north stood a beautiful red barn, and beyond that the big farmhouse where the Halls lived.

Jim and Darlene filled their home with second-hand furniture. Towels and a hooked rug covered the frayed parts of the loveseat. Bushels of garage sale toys and a borrowed upright piano helped achieve a lived-in look. The old house was charming. Darlene especially liked the lovely oak trim.

Jim and Darlene loved the house, but they didn't love being cold. The house had no furnace, and chilly weather came early that year. After shivering in sweatshirts, they were happy to hear Mr. Hall had hired someone to install a furnace.

Over the years, he and his wife made many improvements

to the little house, but they didn't pass the cost on to the church. They charged the church barely enough rent to pay the taxes.

In early November, a handyman came to install an LP gas furnace. As he cut into the wall to run the wire for the thermostat he hollered, "Can you bring me some bags?" Darlene took him some brown paper garbage bags. She watched with interest as he hauled debris from the wall and filled both bags.

"What is that stuff?" she asked.

"It's a rat's nest," he replied. "Haven't you ever seen one before?"

No, she hadn't, and she hoped she'd never see one again. Rats? She looked at the apple cheeks of her toddler and put her hand protectively over her belly where the new baby was growing. She would never, she vowed to herself, live in a house with rats.

You've heard the saying, never say never? Many years later rats invaded again. Jim set traps in the basement. Jim caught six rats that winter, but one of the traps disappeared forever. Darlene didn't like thinking about the size of the rat that had hauled off that trap.

There were no rats in sight when Mom and Dad Peters came from New York for their first visit, and the house was spotless, so their reaction surprised Darlene. They were horrified; all they could see was how old, small, and unfinished the house was.

Jim took his dad for a walk around the property. The yard was a lot like the house, a little civilized and a lot rustic. Dad Peters looked around and suggested they spray the yard for weeds.

"Dad," Jim protested, "if we spray the yard for weeds there won't be a green thing left."

Mom Peters hated the house. She felt her son deserved so much more. Jim and Darlene later found out she'd cried all the way to Georgia on the next leg of their trip to see Jim's sister and family.

Mom had sobbed. "Jim and Darlene have nothing, just nothing."

Mom revised her opinion a few years later, though. "Jim and Darlene have everything."

Good friends from college, Jason and Renee, were even more critical of the church and the house when they came to visit.

Jason looked at the church with disdain. "It's a good starting place, I guess. You can move up from here. It's only the first rung on the ladder. But I think you could have done a lot better than this. I'm kind of surprised you came here. They say location is everything, and what do you have here? Just a place where two dirt roads meet."

Jim visualized Professor Nick Machiavelli nodding in agreement. Jim tried to ignore the uneasy thought that came now and then. Had he made a mistake coming to Corners Church? Should he try to make his ministry here a short one and look for something better?

Jason's opinion of the house was even harsher. "Someone should condemn this place."

By then Darlene had seen the potential of the tiny home and felt defensive.

When Darlene's brother-in-law, Bruce, came to visit he looked around and listened to her plans for paint and wallpaper. "This place will be charming."

*Finally, someone sees what I see.*

However, Bruce was less than impressed with the isolated country location. He was restless and bored.

"Do you want to read the paper?" Darlene asked. "It should be here by now."

"There's a paper? What could the news possibly be? A cow died?"

Darlene indignantly told him the local paper was good. Bruce went to the paper box and came back laughing. He slapped the paper on the table in front of Darlene. "Read that!" He pointed at the headline: "Cow Killed When Hit by Truck."

"Well, would you rather listen to the radio?"

Darlene adjusted the antenna on the radio and put it by the window.

The first story on the radio was about a local judge. The judge had asked people found guilty of minor offenses, "Well, it's almost county fair time, so when would you like to report to the jail to serve your sentence?"

Bruce roared with laughter. "Is this for real?"

Darlene said defensively, "We haven't been to the fair yet, but the sign says it's the most popular fair on earth."

Bruce wiped his eyes. "You two will fit right in here!"

Bruce was right. Jim and Darlene did fit right in. After their first visit to the fair they agreed it might be the most popular fair on earth. They seldom missed a fair after that. When the church almost emptied the Sundays before and after the fair Jim and Darlene understood. The 4-H kids and their parents needed to get projects and animals in the Sunday before the fair and pick them up the Sunday after the fair.

It didn't take long for Jim and Darlene to start falling in love with Corners Church, their little house, and the community. The Corners began feeling like home.

## 8
## OLD JOHN

Old John was a well-known in the community. He lived in a tiny camper in Jim and Darlene's backyard. The camper had no running water, so Old John used an outhouse, also in the backyard. He ate his meals at Halls and helped Kenyon with a few chores. Old John's back was bent, and his speech was slow. He'd hobble over the barn hill to Halls, leaning on his walking stick, always wearing overalls with one strap fastened, the other unhooked and hanging down his back.

It was almost impossible to understand Old John's words, but two sentences were clear: "Pa beat Ma. Pa bad, bad man."

Old John had a remarkable variety of swear words, however, and they came through, loud and clear.

April, barely two years old, liked to sit on the cement stoop next to the red-shingled tenant house with Old John. The two of them laughed and talked like the children they were. Darlene kept an eye on them from the kitchen window. But she soon learned what the rest of the Corners people already knew; Old John was harmless. He and April had each found a friend.

Darlene didn't worry about Old John hurting April. She wondered about something else, though.

"Honey, what if April picks up Old John's vocabulary and cusses at church?"

He chuckled. "We'll deal with that if it happens."

Sometimes Jim and Darlene would wake in the night to hear shouting, laughter, and the sounds of stones pelting old John's trailer. It was too dark to see the tormentors, but Jim knew they were teenagers. Old John would come outside his trailer and yell and swear at them. Not until Jim went outside and hollered would the kids leave. Jim and Darlene refused to believe those teens came from their beloved Corners. Surely, they were teens from somewhere else who had discovered an easy target in Old John.

The bullies didn't try to harm Jim, Darlene, or April. A few times, though, Jim found dead animals in the mailbox, a squirrel or a rabbit. Darlene cried at the cruelty. Why did Old John and those animals have to suffer?

Old John grew older. One day he ended up in a small hospital in Hudson, and Jim went to visit him.

"Will you help us get him in the bathtub?" the nurses begged Jim. "He looks like he hasn't had a bath in years, and he's refusing to get in the water."

That puzzled Jim. He knew Mabel told Old John to take a shower every week. He helped the nurses coax the terrified man into the bathtub. Old John's skin, under the long-sleeved shirt and coveralls he always wore, looked creased and crusted with dirt. Jim helped the nurses scrub him, but it didn't do much good. There were too many layers.

When Old John got home from the hospital and Mabel told him to take a shower, Kenyon followed him and solved the mystery. The steam from the hot water was filling the room, but

Old John was sitting outside the shower, happily looking at a comic book.

It was a sad day when Old John died.

The funeral director pulled Jim aside before the funeral. "Preacher," he said, "I haven't asked anyone this before, but could you keep your sermon short?"

"I can do that, but why?"

"Last night Old John's brother and sister had a fist fight and rolled around on the floor right there in front of the casket. Seems one of them wanted him to wear a black suit, and the other wanted a blue suit."

Old John looked peaceful but remarkably out-of-place wearing a suit in the casket. Darlene's eyes watered as she looked at him. Surely God had welcomed him Home, as He does all children too young to understand their sin and need of a Savior. Now he was happy, his bent back straightened, no longer worried about a pa who beat ma, no longer tormented by thoughtless teenagers.

Jim kept the sermon short. No one seemed to mind.

## 9

## ADVENTURES

Jim, Darlene, and everyone at the Corners missed Old John, but life went on. Jim found the learning curve of being a pastor challenging; he needed help. Now that he was a real pastor with an actual congregation, he wished he'd paid better attention in his college classes. When he heard there was going to be a pastors' conference at a college in Ohio, he longed to go, and he wanted Darlene to go with him. There was one problem; they didn't have enough money.

"We could borrow a tent from Bruce," Darlene said. "He and Eve camp all the time. It wouldn't cost much to camp. April and I could spend the days in the state park, and you could go to the conference."

With creative scrimping and saving, they scrounged up enough for the fee to the conference that covered the sessions and Jim's meals. Darlene packed food for April and herself.

As Jim attempted to pitch the tent at the campsite, he wished he'd accepted Bruce's offer of a tutorial. "I'm in a hurry," Jim had said. "How hard can it be?"

Those old Coleman canvas tents weren't the easiest things to erect.

"Come for a walk with Mommy," Darlene said pointedly, taking April's hand. "You don't need to see Daddy get this mad."

At last, the tent was up, pitched directly over tree roots. Without cots or air mattresses, the three of them slept on the tent floor. A bumpy tree root poked a pregnant Darlene whatever way she turned; Jim didn't sleep well either. April loved camping and slept soundly every night; this became a problem. She was wide awake all day, but Darlene couldn't get through the day without napping.

Early every morning, Jim stepped out of the tent in his suit and went off to the conference, and he didn't return until late evening. As much as he loved the workshops, he felt out of place. It seemed he was the only one from a small country church. Every pastor he talked to was from a much larger church. He heard the other pastors discussing their average attendances and the yearly budgets. Both were much higher than his little church. He tried to laugh it off; *nickels and noses philosophy. That's all it is.* But still, a nagging thought persisted. Had he made the right choice to go to such a small church?

Jim's former college professor, Nick Machiavelli, led several of the workshops, and Jim made sure to go to every one of them. After one session, the professor noticed Jim, pulled him aside, and asked him questions about his church. He listened, smiling and nodding.

When Jim finished, Professor Machiavelli put one hand on Jim's shoulder. "My boy, don't stay at that little church too long. Nothing ever happens where two dirt roads meet. Move on soon. Don't forget what I taught you. You need to climb the ladder to bigger and better things."

Jim attended the rest of the conference sessions but felt

discouraged and defeated. *What if God didn't actually call me to Corners Church? Did I just take the first opportunity that came along?*

He didn't tell Darlene how he felt. She and April seemed to be having so much fun, and he didn't want to ruin that. Though he was discouraged, he couldn't help but smile when he thought of Darlene. He loved the way she made everything an adventure.

Camping was a new and exciting adventure to Darlene. She loved it, until it started raining non-stop. Trapped in the tent, she read to April until one of them was exhausted.

"Mommy has to take a nap. You look at your books now, okay?"

April nodded and smiled, yellow curls bouncing.

"Don't go outside of the tent."

"I won't, Mommy."

She didn't. Darlene woke to find an entire bottle of pancake syrup spread on the canvas tent floor with a tub of oatmeal mixed into it. April was happily finger painting.

Compared to the mess of cleaning up the aftermath of the syrup and oatmeal, going to the dump for the first time was a smaller adventure, but still a memorable experience. It cost to have garbage collected, so most people at the Corners took their garbage to the dump. It was free for those who lived in the township. Old Mr. Lily stood in a tiny booth and checked to be sure cars were from the township.

Mr. Lily was a friendly man who loved conversation. When Jim and Darlene made their first trip to the dump, he was curious. "Aren't you that new young preacher at Corners Church? Park your car over there to the side and come in and chat awhile. Bring the wife and your little girl too."

It was a swelteringly hot day, and the dump smelled like dumps do. The last thing Darlene wanted to do was go in that booth and chat awhile. Had she known how long "awhile" was, she might have refused to get out of the car.

"Come on, Darlene. It would be rude not to go talk to him when he asked us."

"April's sleeping!"

"Wake her up, honey. This won't take long."

Darlene, Jim, and little April squeezed into the minuscule booth with Mr. Lily. There was no place to sit, and the booth stood directly in the sun. It had to be 100 degrees in there. Darlene's pregnant body and swollen ankles wanted to run from the heat, the stench, and even from sweet Mr. Lily, who didn't smell so good himself, and who loved to talk. An hour-and-a half later, they eventually escaped to the car.

Jim snapped his fingers. "I forgot to invite him to church. Oh well, I'll do it next time."

Darlene gave him a look. "There will be no next time for me."

True to her word, Darlene stayed home the next time Jim went to the dump. He didn't return for two hours, even though the dump was only a few minutes from their house.

"I had a nice talk with Mr. Lily, and this time I invited him to church."

"It took two hours to invite him to church?"

"Well, you know how he is." Jim wiped sweat from his face. "I need a shower."

"Yes, you do!" Darlene wrinkled her nose at the stench of the dump that clung to him like nasty perfume.

Jim headed off to the shower. "Oh, he missed you and April. He asked me to bring you with me next time. I told him I would."

It's probably a good thing the noise of the shower prevented Jim from hearing what Darlene said next. But she did go back, many times. She didn't have the heart to disappoint Mr. Lily or Jim.

Mr. Lily grew older, as all dump employees do, and the rest of us too. He never came to church, and when Mr. Lily quit working at the dump, Jim lost track of him.

Years later when Mr. Lily died, his family contacted Jim. "Dad said he wanted you to preach his funeral."

That gave Jim some comfort. Perhaps, sometime, in the quietness of his heart, Mr. Lily had trusted Jesus as his Savior.

## 10
## CLUBBING COUNTRY STYLE

Darlene soon learned people expected her to do more than just attend church. A few church ladies asked her to join the community club, a group of women who met to make quilts for the needy and terry-cloth bibs for nursing home residents. Darlene asked if anyone else from church attended the club. No, they didn't, but they thought as a pastor's wife, it would help her have a good reputation in the community.

Darlene was shy, and she didn't relish the idea of joining a club none of the church ladies attended. She had a fleeting thought of driving to the city and buying short shorts and a bike, like another pastor's wife had done.

Darlene's first community club meeting was unforgettable. She made a ghastly mistake of asking a farmer's wife how many acres they farmed. Silence fell over the room. Someone next to her whispered kindly that asking how much land a farmer worked was as rude as asking how much money he had in the bank. Who knew?

Darlene learned many things from the community club

women. They taught her the Corners' phone manners. It was bad manners to immediately say why you'd called someone. You had to chat about other things before asking if your neighbor knew who the stray dog in your yard belonged to. When you finished talking, you didn't say goodbye. You hung up. That was one Corners' mannerism Darlene couldn't get the hang of.

The community club ladies were patient teachers, and many became her friends, but that first club meeting was awkward. When they asked Darlene if she knew how to tie off quilts, she responded she didn't, but she was sure she could learn. They looked doubtful.

"We'll tie off the quilt," one of them said after a long pause. "Why don't you go over to that cabinet and get us some outin' cloth?"

Darlene went to the cabinet and stared at the neatly folded piles of colored fabric. She looked at the cloth for a long time.

Shirley, the only other younger member asked, "Is something wrong?"

"Yes! They told me to get outin' cloth, and I don't know what that is!"

"Oh! They want material to put on the back of the quilt. Pick anything you like."

Darlene later learned there wasn't much Shirley couldn't do. Her daughter wanted a winter coat from a catalog that cost more than the family could afford. Shirley bought material, looked at the catalog picture, and, without a pattern, cut and sewed a coat that looked exactly like the coat in the catalog.

In those years, no one at the Corners used store-bought baked goods, and Shirley was one of the best cooks. Darlene stopped by Shirley's one day and saw biscuits covering the counters and tables.

"Are you having a family reunion or something?"

Shirley laughed. "That's biscuits for the five of us in our family, and believe me, we won't have any leftovers!"

At the Corners, knowing how to cook was mandatory. People worked hard and needed good food. Matt Little, a farmer who was as thin as a stick, was legendary for eating a dozen eggs and a half pound of bacon for breakfast every morning. He lived to be ninety-six.

The ladies at the Corners had skills Darlene couldn't hope to duplicate, and she began thinking less and less of her college education. She might have book learning, but these women, some who never finished high school, taught her valuable life lessons.

At community club, the ladies often told stories about the old days at the Corners as they sewed; that was Darlene's favorite part of the meetings. She learned in the 1800s prominent families from the east coast had settled at the Corners. The Corners once had two churches, a country store, a post office, and a grange hall.

"Did I ever tell you how the Hall family came to settle here?" Mabel asked one day.

A few ladies laughed, but Darlene shook her head.

"Well," Mabel continued, "Kenyon's great grandparents were on their way west. They stopped to rest at the piece of property where we live now. The next morning, Kenyon's great-grandma stood, looked around, put her hands on her hips, and said, 'Husband, you can go on all the way to Californee if you've a mind to, but me and the kids are staying right here.'"

The ladies laughed. "Us farm ladies don't need women's lib," one of them said jokingly. "We've always known how to speak our piece, and how to do a man's work too."

Shirley groaned. "I'm so tired of driving that dang tractor! I wish I wasn't so liberated!"

The ladies told Darlene when any events had happened at

the schoolhouse or the church, neighbors had come from miles around and packed the places. Sometimes people had even sat around the outside of the church and had listened through the windows.

Annette nodded. "That's what happened when Reverend Milton Wright, Wilbur and Orville Wright's daddy, came to preach. Mama told me all about it. I was a baby. It was around 1905, as I remember her saying. He was part of a group of traveling preachers come to preach a revival."

A few of the ladies looked skeptical. "You mean the daddy of the Wright brothers, the boys who flew the first plane?" Shirley asked.

"It's gospel truth," Annette insisted. "Why Preacher Wright even spent a night with one family right here at the Corners. And he said those two boys of his weren't too keen on going to church."

Mabel chuckled. "Going to church here at the Corners wasn't an option when we were kids. We never thought to question it. We just went unless we couldn't get down the road because of snow or mud."

"Mud?" Darlene asked.

The ladies nodded. "You think these gravel roads are bad now," Mabel said, "you should have seen them back in the day before the county had done anything with them. They were just dirt paths and still a mess when Ford invented that Model T of his. It didn't take long for everyone who could afford a car to get one, except for Henry. He was a stubborn old farmer, set in his ways. We'd pass him plodding along out on Squawfield Road, and the men would laugh and holler out, 'Get a Ford, Henry!' Well, one year the mud was worse than usual, and cars were stuck all over. Henry came along with his horse and pulled everyone out. He smiled, tipped his hat, and said, 'Get a horse.'"

Vivian had a copy of *Pioneer Notes and Reflections*, an essay Ralph M. Lickley had written in 1935 about the previous one-hundred years of community life at the Corners. She sometimes read from it as the other ladies worked, and Darlene loved hearing it. Vivian read, "One early settler wrote back to friends among the New England rocks and said, 'Our soil needs only to be tickled with a plow, and it laughs in wheat and corn.'"

"Jim!" Darlene said after Community Club one day, "I took notes on what Vivian read today from Ralph Lickley's paper. I knew you'd be interested. The first church at the Corners was started by the Baptists in 1854 where the grange is now. Ralph said it was 'a splendid edifice costing two thousand dollars.' They had one hundred and twelve members, and people came from miles around. The building was often crowded. Isn't that interesting?"

Jim sighed. "I wish it was 1854. I'd like to have one hundred and twelve members. Do you think we'll ever have that many?"

Darlene doubted it, but she didn't say so.

She grew to enjoy the community club and was sad when it disbanded because most of the members became too old. They sold the one-room schoolhouse community club to the church for $5.00 to use as a fellowship hall. They wanted to give it to them, but money had to change hands to make the deal legal.

∾

THERE WAS one part of the club meetings Darlene had never enjoyed, and the memory still makes her grin.

When Jim opens his eyes, she reminds him of how she'd disliked the club song.

She sings, "Sew, sew, sewing on our quilts, helps brighten

someone else's world. We are happy as can be because we are community clubbers you see—"

Jim groans and holds up his hand to stop her. That's good because she can't remember the rest.

"Not only did you marry a girl who can't play the piano, an unwritten rule for a pastor's wife back in the day, you also married one who can't carry a tune. But just because I can't sing doesn't mean I won't." She teases him.

He's humming something. She leans in close to hear, and her eyes brim with tears. He's humming a song from a commercial that had been popular when they'd been in college. He'd said it was her theme song: "I'd like to buy the world a coke. . .and teach the world to sing."

She nods. "I still feel that way after all these years, and I know you do too. But when we were so young we didn't have a clue how much that coke and those singing lessons would cost us."

## 11

## SAM AND PETE TEACH JIM A THING OR TWO

When Jim made his first hospital call, he almost gave the patient a heart attack. He walked into the hospital dressed, as he'd been taught in Bible college, in dress pants, dress shirt, suit coat, and tie.

Sam sat upright in bed, face ashen. "So, I'm that bad?"

Jim was confused. "I don't think so."

Sam looked Jim up and down, head to toe. Then he remembered this preacher was fresh out of Bible college and knew little to nothing about country ways. He wasn't dying after all. The new kid just didn't know how to dress.

Sam slumped back on the pillows. His fear of imminent demise had about drained him. With what little energy he had left he told Jim, "Don't you ever come see me dressed like that. If I'm not dying, I'll for sure have a heart attack when I look at you."

As years passed, Jim's visitation clothes downgraded to dress pants and a dress shirt open at the collar, and eventually to clothes that made his people the most comfortable, jeans and a casual shirt. He wore dress clothes behind the pulpit, though.

The people expected that. Had he done otherwise, the congregation would have feared he was trying to make Corners Church into one of those new-fangled contemporary churches where no one used Bibles or hymn books. Sam and the others wouldn't have liked that at all.

Sam taught Jim a lot. Strong, dependable Sam also had an impulsive, fun side, and Betty, his wife, seldom knew what was coming next with him. He might decide to take a trip from Michigan to Florida and ask if she could be packed in an hour.

One blizzardy Sunday the church road was nearly impassable. Sam, well into his late seventies, cheerfully stomped the snow from his boots as he came into the entryway. "Might not have many out today, Pastor," he said. "You know how those old people are. They don't like to get out in this kind of weather."

Sam liked few things better than testing his driving skills on snowy roads, but he also enjoyed a good, haggling car trade. He once dropped Betty off at a grocery store and was waiting for her return when a car pulled in next to him. Sam eyed the car and began talking to the driver about a trade.

When Betty came out of the store, she was puzzled. Their car was gone, and Sam was sitting in a different car. He'd managed to trade vehicles during the short time it took Betty to get groceries.

"That haggling's in my blood," Sam told Jim. "My uncle was a horse trader, and a shyster one at that! He advertised he had a good horse for sale. A guy came to look at it. He didn't trust Uncle because of his reputation, so he questioned him up, down, and sideways about that horse.

"'I tell you, he's a good horse,' Uncle insisted. 'He don't look too good, but he's a good animal.'

"Well, they settled on a price, and the guy took the horse home. Next day the guy comes back, furious to beat the band.

"'You lied to me. You sold me a blind horse!' he yelled. 'I want my money back.'

"'You ain't getting your money back. I didn't lie to you. I told you he don't look too good,' Uncle told him.

"I'm an honest trader," Sam told Jim. "I've never traded anyone a blind car. Did trade one with a headlight out once."

Sam laughed and Jim joined him. No one could laugh like Sam, and sometimes Jim needed a good laugh. He hated when he didn't get things right, and sometimes he didn't.

Jim had preached an entire sermon on "Euodias and Syntyche, those two men at Philippi who couldn't get along."

The next week, Deacon Pete Sanders and his wife, Janet, had invited Jim, Darlene, and April over for lunch, as they often had.

Janet's cooking was wonderful, and Jim and Darlene had a great time. After lunch, Janet brought out some puzzles and toys, and she and Darlene took April into the living room to play. Darlene smiled as she overheard Pete saying encouraging things to Jim. Jim needed that.

Then, in his gentle way, Deacon Pete said, "Pastor, me and Janet were talking. We're thinking maybe those two men you preached about on Sunday were women. We could be wrong, but maybe you could check that out sometime."

"Thanks for telling me, Pete. I sure will check that out."

Darlene looked at Janet. "Oops!"

"It's not a big deal," Janet said. "We just thought we'd say something before someone else did in a way that might hurt his feelings."

*"We could be wrong."* How many old deacons would be that humble about an error a new young pastor had made? And how many new young pastors would accept correction as gracefully as Jim had? Deacon Pete and Jim are going to make a good team.

## 12

## BETTER LATE THAN NEVER

Very early in their ministry, when he was something less than flexible, Jim felt troubled by the congregation's lack of promptness. He didn't accept that sometimes cows didn't cooperate with milking or that a pig escaped and needed corralling before families could come to church.

One Sunday evening, Jim glanced at the clock on the back wall. It was past time to start the song service. "Open your hymnbooks to page—"

"Don't make me do this," Darlene said. No piano player had arrived. The only people in the pews were Darlene and two-year-old April.

"Open your hymnbooks to," Jim continued as though there'd been no interruption. As people trickled in, the piano player went to the platform, and a few more voices joined in the singing. The congregation exchanged amused glances, but no one said anything.

A few weeks later Jim and Darlene visited a church neighbor late on a Sunday afternoon. The neighbor had many questions about the Bible, and Jim lost track of the time. When he and Darlene arrived at church five minutes late, the congregation was already singing with broad smiles on their faces. No one said a word. That was the last time the pastor started a service without the members, or the members started without the pastor.

It took a few years for Jim to get used to country ways, but he grew to love those ways, heart and soul. Eventually, he not only loved country ways he became them.

∽

Darlene looks down at Jim. He has little resemblance now to the young, tanned pastor who had vigorously insisted she and April sing before anyone else arrived at church.

"Jim."

He opens his eyes.

"Do you remember being disgruntled about services starting late? You threatened to paint over the church sign so it read 'Sunday School 10:00ish, Morning Worship 11:00ish, Evening Service 7:30ish.'" He barely smiles. He looks so tired.

# 13
# THE PASTOR LEARNS THINGS NOT IN THE BOOKS

"Pastor," Deacon Pete said, "I sure could use your help doing a job at church."

Jim agreed, and they chose a date and time.

When the day arrived, Jim was gone quite some time, and Darlene wondered what was taking so long. He came home, smelling disgusting. His hand was red and swollen, and he forced a grin.

"Well, that's one job I didn't learn about in Bible college. Pete and I had to tip over the outhouse and get a bee's nest out."

He held up his hand. "I need to put something on these bee stings, and I think I need a shower."

Darlene thoroughly agreed.

A few weeks later Jim asked Darlene, "Have you noticed there's no mailbox at church? The mail goes to several members, and they bring it to church when they come. I think we need a mailbox."

Jim bought a mailbox and a six-foot wooden post. He had no saw, but he borrowed a posthole digger. It took a long time to dig a hole deep enough for the post, but he came home satisfied with his afternoon's work, and he was sure the congregation would be happy.

When Sunday came, Jim couldn't wait to show Darlene the new mailbox.

"What?" he asked, puzzled as he pulled into the parking lot. The mailbox was tipped on its side, and a mountain of dirt sat next to it. He learned he'd cut through a cable and disrupted phone service for the entire nearby town of Ransom.

It took days to repair the phone lines. Everyone remembered that for a long time; he made an instant reputation for himself in the community.

A month after the mailbox incident, Deacon Pete asked Jim to go for a walk. Pete looked sad and uncomfortable.

Jim felt alarmed. Had he done something wrong? He thought of a story he'd heard about a young preacher who'd gone to a country church. His preaching was terrible. The patient people waited for him to improve, but he only got worse. Eventually, the congregation told their deacon he had to talk to the young preacher. They couldn't stand anymore awful sermons.

The deacon took the preacher for a walk. What could he say without crushing the young man's feelings? After several minutes of silence, the old deacon asked, "How were you called to the ministry?"

"Oh, that's easy. I was out on my tractor one day, and an airplane flew overhead. The exhaust spelled letters in the sky, 'P' 'C.' I knew right away that meant 'Preach Christ.'"

"Humph." The old deacon scratched his chin uncomfortably. "Don't you think maybe it could've meant 'Plant Corn?'"

Deacon Pete wasn't saying anything. Jim wished he would. *Is he going to tell me the congregation isn't happy with me? I know I've made more than a few mistakes.*

Pete cleared his throat. "Some of us at church are worrying.

You're such a nice young man, and we know that a first church can make or break a preacher. When we run out of money and can't pay you, and you have to leave, we don't want you to think it's your fault."

Jim assured Pete he didn't expect the church to run out of money, and should it happen, he wouldn't give up on the ministry or blame the church. If he'd only known then how difficult it was for the church to provide his salary, he might not have answered so confidently.

## 14

## MAKING ENDS MEET

The church congregation paid Jim more than they could afford—$110.00 a week. That was 1974. The average yearly income then was $13,900, about $267.00 a week. Jim and Darlene later learned that on many Sundays, when the treasurer counted the offering and it came to less than $110.00, the board members quietly dug deeper into their almost empty pockets to make up the difference.

At first, Jim and Darlene thought they could manage fine with $110.00 a week. The cost of a stamp was only $.10, bread $.28, milk $1.39 a gallon, and gas only $.53 a gallon. True, the pay was only a third of what Jim had been making working in a factory, but here they didn't have to pay rent.

When the first month's electric bill of over $100.00 came, they looked at each other and swallowed hard. Then came the bill to fill the LP gas tank; it was over $300.00.

"That's not too bad," they said to each other. "That'll probably last a whole winter."

"That'll last only three or four weeks in the winter, if the weather isn't too cold," Kenyon told them.

Professor Nick Machiavelli sent Jim a postcard. "A workman is worthy his hire. I'm guessing you're having trouble making ends meet. Tell that little dirt road church of yours you need a raise. N.M."

Jim tossed the postcard in the garbage. He felt embarrassed. What if someone read that postcard and thought he'd complained to his professor about his wages? He'd never ask the church for anything, he vowed to himself. But he reached into the garbage, pulled out the postcard, and filed it. For some reason he couldn't part with anything Professor Nick Machiavelli sent him.

Inflation was pretty high the next five years. By 1979 stamps cost $.15, bread was $.40, milk increased to $1.62, and gas jumped to $.86 a gallon. Many more years would pass before the church could give Jim a raise. That gave God many opportunities to do miracles and to prove to His servants they could trust Philippians 4:19: "But my God shall supply all your need according to his riches in glory by Christ Jesus."

## 15

## FOOD SHOWERS

There was never enough money, but Jim and Darlene were seldom hungry. Almost every year, the Corners Church held a Thanksgiving food shower for Jim and Darlene. The first year, when Jim and Darlene arrived home after prayer meeting the night before Thanksgiving, they were puzzled to see so many cars in their driveway. Everyone who'd been at prayer meeting and some who hadn't were there waiting for them.

People began piling out of their cars and following them inside, carrying boxes and bags of food. They filled the table with the food and smiled expectantly.

"Well, aren't you going to open everything?" someone asked.

Jim and Darlene unpacked many pounds of flour, sugar, brown sugar, powdered sugar, meat for the freezer, hunks of cheeses, milk, eggs, and canned goods. People chuckled when they noticed almost everyone had given pasta.

"Guess you won't run out of spaghetti anytime soon," someone remarked to Darlene.

Jim had often mentioned in his sermons that being married to an Italian meant you had to eat spaghetti once or twice a week, whether you wanted to or not! That may have been a slight exaggeration.

Those food showers continued every year. As Jim and Darlene's children were born and grew older, they loved to help unpack the bags and boxes from the Thanksgiving food showers. They knew they'd find a few treats especially for them.

∼

EVERY HOLIDAY WAS *special at the Corners*, Darlene thinks. This will be the first year Jim won't be with her to celebrate Thanksgiving, but she'll keep thanking God for him as long as she lives. What a joy it has been to grow old with this man, to serve God together, to give until they had nothing left to give.

*Would they do it all over again? If we had one-hundred lives, Lord, we'd give them all to you and laugh with the joy of doing it. Thank you for letting us live, love, and grow old at the Corners.*

## 16

## DILEMMAS AND TREASURES

Darlene had been expecting Jimmy when they came to Corners Church, and all nine pounds nine ounces of him was born two days after Christmas. He came home from the hospital in a Christmas stocking. Jim and Darlene had no dryer, so all winter Darlene hung wet cloth diapers and the rest of the laundry all over the house to dry. When spring came, she couldn't wait to use the outside clothesline. Her OCD had experienced more than its fill of wet laundry drying in conspicuous places.

The first remarks from the congregation about Darlene's laundry were positive.

"You're well respected in the community," Betty said, nodding approval. "Only Linda Travis hangs her laundry out earlier than you do."

*People are noticing what time I hang out my laundry?* Still fresh out of college, where respect earned had nothing to do with clotheslines or laundry, Darlene accepted the compliment with a gracious but puzzled thank you.

The next response from the congregation to Darlene's

laundry was less favorable. Janet asked Darlene not to hang laundry outside on Sundays, because doing laundry on the Lord's Day was a bad testimony to the community. Some people didn't approve of working on Sunday.

By then, the cloth diapers were yellow instead of white because the Corners had the highest concentration of rust in the water in the county. The Sunday Janet asked Darlene not to hang laundry out on Sundays, Jim's closing hymn was "Whiter Than Snow." That didn't apply to the diapers.

Darlene already knew how to solve the laundry problem. She planned to be a secret sinner. She didn't have enough diapers to get through more than a day, so she'd still do Sunday's laundry and hang it in the house. She only hoped no one would come over after church. No one came. Apparently, "Be sure your sins will find you out" doesn't apply to Sunday laundry.

A few years later, Darlene's laundry dilemma became even more difficult. The old, second-hand washer clunked its last clunk, and even Jim couldn't repair it. Jim could fix most things; his years of being a country pastor with little pay encouraged him to learn skills, and he was an amazing handyman. He fixed cars, washers, dryers, furnaces, and stoves. Darlene admired him for it, and often thought a lesser man wouldn't survive as a country preacher.

It helped that Jim collected rubber straps as a hobby. Those came in handy; they held the vacuum together and pulled the screen door shut when the spring broke. In later years, a rubber strap kept the door to the second-hand dryer closed so it would spin. Jim fixed all kinds of things.

When, to her disappointment, Jim couldn't fix the washer and had to give it a funeral service instead, Darlene did laundry for months in the bathtub, scrubbing and wringing out clothes as people must have done on that land for hundreds of years before her.

*At least I have hot, running water,* Darlene often reminded herself. *Pioneer women probably had to carry water from the St. Joe River, boil it, and then do laundry.*

As she scrubbed, her hands got red, raw, and infected. She could hear her mother's voice saying as it had so often, "Use it up; wear it out; make it do, or do without."

*Well, I'm doing without now, Mom,* she thought. Mom would approve. Mom had allowed no self-pity in herself or her children. Darlene wished she could hear her mom's voice one more time.

The final time Darlene's mom had called, she'd asked how Jim was. Darlene had told the truth. "He's discouraged. He graduated from Bible college nine months ago, and he hasn't had a single contact from a church yet. He's starting to wonder if he's supposed to be a pastor."

"Tell him I said he'll be a pastor. I've known that since he was a little boy."

Mom died soon after that phone call, and two months later, Jim preached for the first time at Corners Church.

Darlene tried to be a brave and cheerful pioneer wife, but when Mom and Dad Peters came to visit and offered to buy her a washing machine, she didn't say no.

Mom and Dad Peters came to visit at least once a year usually towing Dad's little utility trailer. Once, Mom and Dad brought a little, pink refrigerator. Mom was disappointed when it didn't survive the journey. Darlene looked at the size of the refrigerator, perfect for a tiny elderly lady, but not so right for a growing family who often fed "half the county" as Jim said. She wasn't as disappointed as Mom.

The utility trailer came filled with all kinds of treasures. Often it had bags of toys and stuffed animals Mom had collected at garage sales. The kids adored their grandparents, not because of what they gave but because of who they were. When they were older, the children waited on their bikes on Squawfield Road, not far from the house. Sometimes they waited for hours for the first sight of their grandparents' car. Then they'd pedal furiously home.

"Mom! Dad! They're coming! They're coming!"

Dad Peters insisted on helping Darlene do anything that needed to be done, and she adored him. Everyone did. A little girl at his church told her mom she loved him because "He lives happily ever after." Much later, when he was on kidney dialysis, the nurses and the other patients called him "Mr. Sunshine."

Tired and happy one night during a visit, Darlene said to Jim, "Sometimes I wonder if your dad is even human. I think maybe he's an angel in disguise."

Jim yawned. "No, he's not. You haven't been alone in the car with him like I have. Angels don't call every other driver an idiot or a jerk."

They fell asleep laughing, as they did many nights when they lived in the little house that was stuffed full, not only with love and laughter, but just plain stuffed full.

Darlene woke up. "Honey! Where are we going to put all those toys and stuffed animals your parents brought the kids?"

"Go back to sleep and don't worry about it. After Mom and Dad go home, we'll give the toys to Goodwill."

"We can't! You know that would break the kids' hearts."

Somehow, they always found room for all the treasures Mom and Dad brought and kept the memories of those happy visits in their hearts.

## 17
## A NO AND A YES

A dimpled, blond boy joined the family in 1977. With Davey's birth, the family grew to five, but the paycheck grew not at all. Jim and Darlene decided to solve the problem. Darlene looked for work and was thrilled when she found a job working in a bakery at Market Home. The store wasn't open on Sundays; in those days, in that rural area, few stores were. Darlene explained she couldn't work on Wednesday nights because of prayer meeting, and the store manager agreed.

There were few things Darlene liked better than baking, so the job seemed a perfect fit. At Wednesday night prayer meeting, Darlene shared her excitement about her new job.

"I'll be starting on Monday," she said.

Have you ever heard the old saying, "If you want to make the angels laugh, tell God your plans?"

The next morning one of the deacons called Jim.

"The board talked about this," the deacon said, "and we don't want Darlene to take that job. We think it's important for her to be available for the women who may need her.

Besides, how will she make hospital calls and do counseling with you?"

Jim repeated the conversation to Darlene.

"Are you serious? They really don't want me to take the job?"

She was shocked. It hadn't occurred to her the board would have an opinion about her working. It wasn't like Jim was getting another job.

Jim and Darlene could have ignored the board's wishes, and at first Darlene was tempted. In today's world, she might have taken the job she wanted, but back then, as Darlene quickly discovered, it was unspoken but well understood, that a pastor's wife was expected to serve wherever needed, and since Corners Church was so small, they needed her everywhere. She counseled, made hospital and nursing home calls with Jim, taught Sunday school and children's church, organized potlucks, and planned church events like Vacation Bible School. It was a lot of work, but Darlene loved the people, and she liked a challenge.

When Darlene got tired, she rested when she could. When she couldn't rest, she repeated to herself what Samuel Rutherford had written back in the 1600s, "When I lose breath climbing the mountain, He maketh new breath."

Darlene wasn't working for God; she was making herself available for God to work through her, and it's a good thing she learned that lesson early, because the load got heavier before it got lighter.

The original few people at Corners Church were sturdy and self-sufficient, but God sent some new ones who needed more time and care. One woman decided to do all her sewing at Darlene's house so Darlene could babysit her children. Sometimes people requested Darlene to clean for them, give their children haircuts, or make them meals. It was an incredibly busy life, but Darlene thought she could still fulfill her church obligations and take the job she wanted at Market Home.

What should they do about the job? Jim suggested they pray about it and make their decision the next day.

Reluctantly, in order to keep the peace, they decided to abide by the board's wishes.

"Okay, I won't take the job, but how are we going to keep paying these bills?" Darlene asked.

"Go ahead and worry." Jim smiled. "I would if I were you. After all, God has let us down so many times before."

"I could use that bike, shorts, and sunglasses right about now," Darlene replied.

Darlene had never sympathized more with the young Presbyterian pastor's wife she'd read about in the paper who'd grown beyond frustrated with all her church's unspoken rules. According to the paper, she'd been discovered across town, far from her parish, bike riding with sunglasses and scandalously short shorts. This was unheard of behavior by a Presbyterian pastor's wife or even a Methodist one. Apparently, whenever she'd felt the need to get away, she'd thrown her bike in the back of the family station wagon and had headed for the opposite side of town where no one knew her.

When the newspaper reporter had asked her husband if he'd known about his wife's behavior, he'd replied, "No comment."

As Darlene had read the article aloud, she'd said to Jim, "Too bad she fell and broke her ankle and got caught."

When asked how many times she'd been in that part of town biking in her scandalous shorts, she'd replied, "I'm not saying."

Jim and Darlene later heard how area churches had responded to the saga of the scandalous shorts. The Presbyterian pastor and wife had suddenly been sent to another church out of state.

The Methodists had held a rather solemn meeting and discussed rules of conduct for their own pastor's wife. After pie, coffee, and a two-hour debate, the meeting had adjourned when one board members had mildly remarked they probably didn't need rules of conduct for Mrs. Dodds, who was a mature, stately sixty, and had, according to older members, been mature and stately at six. They had decided that should the Methodist district ever appoint them a young pastor and wife, the board would readdress the subject, with appropriate pie and coffee of course. The youngest board member had facetiously remarked that at least the event gave the Presbyterians free publicity, whereas the Methodists had never been in the paper.

Later, Mrs. Dodds had been overheard humming a tune the Royal Teens had made famous in 1957, "Short Shorts." The members of the Women's Missionary Society who'd overheard her had whispered to the rest of the society that perhaps Mrs. Dodds had not always been as mature and stately as previously supposed. They'd agreed to keep a good eye on her.

The Catholic priest's housekeeper had reported his reaction to the story. He'd read the news in the small living room of the rectory and had shaken his head. He'd remarked that the Catholic Church was the only one with enough sense to prohibit clergy from marrying, and he, for one, was grateful not to have a wife.

He'd pulled out his rosary to begin evening prayers and had muttered, "Short shorts indeed!"

The people at Corners Church had been very kind to Darlene the Sunday after the story of the bike and short shorts had livened the news. Several of the older members had remarked they were happy their sweet pastor's wife wouldn't do anything scandalous. She'd thought of a few scandalous things she'd been tempted to do, but wisely, she hadn't shared them.

∼

"Honey, do you remember that young pastor's wife who used to drive across town where no one knew her and bike in her short shorts?"

Jim nods.

"I guess she'd be our age now. Well, wherever she is, retirement home or heaven, I hope she has her bike with her!"

Jim sighs.

Darlene laughs. "Like I told you over fifty years ago when we started out in the ministry, you should have married someone who played the piano and shared your strict standards."

"Teeter totter," he mutters.

Darlene's puzzled. *Is Jim delirious?* She glances at him, but he looks alert and has a half-smile. Suddenly, she remembers. The teeter totter! They'd been about six years old at the Sunday school picnic. They'd each sat on one end of a teeter-totter and kicked it up with their feet. Stuck, they'd sat suspended in mid-air; the teeter-totter had refused to go up or down.

One of the men from the church had come to their rescue. After he'd lifted them down, he'd adjusted the board so it was longer on one side.

"You must weigh exactly the same," he'd explained. "The teeter totter was perfectly balanced."

"You mean you think after all these years we still perfectly balance each other?" Darlene asks.

He nods and tightens his grip on her hand. Oh, but his hand feels cold.

To keep from crying she asks, "Do you remember that first week at Corners Church when you came out of your study? You asked me to do you a favor. You said if anyone asked me what I thought about movies, or dancing, or music not to answer them, but send them to you. At first, I was insulted, but then I thought it was probably wise, so I agreed. A half hour later you came out of your study again with that worried frown and another request. 'If anyone asks you what you think about *anything*, please don't answer. Send them to me.' Then you read me Romans 14:22; I think you yanked it from its context for the occasion, 'So whatever you believe about these things keep between yourself and God.'"

He looks apologetic.

"It's okay, honey," she assures him. "You wouldn't have been able to stay at Corners Church for fifty years if I'd told them everything I thought that first week!"

∼

DARLENE CONTINUES THINKING about the bakery job she'd wanted as Jim slept. Soon after she'd declined the job, a woman who hadn't known anything about the job offer had given Darlene an ad she'd cut from a Christian magazine.

"You've told me you like to write," she'd said, "so when I saw this, I wondered if you might be interested."

Darlene had looked at the ad. "Christian publishing house needs curriculum writers. Please send resume."

The lady had looked shocked when Darlene had jumped on the nearest pew and had done a happy dance. Okay, that hadn't really happened. What had happened was a quickly mailed resume and a work-from-home job that had helped pay the bills for many years.

## 18

## EARLY MUSIC

Almost everyone at Corners Church sang well, and Darlene loved the singing. A few of the early songs faded as time passed. They stopped singing "A Christian Welcome Here," and that probably wasn't a bad thing. Imagine wandering into a country church of fifteen people and having everyone look at you, smile, and sing:

> There's a welcome here, a welcome here
>    A Christian welcome here, Hallelujah!
>    There's a welcome here, a welcome here
>    A Christian welcome here!

The birthday song, however, remained through the years. When someone had a birthday, the congregation recited:

> Many happy returns
>    To the day of thy birth
>    May sunshine and gladness be given.
>    And may Thy dear Father

Prepare thee on earth
For a beautiful birthday in heaven.

They then sang together: "Happy Birthday to you, happy birthday to you. May God bless and keep you; happy birthday to you."

The birthday person, whether eight or eighty, then chose a small gift from the birthday box.

Darlene was one of the few people in the church who couldn't sing on key; although, the congregation lovingly insisted her voice was beautiful. They begged Darlene and Jim for a duet. With pounding heart and shaking knees, Darlene finally agreed. They sang, "How Long Has It Been?" written by Thomas Mosie Lister.

> How long has it been
>> Since you talked with the Lord
>> And told him your heart's hidden secrets?
>
> How long since you prayed?
> How long since you stayed
>> On your knees till the light shone through?
>
> How long has it been
>> Since you knew that He cared for you?
>
> How long has it been
>> Since you knelt by your bed
>> And prayed to the Lord up in heaven?
>
> How long since you knew
> that He'd answer you and would
> keep you the long night through?
>
> How long has it been
>> Since you woke with the dawn
>> And felt that the day's worth the living?

> Can you call him your friend?
> How long has it been
> Since you knew that he cared for you?

Darlene hoped the duet was a onetime event, but the congregation enthusiastically requested the same duet several times a year. Darlene obliged, but every time she sang "How long has it been?" she thought, *not long enough!*

Once the church grew and the congregation had more people to choose from for special music they never again asked Jim and Darlene to sing a duet.

∼

DARLENE LOOKS at Jim in the hospital bed. She'd give anything to be young again for a few minutes, holding hands behind the pulpit and singing, "How Long Has It Been."

No matter how long we have those we love, it's never long enough.

## 19
## SINGING

"I always loved the singing," Jim says.

"So did I, as long as I wasn't up front doing it."

"I wonder if Davey knows how much I appreciated all the song services he led for us after he grew up. Remember how he closed every one with, 'In my life, Lord, in my song, Lord, in your church, Lord be glorified'? That became the church theme song because of him." Jim stopped to catch his breath. "Came to be my theme song too. Like to have Corners Church sing that at my memorial service."

Darlene nods. "We'll tell Davey in the morning. You know our son. He'll be here early."

∼

SINGING WAS a colorful part of the fabric that was Corners Church. Darlene's eyes widened the first time she heard the small congregation sing, "I've got the Corners Church enthusiasm down in my heart. Where? Down in my heart. Where?

Down in my heart. I've got the Corners Church enthusiasm down in my heart. Where? Down in my heart to stay."

Deacon Pete had a beautiful voice and a mellow guitar. Everyone loved it when he sang a special. The church favorite was, "I cannot come to the banquet, don't trouble me now. I have married a wife; I have bought me a cow."

The church kids purposely turned the song lyrics around and sang loudly, "I cannot come to the banquet, don't trouble me now, I have bought me a wife; I have married a cow."

The kids misquoted on purpose, but Jim accidentally misquoted a hymn in one of his sermons, "I've built my hope on nothing less than Jesus' blood and righteousness . . . all other ground is *stinking* sand."

When Jim saw grins and heard smothered giggles, he asked Darlene after church what he'd said.

"You said stinking sand instead of sinking sand."

"Well, all other ground really is stinking sand."

## 20
## BOARD MEETINGS

There really wasn't much business to conduct at the early meetings, but the church board held them religiously anyway. Meetings often consisted of laughter and recounting old stories.

"Did we ever tell you about the time we went on vacation together?" Pete and Sam looked at each other and laughed. Betty, Sam's wife, started shaking her head.

"We decided to take a road trip from Michigan to Florida. Well, we didn't have much money, so we got the idea the wives should take their home-canned goods with us to save on food costs," Pete said. Sam started laughing as Pete continued. "They packed boxes of tomatoes, green beans, applesauce, all kinds of stuff, and we tied the boxes on the running boards, because there wasn't enough room for them in the car."

Betty interrupted. "Janet and I told you that you didn't tie those boxes on good enough."

Pete looked at her and grinned. "They stayed on quite some time."

"Not long enough," Betty said.

Between chuckles Sam added, "Made quite a crash when they fell off and broke all over the road."

"What did you do?" Jim asked.

"What could we do? We didn't have a broom or nothing. We kept going."

"Did we ever tell you about the time before we were saved when we tried to keep someone from drowning?" Sam asked Jim.

Jim shook his head, and other board members grinned; they'd heard the story several times. Mary Beth laughed out loud.

"Well, we were driving past the lake when we saw all these people standing at the shore, looking at the water," Sam began.

"We slowed down to take a look," Pete continued, "when Sam says to me, 'Pull over quick! I do believe someone's drowning!'"

Sam nodded. "We were both good swimmers back in the day. So, Pete pulls over, and we go racing through the grass to the crowd standing by the water. 'Move aside!' we yell. 'Who's drowning? We'll rescue them!'"

Pete laughed. "There we were, kicking off our shoes, yanking down our suspenders, and those people were looking at us like we'd lost our minds. Then, one of them says to us, 'No one's drowning. We're trying to have a baptism here.'"

The two would-be rescuers reddened a bit, even all those years later, thinking about how funny they must have looked, hurrying away, wearing one shoe each, holding the other shoe, and pulling up their suspenders.

Jim and the rest of the board members laughed.

The few family members not part of the board waited in the auditorium for the meetings to end so they could go home.

Those meetings would have been a lot shorter without the stories, but those waiting half-wished they were on the board too, so they could be part of the fun. Hearing the stories secondhand was good, but it wasn't quite like being there.

## 21

## COUNT THEM ALL

There was a big push to get the Sunday morning attendance to twenty-five. A church member told Jim about an area pastor who promised to sit on his church roof and swallow a goldfish if their church attendance reached 100. The attendance hit 100, and the pastor did sit on the church roof and swallow a live goldfish. The newspaper sent a reporter to cover this exciting event, and the church got its name in the paper.

Jim desperately wanted not to sit on the church roof and swallow a live goldfish. He loved his fish at home, even if the aquarium had leaked on his Bible and several of his best commentaries. He'd named every goldfish. To sit on a church roof and swallow a goldfish that looked like his own Charles Sturgeon would not only be undignified; it would feel almost like cannibalism. How would he ever again look Charles Sturgeon in his fishy eye?

Jim firmly vetoed the goldfish idea, but he did want the church to grow and had been praying about it. He'd even recently attended a church growth seminar. Professor Nick

Machiavelli had been the keynote speaker, and Jim's old college friend, Todd Pritchard had been there. The three of them had gone out for coffee after one of the meetings.

Todd and Professor Nick Machiavelli were kindred spirits. Jim admired their go get 'em philosophy, but he felt uneasy. *It seemed like all they cared about was nickels and noses—the amount of offering and how many butts were sitting in the pews, but that couldn't be.* Surely the professor he idolized held ministry to a much higher standard than that.

"You're going places, my boy," Professor Nick Machiavelli had said, shaking Todd's hand. "I'll see *you* at the top!" Then he'd smiled his charming smile and patted Jim on the shoulder, still looking at Todd. "Now if we can get this one to start climbing the ladder!"

Todd had smiled broadly. "Thanks, Nick! I keep asking Jim to let me preach at that little going-nowhere church of his. I could light a fire under those people."

*Why does he call him Nick? That's not respectful. I guess Todd thinks he's on an equal rung of the ladder.*

Jim didn't get much out of the church growth seminar except an uneasy feeling he should be doing more than he was. When he came home, he did reluctantly agree to shave his mustache, should the attendance ever hit twenty-five. He'd grown facial hair in a futile attempt to look more mature.

The congregation invited everyone they could think of to church, and Sunday after Sunday the attendance almost reached twenty-five. One hot summer day someone propped the heavy, white wooden doors open to let in humid air. Jim was on point three of his sermon, and people wiggled restlessly in the pews. Grandmas fanned themselves with bulletins. Fred was, as usual, asleep and snoring. Suddenly, through the open doors, a skinny stray dog wandered up the aisle, stopped at the pulpit, and looked at Jim with sad eyes.

"Count that dog!" a lady shouted enthusiastically. "He makes exactly twenty-five."

Jim glared at the lady. He knew she hated his mustache.

"Love one another," he muttered under his breath. That mustache was hot and itchy in the summer anyway, and he could regrow it.

In a grand and humble gesture, Jim nodded at the congregation. "The mustache goes!" he said. The following cheers made him feel less than charitable, but he went home and shaved. Then for the next few weeks he had to endure smirks from the congregation as he preached on serious topics of heaven and hell, and they noticed his upper lip was as white as a bedsheet and sharply contrasted with his tanned face. He studied as much as possible in his lawn chair in the sun for the next few weeks. When winter came, Jim not only regrew the mustache, he added a beard.

## 22
## A SISTER'S VISIT

A visit from out-of-town family often meant an invitation to a church member's home and those farm wives sure could cook! When Jennifer, Darlene's sister, came, an invitation to dinner even included a tour of the farm.

As they walked through fields of ripening grain, Jennifer noticed the cows grazing contentedly.

"I've been reading about cows," she told the farmer. "Yours are black and white. So, they are holster cows, right?"

A trace of a grin tugged at the farmer's lips. "Close. They are Holstein. Good for milking. Over ninety percent of cows on U.S. dairy farms are Holstein cattle."

Jennifer spotted one with horns, fenced off from the others. "Why is that one by herself?"

"He," the farmer corrected. "He's a bull."

"Oh," Jennifer said brightly. "Well, I don't understand. It looks like you have at least one-hundred cows. Why do you have only one bull?"

Jim groaned. "Can you shut your sister up?" he whispered to Darlene.

"Doubtful," she whispered back.

When the farmer didn't answer right away, Jennifer repeated the question. "Why is there only one bull?"

The farmer glanced up, as if asking for help. He cleared his throat. "Most generally, one's all you need."

"All you need for what?"

Jim elbowed Darlene. Darlene pulled Jennifer back to walk with her as Jim stepped up to walk with the farmer.

"I'll explain later," Darlene said to Jennifer.

"Well, I don't know why you can't tell me now. It's a simple question."

The dinner bell rang. Jennifer paused, horrified, next to the milk cans on the porch. Flies buzzed and covered the cheesecloths tied over the cans.

"They better not expect me to drink any of that milk!" Her whisper was a bit too loud.

"That's not for drinking. It will be picked up and made into cheese." Darlene tried to whisper quietly.

"What?"

Supper tasted even better than it smelled. They had roast beef, steaming mashed potatoes and gravy, bread and butter pickles, warm homemade bread, strawberry freezer jam, and for dessert, cherry pie and ice cream. Fortunately, the drink choices were iced tea or lemonade, so Jennifer didn't say anything about the milk, and in enjoying the food, she forgot to ask any more questions about the bull.

On the way home Darlene said, "Hey Jennifer, to answer the question you asked about why there were so many cows but only one bull, do you remember the Bible story about Solomon who had seven-hundred wives, three-hundred concubines, and who knows how many kids?"

"Sure, but I don't see what that has to do with one bull and one-hundred cows."

"Yes," Darlene said firmly, "you do."

Jennifer thought with a puzzled frown; then she groaned and slid lower in her seat. "I can't go to church with you tomorrow," she said, blushing. "I don't think I can ever face that farmer again."

~

DARLENE SMILES as she thinks of her three sisters, the sister reunions, the laughter, the long phone conversations, and the shared joys and sorrows. Only Lou and Jennifer are left now; God had called Eve Home to Heaven. Eve had been a light to the other three, showing them how to live and even how to die. Darlene closes her eyes and pictures the faces of her beautiful sisters. They're laughing and young, and they throw their arms around her in a group hug.

"Someday soon," Darlene says, "soon."

## A TOUGH LIFE LESSON

When people remarked Corners Church must be a lot like *Little House on the Prairie*, Jim and Darlene smiled. In some wonderful ways, it was. But people at the Corners had the same problems as people everywhere; there just weren't as many people.

In years to come, Jim and Darlene would face every type of counseling. One of their earliest counseling experiences was like being dropped into an icy lake in the winter. The shock, once they survived it, taught them a needed lesson. They learned to know when they were in over their heads.

They should have known right away to send Jessica to a more experienced, trained counselor. When she invited them over, they went gladly, expecting the usual good refreshments and interesting conversation. Jessica was a kind, godly woman who lovingly cared for her elderly mother who lived with her.

Jessica smiled her usual beautiful smile. "Sit down," she urged them. "I don't have any refreshments today. I have something very important to talk to you about. Frank is at work, and he didn't understand this at all, but I'm hoping you will."

With great excitement, Jessica pulled out a large blackboard on wheels. "I'm God," she abruptly said. "I'm Jesus. I'm the Holy Spirit, and I can prove it."

Jessica animatedly wrote words and drew complex diagrams on the chalkboard. None of them made any sense. She talked on and on, and Jim and Darlene looked at each other with wide eyes when Jessica turned to the blackboard.

When Jessica stopped to catch her breath, Jim gently explained she couldn't be God.

"I thought you of all people would understand," she said angrily. "Well, come outside with me. I can prove it."

Jim and Darlene followed Jessica outside.

"Here, kitty, kitty, kitty," she called.

The barn cats came running.

"See?" she said triumphantly. "That proves it. See how the cats come when I call them?"

"What's wrong with her?" Darlene asked Jim on the way home. "Do you think she's had some kind of psychotic break?"

"I don't know," Jim answered, "but I'm calling Frank at work."

"Jessica's had mental problems before," Frank told Jim. "This time it seems worse. She hasn't slept for days."

A week later the phone rang around 2:00 a.m.

"No!" Jim exclaimed. "Please, don't do that. We'll be right over."

"Hurry and get dressed," Jim told Darlene. "Frank's working the night shift, and Jessica's alone with her mother. She says she's going to kill her and then herself. She's holding a knife to her mom's throat. I told her we'd come right over, but first I'm calling Frank and the police."

The police ordered Jim not to go to Jessica's. The officers got to the house about the same time Frank did. Jessica was calm, serene, smiling, and holding a large knife to her mother's throat.

The police were able to convince Jessica to put down the knife. They took her to a hospital where doctors gave her medication that made her sleep for seventy-two hours. When she woke, trained counselors treated her.

After a long time, Jessica came home. Jim and Darlene knew her for many years after that, and she never had another episode.

## 24

## FRANKIE COMES TO CALL

Frankie, Darlene's friend from community club, was crying when Darlene opened the door.
"What's wrong? Is Toby or one of the kids sick?"
Through tears, Frankie spilled her heart. She'd fallen in love with her boss, a married man who had three young children.
Darlene listened and let Frankie talk.
"Toby rarely goes to my church with me. He never wants to talk about God or spiritual things. If he stops watching TV long enough, he only wants to talk about his truck, guns, hunting, or fishing. We never talk about anything important." Frankie blew her nose and looked at Darlene. "My boss actually listens to me and cares about how I'm feeling. We talk about everything. I want to tell him I'm in love with him."
"He doesn't know how you feel?"
Frankie shook her head. "I don't think so, but I want him to know."
"I'm sorry you're hurting, but if you do this, you could ruin

your marriage and his. Think about your family and his. And I'm guessing you know exactly what God thinks about this."

"But I love him; I really love him," Frankie said, crying again.

Darlene's heart ached for Frankie. She hugged her, but she knew she had to be firm, as hard as it was. "Love is more than an emotion; it's a choice. Didn't you promise before God to love Toby?"

"Yes, but what do I do about how I feel?"

"You don't have to let your feelings be in charge; you can choose to do the right thing."

"But I don't think I can stand to live like this; I have to do something with these feelings."

"You can do something. Quit your job. And pour all that love you have into praying God will bless your boss's marriage and yours."

Frankie shook her head and left crying. She wasn't at the next community club meeting and never came again. Darlene often wondered what Frankie had decided. She thought for sure in such a small community she'd hear something about Frankie or run into her somewhere, but it didn't happen.

Twenty years later, Darlene saw Frankie after a school play. Her hair was gray, and there was a soft contentment in her eyes. She and Toby held hands with a skipping grandchild.

She nodded at Darlene and mouthed, "Thank you."

"Do you know that lady, Grandma? We should go talk to her."

Frankie smiled at Darlene. "I don't need to go talk to her, honey. She can hear what my heart is saying."

"I can hear what your heart is saying too, Grandma. It says you love me and Grandpa Toby. Your heart is happy."

"You're right, honey. My heart is very happy."

## 25

## SPONTANEOUS NOT SCHEDULED

Darlene looks at Jim, sleeping so soundly, and thinks about the countless nights they'd gone without sleep to be there for the people they'd loved. She remembers the time they'd prayed in the middle of the night with a dad whose teenage son had run away. He'd eventually returned but not every situation had ended so well.

She recalls many nights when they'd jumped out of bed, dressed quickly, and hurried to a hospital or a home. Sometimes the people recovered, and sometimes they were healed forever as they opened their eyes and found themselves at the feet of Jesus.

*That's what you'll do soon, honey,* Darlene thinks, looking at the man she loves.

She remembers some of their counseling sessions. Some were humorous, in retrospect.

∽

ONE MAN CAME to talk in the early evening and stayed all night. He'd asked Darlene to fix him breakfast before he went to work in the morning.

Another time, a neighbor stopped by to ask for advice while Jim and Darlene were eating lunch.

"Do you want to have lunch with us?" Darlene asked. "We'd love to have you."

"No, thank you," the neighbor replied, as he continued talking, standing in the kitchen while the food got cold.

After several more minutes of standing and talking, Darlene repeated her request. The neighbor again politely refused and kept talking.

After almost an hour, Darlene was getting tired of standing. "Are you sure you won't join us for lunch?"

"Well, okay!" the neighbor responded enthusiastically. "I have a rule; I never accept an invitation unless it's given three times. If someone asks me three times, I know they mean it!"

He took off his coat, handed it to Darlene, and sat at the table. She warmed lunch, and they all lived happily ever after.

Usually, counseling sessions were spontaneous and not scheduled. People often asked to talk after the morning or evening services. As soon as the kids got old enough, they hiked home, so they didn't have to amuse themselves at church for hours.

"You shouldn't let people take advantage of you like that." Professor Nick Machiavelli scolded Jim on the phone. "Set counseling hours on specific days, and tell people they have to come then and only then."

"Thanks for your advice," Jim replied.

They wouldn't take that advice. That would be like telling a crying son or daughter to come to the office next Wednesday at noon. Jim was surprised to realize the people at Corners Church were starting to feel like family.

"Maybe we counsel at odd hours," Jim said, "but at least we don't have all the committee meetings larger churches have. We don't have a single one. What's that thing Sam says about committees?"

Darlene laughed. "A committee is a group of people who can't do nothin' alone, so they get together and waste time deciding nothin' can be done."

## A LATE NIGHT CALL

When the phone rang at 10:00 p.m., Jim and Darlene looked warily at each other. A late evening call was seldom good news.

"Pastor, I know it's late," Gary said, "but I'm desperate. Mandy wants to leave me. I've tried everything. She says she'll come talk to you first, but she's going tonight. Can we come over?"

Darlene hurried to take off her pajamas and get dressed. *I hope the kids sleep through this.*

Gary and Mandy liked tea, and Darlene hurried to brew a pot before they knocked on the door. Darlene hugged Mandy; it was like trying to hug a board. Gary's face was red, his eyes swollen from crying. *I don't think that one box of Kleenex on the coffee table is going to be enough.* She put her hand on Gary's shoulder in wordless sympathy.

It was a long night. Mandy refused to say a word. She rejected the tea too. Darlene was surprised; Mandy had never declined a cup of tea. Gary didn't want tea either. He said he couldn't swallow it.

As Mandy stared without blinking at some spot on the wall, Gary explained what had happened. "I thought we were happy," he said brokenly.

Darlene glanced at Mandy. No expression. *She looks like a store mannequin.*

"About two months ago we were at the girls' game, and we ran into Mandy's high school boyfriend. She hadn't seen him for twenty years. She introduced him to me, and we talked quite a while. Seemed like a nice guy—at the time," Gary said bitterly. "Come to find out, she met him at a motel the next day when I was at work and the girls were at school. She wants to leave me and the girls."

He turned to Mandy, who was sitting as far as possible from him on the couch, her hands folded in her lap. "Please, Mandy, I love you," he begged, crying again. "I forgive you. Please don't leave me." He moved closer and tried to put his arms around her.

Mandy's expression didn't change. She blinked a few times, sat with her back rigidly straight, and kept staring at the invisible spot on the wall.

Jim and Darlene tried everything. They read the Bible; they prayed. They told Mandy they loved her. The Kleenex box was empty, and Darlene handed Gary a roll of toilet paper.

"Don't do it, Mandy," Darlene said. "You're going to jump right off a cliff and take those girls with you."

Mandy didn't respond. At 3:00 a.m., she said the first words she'd said all night. "Ok, Gary, I said I'd come, and I came. Can we leave now?" she asked, her voice flat and expressionless.

Jim and Darlene stayed up awhile longer, holding hands, asking God to speak to Mandy's heart, since their words hadn't reached her.

"Maybe she'll think about the verses you read her and change her mind."

Jim shook his head. "I don't think so."

When Gary and Mandy got home, Gary fell asleep out of sheer exhaustion. When he woke at 6:00 a.m. to go to work, Mandy was gone.

Mandy went to live with her boyfriend and filed for divorce. Gary got custody of the girls; she said she didn't want them. Years later, Gary met and married a lovely woman. Mandy's boyfriend grew tired of her and dumped her.

Darlene saw Mandy sometimes after that at Market Home. Darlene smiled and tried to talk. Mandy looked at an invisible spot over Darlene's head and said nothing.

Not all stories end happily ever after.

## 27
## SOME VERY SPECIAL MEETINGS

Excitement was in the air because the county churches had decided to hold special meetings at the fairgrounds. Most of the participating churches were small, like Corners Church, so money was in short supply. Each church took special offerings for weeks to cover the expenses of the meetings. The pastors met frequently, discussing who to ask to come preach. They decided on Reverend Naught, a well-known speaker, and contacted him. They hoped he would agree to come for a love offering, but he insisted on a guaranteed sum. The pastors swallowed hard, went back to their small churches, and asked for more money.

The pastors nominated Jim to drive two hours to pick up Reverend Naught at the airport in Grand Rapids. The reverend complained most of the way back to the fairgrounds. Why had they sent someone with such a small car to transport him? Who'd ever heard of driving a special speaker in a car with no air-conditioning? He questioned Jim about the expected size of the crowd and grumbled that he hoped the endeavor would be worth his time. Jim could think of a few things to say, but he prayed silently instead.

"Kind of a quiet sort, aren't you? I can't imagine too many people come to hear you preach. How many people come to your church?"

"Twenty-five, maybe thirty on a good Sunday."

Reverend Naught snorted with laughter. "And you think *that's* worth your time?"

"Well, now," Jim said with a trace of a grin, "didn't Jesus often preach to twelve? And one of them didn't get a thing out of it."

"Humph!"

Jim smiled, but Reverend Naught's remarks stung. They reminded him once again of the rungs on the ladder he'd often been advised to climb.

It was a long two-and-one-half hour drive to the fairgrounds. Jim later told Darlene it felt more like twenty hours.

"How did you keep from getting furious with him?" Darlene asked.

"Well, I mostly felt sorry for him. Seemed like all he cared about was nickels and noses. Was he for sure going to get the money we'd promised him? He hoped we'd done good advertising so he'd have a good crowd. I prayed God would use him in spite of himself."

Reverend Naught rolled his eyes when he saw the sparsely populated stands at the fairgrounds. "Isn't this a county-wide meeting? I expected a better turn out, even in this hick town." He frowned at Jim. "Don't you have a family? Where is your family?"

Jim nodded at the grassy section next to the stands. "My wife and kids are sitting down there on a blanket."

"What!" Reverend Naught's frown deepened. "That isn't a

good example. I suggest you go down there, and tell your wife to come fill an empty seat in these stands."

Jim ignored him. He had a hunch the sermon was likely to be lengthy, and he knew Darlene had her hands full keeping the kids occupied, even on a blanket. Keeping them quiet in the stands was more than he would ask her to do.

Reverend Naught preached for ninety minutes. He paced. He roared. He whispered. He cried and wiped his face often with a large, white handkerchief. At last, he gave the altar call. No one came forward. He extended the altar call to the point of embarrassment. Still, no one moved. Jim wasn't surprised. Country folk can tell a glue factory horse from a thoroughbred a mile away.

Reverend Naught was in a foul mood on the way back to the airport. "I've never preached in such a hard-hearted place. Don't ask me to come preach here again, because I'll have nothing to do with this county."

Jim drove quietly. He didn't tell Reverend Naught he didn't have to worry about another invitation.

Finally, they got to the city. "Take me to a restaurant before we go to the airport," Reverend Naught demanded. "And take me somewhere nice. I don't eat at any greasy spoons."

Reverend Naught chose the restaurant and ordered steak, the most expensive item on the menu. Jim ordered a glass of water and fries. He used all his grocery and gas money for the week and had barely enough money to cover the bill and the tip.

"What did you say when he asked why you only ordered water and fries?" Darlene asked when a weary Jim arrived home.

"I don't think he even noticed." Jim yawned as Darlene made him a sandwich. "He was too busy enjoying his steak."

"Well he better enjoy steak here," Darlene said, "because

when he gets to heaven, I know who will be having the glass of water and fries. If he gets to heaven," she added darkly.

"Now, Darlene—"

Darlene interrupted him with a hug and a kiss. "Do you know what a good man you are?" she asked. "Probably not. I better enjoy your company here, because when I get to heaven, I'll probably have to share a glass of water with Reverend Naught."

"Don't forget about God's grace—"

"Shh." Darlene smiled. "I know about grace. It's my favorite word. Now, eat your sandwich, and come to bed. It's been a long day."

Jim didn't argue. After ten hours of driving plus the time at the fairgrounds, he was more than ready for bed.

∽

DARLENE'S STARTLED from her memories when Jim reaches for her hand from his hospital bed.

"Come to bed, babe. It's late. Don't be long."

"I won't," she promises. "You sleep now."

## DOG ADVENTURES

A country pastor quickly learns the dangers of lurking dogs. Jim was passing out information about Vacation Bible School. He pounded on the door of a farmhouse, but no one was home. He turned to leave when an ominous looking dog came slinking out of the shadows. You really have to watch out for the ones that don't bark. Without a sound, the dog lunged, sinking his teeth into Jim's leg, right above the top of the cowboy boots he usually wore. He shouted a few slang words at the dog that he didn't use in front of the deacons and shook his leg. He was afraid to cuff the dog on the head, fearing it might let go of his leg and go for his hand.

Jim looked up. "Lord, if this is how you treat your country preachers, it's no wonder you don't have any more of them! Please, if you've ever helped me, help me now!"

In what he thought was a sure answer to his prayer, a truck pulled into the driveway, and a lady got out and started walking toward him. She stopped, looking alarmed when she saw the dog.

"Lady," Jim begged, as he felt warm blood trickling down his leg, "please call off your dog."

"I don't live here," the lady replied. "I stopped to ask for directions, and that isn't my dog. I've never seen him before in my life."

"Not funny, Lord," Jim muttered.

"What's that you say?"

"Nothing."

The two of them looked at each other helplessly.

"What are you going to do?" she asked.

"Why don't you go see if you can find a neighbor to come help me?" Jim asked, not saying *preferably one with a shot gun*.

She was only too happy to escape to the safety of her truck, but before she could back out of the driveway, another truck pulled in next to hers, and a woman jumped out.

"Buster!" she yelled at the top of powerful lungs. "Let go!" The dog let go of Jim's leg and slunk back into the shadows, tail between his legs.

"Who are you? And what are you doing here?" She glared at Jim.

"I'm a pastor, and I came to invite you to Corner's Church," he said, wondering why she didn't ask if he was okay.

"Church and me don't get along," she said abruptly, as she edged past him and went into the house. Before she slammed the door, she stuck her head out and said, "You preachers ought to have enough sense to read the sign." The door slammed.

That's when he saw the Beware of Dog sign nailed to the side of the house. As he limped away to go to the doctor, he wondered about her remark of *you* preachers. Others must have come calling before him. Apparently, that was one country dog that had a taste for clergy.

## 29

# THE DOG DAYS OF SUMMER

The summer day was perfect; a rarity in Michigan where Michiganders usually complain it's too hot, too cold, too wet, or too dry. This day was just right.

"I wonder if this is what the weather's like in heaven," Darlene remarked.

"I wouldn't be surprised." Jim smiled at her.

Her heart still did a little flip when his eyes lit up like that.

They were handing out Vacation Bible School flyers. After Jim's last experience handing out flyers, they'd decided maybe it was better to go in pairs. Jim's leg still throbbed when he thought about that dog. They took turns at each house, knocking on a door, or chatting with someone out in a yard. Covering the three-mile radius around the church took many days.

Jim pulled up a long dirt driveway to the back door of a house. Only city people knock on the front door of a farmhouse.

"You have to get out here," he said abruptly, turning away from Darlene and staring out his window.

"Why? I got out at the last house. It's your turn." She glanced around the yard. "Oh, you're afraid of the dog."

"It's not the dog."

*What?* Darlene was puzzled. Looking closer she noticed a young woman sunbathing, lying on her stomach in a lawn chair. She obviously was not dressed for visitors.

"Never mind," Jim said. "Let's leave."

"We can't. She's waving at me. I'm getting out."

The young woman was friendly and surprisingly not at all embarrassed to be caught wearing too few clothes. She remained lying on her stomach talking to Darlene and kept her large dog close to her chair. Darlene wondered why she kept such a tight hold on her dog's leash, but she found out when she tried to hand the woman a flyer. The dog went crazy, snarling, barking, and lunging at her. The under-dressed lady hung unto the leash with both hands, as the big dog spun the lawn chair ninety degrees.

"I guess I better go," Darlene said.

"Maybe," the lady replied.

They were both laughing. Halfway to the car Darlene turned back. "Nice meeting you," she hollered, still laughing.

"Maybe I'll visit your church sometime," the lady said.

"I hope you do."

Darlene climbed into the car. Jim was still studiously looking out of his window in the opposite direction.

"So, what happened?" he asked once he'd backed out of the driveway.

"Well," Darlene replied, "her dog almost ate me, and you didn't come to my rescue.

And she said she might visit our church sometime. Isn't that great?"

"I don't know." Jim sighed. "I guess it depends on what she wears."

## 30
## THE WILD DOGS

People think they can drop off any animal they get tired of near a farm, and someone will care for it. Country people adopt many pets cruel, uncaring owners abandon, but they can't care for all of them.

Jim and Darlene adopted so many stray animals that Darlene once dreamt someone left an elephant tied to their mailbox.

Some dogs, who don't find homes, form packs, turn wild, and attack sheep, chickens, anything they can get for food.

Jim and Darlene were visiting neighbors around the church to invite them to a service when they pulled into a driveway and heard howling dogs and what sounded like a child moaning in agony. They rushed out of the car, ran behind the house, and discovered a calf tied to a rope with three wild dogs attacking it, chewing into its sides.

Adrenaline pumping, they forgot they were afraid of strange dogs and ran, shouting, waving their arms. The dogs snarled but fled. No one was home, and Darlene flatly refused to leave the calf. What if the dogs returned? She looked at the calf helplessly, and it looked back at her. What could she do for it? Blood was streaming down its sides.

"We can't stay here all day," Jim said, "and we can't leave one of us while the other goes for help. Those dogs might attack just one of us."

"I guess we both have to stay then."

"We should pray," Jim said. And they did.

After what seemed like forever, the farmer pulled into the driveway. He thanked them and ran to call the vet and get help for the calf. Surprisingly, the calf survived.

Jim later preached at Corner's Church: "That helpless calf being attacked by those dogs broke our hearts. It made me think; that's how Jesus must have felt about us. There we were, tied by sin to a stake, with the devil chewing into us, ready to make his killing lunge, when Jesus said, 'Oh no you don't. They're mine.' He gave His life for ours and let Himself be nailed to a cross. He took our sins into His heart. He felt our guilt and shame and took our punishment. When He died, I imagine the demons howled with glee, the way those wild dogs snarled at that calf. Resurrection morning told a different story. The demons slunk into the shadows then. The sin that ties us to the stake is gone when we accept His sacrifice as ours. We are forever free; rejoice in your freedom!"

Nobody fell asleep in that sermon, not even Fred, and he was famous for snoring through sermons.

## 31

## THE OLD DOG

"I have flyers about the county-wide youth rally at the fairgrounds," Jim said to Mrs. Kregel, a pastor's wife from a neighboring church. "Do you folks want some to pass out at your church?"

The two were chatting in an aisle at the small Market Home, a grocery store where you were sure to meet your neighbors. Back in the day, you didn't go to Market Home if you were in a hurry. There was no running in there just to grab one item and scoot. You had to allow chatting time.

You also had to allow time for the always-friendly-never-in-a-hurry clerks. They didn't care if the line extended to the back of the store. As they slowly punched the price of each item into the register, they still asked you how your brother-in-law's Aunt Sophia was doing after her hip replacement. At first, the slow speed drove Darlene crazy, but in years to come, after she became so country herself you'd think she'd been born at the Corners, Market Home became her favorite store.

"Sure, we'd love some flyers! Dylan is really excited about

that youth rally. Bring them by the house. If we aren't home, leave them on the kitchen table. We don't lock our doors."

After more chatting about the weather, gardens, and the Kregel's nine children, the two said goodbye.

A few days later Jim stopped by the Kregel's house. No one was home, so he followed instructions, went in, and left the flyers on the table. He was leaving when he heard a bark and saw a dark furry lunge.

"Oh no, not again!" he yelled. "Lord, if you keep letting these dogs attack me, I think I'll quit the ministry and go back to working in the factory."

As he furiously shook his leg, trying to dislodge the dog, he thought about his past factory job. After Bible college, he'd worked at American Motors before coming as pastor to Corner's Church. When he'd left that job with its excellent salary and benefits, his coworkers had asked how much the church would pay him. He'd told them.

They'd laughed. "Good luck living on that," they'd jeered. "You'll be back in six months."

No, he wasn't going back to American Motors. He was learning to love Corners Church. But why did God have to keep blessing Him with all these dogs?

"*In everything give thanks,*" the verse came to mind.

"I'll thank you, you jerk of a dog," he yelled in his most commanding voice, "to let go of my leg!"

Jim was shocked when the dog let go. The dog and the preacher stared at each other as the preacher backed out of the door.

A few days later, Jim again saw Mrs. Kregel at the Market Home. With nine children, she had to shop often.

"Did you find the flyers on your table?" Jim asked.

"We did find them. Thank you!"

"Well maybe you shouldn't tell people to go in your house when you aren't home, because your dog bit me."

Mrs. Kregel bent over laughing. "Oh Jim," she said, between laughs, "our dog couldn't possibly have bitten you. She's so old, she doesn't even have any teeth."

Indignant, Jim pulled up the leg of his jeans and showed her his black and blue calf.

She still couldn't stop laughing. "You notice your skin isn't broken. My dog didn't bite you. She may have gummed you a little bit!"

## ADDITIONS

"We're all used to the outhouse, don't you know," Sam said, "but maybe our visitors won't feel the same way we do. If we want our congregation to grow, we should think about adding on a bathroom with indoor plumbing."

"Where would we put it?" Deacon Pete asked.

"I've been thinking. If we bumped out the space in the backroom that's part of the entryway to the basement, I think we could fit a small bathroom in there."

No one ever accused Corners Church of hasty decisions. The board talked about and prayed about new bathroom for quite some time. The main question was how to pay for it. Corners Church had a strict policy they never violated: Don't borrow money.

One day, Deacon Pete saw a garage sale advertised. He called the other board members and Jim, and they set off on an adventure to buy a used toilet for the planned indoor bathroom. They had quite a good time at that garage sale. They left with a furnace, duct work, registers, door, sink, toilet, plastic water lines, and kittens. The kittens weren't for the church; Deacon Ken took them home.

At last, the men completed the bathroom, and no one was happier than Darlene. She wanted to make a sign for the unisex bathroom door with the three musketeer's motto: *One for all, and all for one,* but Jim refused her offer.

Other additions came later, a second bathroom and a nursery, an addition to the tiny auditorium, two more Sunday school rooms, and near the end of their ministry a fellowship hall that had running water, more bathrooms, a larger nursery, and more Sunday school rooms.

But none of the additions were celebrated with any more enthusiasm than the new indoor one-for-all bathroom. Suddenly, all the children had to go at least once during every service. Some of the kids forgot to close the door and sang loudly as they used the new facilities. That didn't bother anyone. Jim was oblivious to everything when he preached, and the church members smiled tolerantly. This was, after all, Corners Church, where love covered a multitude of sins, and noises.

Darlene thought it would be fun to have a church fellowship and toast marshmallows in a grand burning of the outhouse. Jim didn't much like that idea. He'd seen the underside of that outhouse when he'd helped Pete turn it over and had gotten stung by bees. One day, Jim disappeared for a while and came back smelling like smoke and other things.

"Where have you been?" Darlene asked, wrinkling her nose.

"I went to church and burned the outhouse. And no bees stung me!"

"I thought we were going to have a fellowship and toast marshmallows when we burned it!" Darlene protested.

"And I thought we weren't," Jim grinned and went to take a shower.

Darlene watched him leave with her hands on her hips. She'd been trying to tell him what to do since they'd been preschoolers. It still hadn't worked.

∼

DARLENE LEANS over the hospital bed. "Honey, when's it my day to be the boss?"

Jim smiles. "Today," he whispers. "You can be the boss today."

*If I really could be boss, I'd tell you not to leave me. Not yet.*

## 33
## LESSONS IN HUMILITY

Before the first addition was built, Corners Church had no room for a nursery. This was sometimes good, sometimes bad, but always interesting. On the plus side, the babies learned to sing hymns as soon as they could talk. Darlene knew the negative side well. She cared for all four of their babies alone in church because, for some reason, Jim seemed to think it might be a slight distraction to preach with a screaming baby in his arms. Darlene often left church feeling as exhausted as a participant in a wrestling match.

If Jim and Darlene learned humility, their children had a lot to do with it. April once scowled and stomped her two-year-old foot before the service started. "Don't like church!"

Right then a sweet older couple entered the auditorium.

White-haired Mrs. Hartsell smiled at April. "Oh, that's because it's hard to sit still when you're so little. But you like Hartsells, don't you?"

"No!" April hollered loudly and firmly. "Don't like Hartzo!" She began pointing at others as Darlene hurried to remove her. "Don't like Smith. Don't like 'nother one Smith. Don't like

Fee. Don't like 'nother one Fee." Darlene eventually managed to get April out the door.

Another birthday rendered April easier to handle, a good thing, because by then baby brother Jimmy added his own contributions to the services. Once he yanked his glass bottle out of his mouth and slung it in a neat overhand. It whizzed so close to Mary Beth's head she could feel the breeze. The bottle, still unbroken, rolled under the pews, following the uncarpeted boards almost to the front of the auditorium—clunk, clunk, clunk-clunk. Grinning, people handed the bottle back over the pews to where Darlene sat in the back.

After Davey arrived to add to the confusion, a well-meaning church member suggested Darlene might be a better example to others if she sat up front. Darlene agreed, against her better judgment, to give it a try. Davey's behavior during the service graduated from bad to worse until a fast exit was the only solution.

As soon as Darlene stood, Davey anticipated what was coming and hollered, "No! No! I'll be good!" He continued shouting even after Darlene was all the way to the back and out the door.

Jim later told her that even after the heavy wooden door was shut, he could still hear the faint echo of, "No! No! I'll be good!"

Jimmy was about five when a missionary visited their home for the day. It had been a long day; Jimmy was tired, and when warnings didn't work, Jim took him to another room to correct him. It was almost time for the evening service. All afternoon Jimmy had admired the missionary's Stetson hat, so the missionary, trying to make him feel better, asked him if he'd like to go get his hat for him.

Between sobs Jimmy replied, "Go ... get ... your ... own .. . stinkin ... hat."

As the kids grew, Jimmy became the quiet peacemaker, unless one of his siblings pushed him too far. One day, when Jim and Darlene were gone, April did a little too much pushing, and Jimmy told her exactly what he thought of her. April grabbed a flimsy plastic TV tray and started chasing him. When Jimmy ran outside, April followed him and whacked him over the head with it.

Instantly, Jimmy collapsed into Darlene's flower bed.

April thought she'd killed him.

"Davey, what are we going to do? I think he's dead! Should I call an ambulance? Mom and Dad are going to kill me."

"I don't think he's dead. Look, he's breathing."

When Davey couldn't rouse Jimmy or get him to move, he got worried too. "I think you really hurt him bad! You better call an ambulance!"

April started sobbing.

Jimmy stood and calmly brushed off leaves and dirt. "There. I guess that'll teach you not to go around hitting people over the head with TV trays."

Of course, everyone at church heard about it. The boys thought it was too funny not to tell.

∼

DARLENE CHUCKLES SOFTLY, remembering so many things the kids had said and done that hadn't seemed as funny then as they did now. *How had they grown up so fast? Where had the years gone? Every parent wonders that.*

Did their children and grandchildren have any idea how much it meant to them that they all still loved the Lord and attended church? Some of them still attended Corners Church. Darlene thinks of a verse dear to her heart. *I have no greater joy than to know my children walk in truth.*

## 34

## CANNONBALL!

Corners Church had no baptistery, so they used a lake. In an early baptism, Jim baptized his older two children and a teenage convert. The teenager had never seen a baptism and had no idea you were supposed to be serious and reverent, and it hadn't occurred to Jim to tell him.

Jim called the teenager to come into the lake first. Instead of wading out into the water, the young man ran down the dock and did a cannonball, soaking Jim. Church people on the shore chuckled.

Jim asked the teen the usual questions: "Have you accepted Jesus as your Savior from sin? Is it your desire to follow Him in believer's baptism?"

The young man nodded vigorously.

"Upon this, your public confession of faith in Jesus Christ, I baptize you in the name of the Father, the Son, and the Holy Spirit."

After Jim brought the young man up out of the water, he expected him to walk to shore where he'd be greeted with handshakes and hugs, but no. He stayed in the water doing the backstroke and spitting fountains of water, much to the entertainment of the watching congregation, while Jim baptized the others.

"Why didn't I think to baptize him last?" Jim groaned later to Darlene.

"Well, it was a baptism everyone will remember!"

In later years, they stopped using the lake and started using a baptistery in an area church. Once, the pastor of the church forgot to heat the baptismal water. As Corners Church families occupied the pews of the borrowed church, they sat solemnly and quietly. There was always, okay, *usually*, something precious and holy about a baptismal service.

Jim stood in the icy water, shivering. He'd warned those being baptized that the water was cold. He reached out his hand to help one boy walk down the steps into the water.

"Holy cow this is cold!" the boy yelled. That service wasn't quite as solemn as some of the others.

Many years later, when the kids were grown, Jim climbed out of a baptismal and was barely out of sight when the congregation heard a loud noise. Jim and Darlene's son was leading the singing.

Davey paused when he heard the noise. "I hope that wasn't my dad falling!" he said.

It was.

## OLD MAN WINTER

Jim opens his eyes. "What day is this?" His speech is clear. "If it's Sunday, I want to get to church early. I need to fix that loose board on the ramp before Grandma Roseheart or someone else trips on it." He closes his eyes, and then suddenly opens them again. "What month is it?"

"It's July," Darlene replies.

"Oh good," he says, slurring his words. "I'm glad it's not January. I'm too tired to shovel at church today."

"Me too!" She shakes her head, remembering a long-ago January. *Had it been the blizzard of 1978?*

∼

OLD MAN WINTER came with a vengeance that year, and he came to stay. Snow piled up, and blizzard winds howled. The snow whipped across the empty fields and settled in the road. Some parts of the fields were almost clear, but there was a good four feet or more of snow in the roads. The snowplows tried repeatedly to clear the road, to no avail. That wind-driven snow was packed solid.

Snowed in, Jim, Darlene, and the kids ate what they had in the freezer. Thanks to their generous church family, they had a plethora of steaks, hamburgers, and roasts. They also had all of Darlene's frozen and canned fruits and vegetables, but they quickly ran out of store goods like pasta, rice, flour, and sugar. Soon the cereal was gone too. They ate beef for breakfast, lunch, and supper.

"I'm sick of steak, I want a casserole!" April complained.

"Mac and cheese!" Jimmy added, pounding his spoon.

"Kids," Darlene said, "lots of people in this world never even get to eat a steak."

"Well I wish we were one of them!" April replied.

Jim and Darlene looked at each other, amused, and secretly agreeing. Beef three meals a day was too much of a good thing.

More than food, they missed people. When a snowmobile sunk in the deep snow in their front yard, Jim helped the driver dig it out, and Darlene invited him in to warm up with a hot chocolate.

"What's open in Hudson?" she asked.

He shook his head. "Nothin'."

When the plows began to clear the main roads, Darlene and Jim's side road was still impassable. They hadn't been able to have church or get out for three weeks. When someone pounded on the door, the kids ran to open it. *Who could it be?* Darlene wondered. Their road was still solidly blocked.

Sam stood there, grinning, his face covered with snow. "I parked on Squawfield Road and walked in," he said. "Pastor, I came to bring you your pay. I figured with three weeks of no church, you might be needing some money."

Jim was shocked. Back then, the church was still too small

to have any money in the bank. There had been no church services, hence no offerings. Where had the money come from?

"It's okay," Jim told Sam. "We haven't been able to get out to spend money anyway. But I'm curious. Where did you get the money?" *Had it come right out of Sam's pocket?* Jim wouldn't be surprised.

Sam shook the snow off his coat and laughed. "I went to the church families who live on main roads and asked them, 'You got any money to give the preacher?' And I got this." He shoved a wad of bills into Jim's hand.

Bless Sam, bless them all, those first and most faithful friends from Corners Church. They never gave Jim and Darlene a reason to doubt their love.

Darlene often prayed Christina Rosetti's prayer for them, "O Lord Jesus, when Thou rewardest the saints, remember, we beseech thee, for good, those who have surrounded us with holy influences, borne with us, forgiven us, sacrificed themselves for us, loved us; nor forget any."

"I got an idea too," Sam said. "The church road is still as packed with snow as your road is, so we can't have church there. But if you'll walk out to Squawfield, I could pick you up on Sunday, and we could have church at Ken's for those who can get out. His road is plowed now."

Sunday came, and with it, the bitter winds increased. Jim and Darlene walked through the fields because there was less snow there than on the road. Jim trudged ahead, carrying a heavy box of hymnals in one arm and pulling a sled with Jimmy on it.

Darlene carried Davey and held April's hand as they trudged through the snow. Even with heads lowered, the bitter wind was almost unbearable. Tears froze on cheeks.

"I can't do this!" Darlene hollered to Jim over the wind. "I'm going home."

"No!" he yelled back. "We're closer to Squawfield Road than we are to the house. I can see Sam's car. He's waiting for us. Just keep walking."

Darlene tried to remember stories she'd heard about people in other countries walking miles through all kinds of weather to go to church. It didn't help. She'd never wanted to go to church less. She looked with pity at six-year-old April who was sobbing.

Once they got to Ken and Ellen's they thawed out, and Darlene's cold heart warmed. It was wonderful to see church family. Ken and Ellen were good friends. Ken was the youngest deacon, and years to come would prove him a wise, faithful man.

When the passing of years left Ken the oldest deacon, Jim and Darlene reminisced with him when they visited him in the hospital after a fall from his planter left him with three broken ribs.

Years earlier, when they had all still been young, Darlene had fallen down a flight of stairs. Ken and Ellen had given her a spring from a ball point pen and a note explaining the spring was a "helper-upper" she should attach to whatever part of her anatomy was going to hit the floor first if she planned to keep falling.

"I guess you're the one who needs the 'helper-upper' now," Jim said.

The laughter in that hospital room probably didn't help Ken's broken ribs as they recalled the time Ellen had sent over a peach pie but had forgotten the sugar, and Darlene had invited them for supper a few weeks later and forgotten the sugar in the Kool-Aid. Ken had accused Darlene of trying to get back that cup of sugar Ellen had forgotten.

Darlene wasn't laughing when they walked home from Squawfield Road in the winter storm. It wasn't as bad as walking out had been because the wind was at their backs. Still, Darlene wondered if she should give Jim the silent treatment the rest of the afternoon, just on the principle of the thing.

∼

Darlene gets out of her chair next to Jim's hospital bed and walks to stretch her stiff legs. She chuckles, remembering that snowy day. The silent treatment hadn't lasted long; it was one thing she'd never been able to master. When she'd been a little girl, her dad had offered her a whole quarter—a lot of money back then—if she could go fifteen minutes without saying a word. She hadn't gotten the quarter.

## THE BEST OF NEIGHBORS

Kenyon and Mabel bought new wallpaper and indoor-outdoor carpeting for the little house. Mabel let Darlene pick out the carpet color.

At the carpet store, Mabel saw Darlene glance wistfully at a plush, teddy bear brown carpet sample. "That wouldn't be practical with the number of people you'll be having in and out," she said gently, "especially with all the mud we have on the farm."

Jim and Darlene had never seen so much mud, especially in the springtime. March was the month of mud and manure; that was when many farmers spread the winter's accumulation of manure in the fields.

The Halls were the best of neighbors. Mabel often sent over a warm batch of cookies with instructions to "give them to the dog if you don't like them."

Not only were Kenyon and Mabel generous, they were also intelligent and well read. Even though they, and others from the Corners, said "gardeen" instead of "guardian," "gee-tar" instead of "guitar," and "choir-practor" instead of "chiropractor," they were far from uneducated.

"Guess what I found out?" Darlene asked Jim.

"What?"

"Mabel and Kenyon read *The Wall Street Journal* six days a week. Every page."

"You serious?"

Darlene nodded. "I guess lots of Corners people do. I'm sure they know more about news, politics, and finances than we do!"

Halls answered many questions for Jim and Darlene, especially when Darlene began gardening. The first spring Darlene had a garden, she was hoeing the large clumps of clay soil that had hardened into near cement when she found it. A carrot! *Who'd had a garden there before?* Darlene grabbed the carrot and ran next door as excited as a kid.

"Mabel! Look! I found a carrot! Can you tell me about the people who had a garden in that spot before? And do carrots come back by themselves every year?"

A smile tugged at the corners of Mabel's lips. "That's a wild carrot, Queen Anne's lace, a farmer's pest, a weed. And no, carrots don't come back every year. They are annuals, not perennials. You plant them every spring, but they don't grow well in our heavy clay soil."

~

ONE DAY KENYON rode his lawn mower over to the little house. "Jim, can you come over to my house?" he asked.

Jim noticed Kenyon's usual cheerful smile was missing. "Is anything wrong?"

"You might say I have righteous in-dig-nation," Kenyon

replied grimly, as they crested the barn hill and headed to his home, affectionately called "the big house."

"Look at that!" Kenyon pointed at his garage door. "Do you know where I can get me a new wife?"

Jim stared at the garage door. Only half of it remained. It looked as though a car had driven through it.

"Yep." Kenyon nodded. "Mabel backed the car right through that door. She was on her way to speak at a Women's Christian Temperance Union meeting, and she was running late. You know what her speech was about? It was about the bad things that can happen when you're in too much of a hurry!"

Kenyon's face warned Jim it wasn't the best time to laugh. He laughed later though when he told Darlene. She chuckled with him.

∽

THE KIDS LOVED Mabel and Kenyon.

When Davey, was two, Mabel asked him what he wanted for Christmas.

"Want tractor."

"A little tractor?" Mabel smiled. "I can get you that."

"No!" Davey shook his head. "Want big tractor like Misse Hall's."

Mabel chuckled. "I don't think I can do that. What else would you like?"

"Silo!"

"Maybe I could find a little silo."

"No! Big silo, like Misse Hall's."

Davey didn't get the big tractor or silo that year, but he grew up to own a few acres and some tractors. He never did get a silo.

## EASTER ICE STORM

"Honey," Darlene squeezes Jim's hand. "Do you remember the Easter ice storm?"

He smiles. "*Fiends* from church," he says.

Darlene laughs. She'd written an article about the ice storm, and, to her delight, the paper had printed it on the front page. Her delight had turned to mortification when she'd discovered that every time she'd written, "friends from church," the paper had misprinted it as "*fiends* from church."

∼

Darlene and Jim wouldn't forget Easter Sunday, 1979. Freezing rain started pelting the windows the night before. The kitchen lights flickered a warning. The three small children slept soundly, and Darlene started warming soup.

"Let me read my sermon to you before you fix the soup," Jim said. He really wanted to practice his sermon, and his fish refused to look interested.

Jim finished, snapped his Bible shut, and asked, "What do you think?"

The lights flickered again and went out.

"I think I don't like cold tomato soup."

The temperature inside the little house dipped low that night.

In the morning, Jim slid on four wheels to church. The white frame building shivered with no heat. Branches and downed wires littered the dirt roads, and it would be many days before power returned. Jim shut off the furnace so it wouldn't come on needlessly if the power did come back on. They only heated the church for services.

"Jim, I'm sorry no one but me heard your good sermon," Darlene said when he got back home.

Jim grinned. "Probably you were the only one who needed to hear it!"

After a cold breakfast, the family wrapped in blankets and celebrated Easter. Their four voice choir plus one coo did feeble justice to "Christ Arose!" Jim read the resurrection story and reminded them that they had the promise of eternal life because Jesus died and rose again. Suddenly, it felt like Easter, even though April wore no Easter ruffles and Jimmy's and Davey's cute little shirts and ties stayed in the closet.

Jim and Darlene stuffed the kids into snow suits, and the five of them took an Easter walk around the yard.

Easter morning was beautiful! No crocus, green grass, or golden daffodils greeted them, but they didn't miss them. The beauty of the branches reflected the glory of the sun. Each twig wore a solid coat of gleaming ice; they could only look at the trees a minute at a time because the breathtaking glitter of ice hurt their eyes. The sky was a brilliant blue, and the sun felt warm.

Darlene cherished the memory of that long-ago Easter day

when appearances said it was January, but the calendar said it was Easter. Despite how things looked, spring was on the way.

Isn't that what Easter is all about? It's light from darkness, joy from pain, life from death. Christ died so we might live and live more abundantly. Anything less than abundant life denies resurrection power. That day taught Jim and Darlene a lesson: If it doesn't look like Easter yet, just wait for it.

~

DARLENE LOOKS at Jim and feels the sweetness of the resurrection promise. Winter grips them now, but eternal spring is right around the corner.

Darlene remembers how they'd ended that Easter.

~

ONCE AGAIN, wrapped in blankets, they listened to Jim read from *Little House on the Prairie*.

"Hey!" Jimmy interrupted. "They had lanterns too!"

Darlene looked gratefully at the kerosene lantern and thought, *We never appreciate light so much as when it's dark and stormy. We have Easter's light for each dark day of life.* That was God's promise, she knew. But would she remember it? It was a truth that would take a lifetime to learn.

~

EVEN NOW, when the love of her life is dying before her eyes, she feels God's loving-kindness, His tender mercy, His resurrection power lifting her above circumstances.

*You, Lord, are my strength and my song, the song of perpetual spring.*

## PERFECT KIDS

"Honey," Darlene says, lightly touching Jim's shoulder. He wakes and smiles at her. "We were lucky to have such perfect kids, weren't we?"

He raises an eyebrow.

"Ok," she admits, "so they weren't perfect, but they sure were a lot of fun, and a big help in the ministry, weren't they?"

Jim nods and closes his eyes. Darlene tries to remember stories about the kids. She wishes she could remember more.

∼

WHEN DAVEY WAS TWO, he had a perfect best friend. Tommy never talked in church, never argued for a window seat in the car, never fought over toys. Tommy's main drawback was he wasn't real. He existed only in Davey's imagination.

Darlene remembered the time Davey yelled in the car, "April threw Tommy out the window!"

April looked defensive. "Davey kept telling me to move over because Tommy needed more room. I'm sick of it."

Darlene scolded, "April, you get Tommy back right now."

"How am I supposed to do that? You know he's not even r—"

"You threw him out; you get him back."

April shrugged, reached out her window, grabbed a handful of air, and handed the emptiness to Davey. His sobs turned to sniffles, then to smiles. Tommy was safe, and Davey's world was whole again. By the next year, though, Tommy had been long forgotten and replaced with real friends.

∽

DARLENE SMILES as she remembers another story.

∽

THE KIDS WERE VERY small when they learned to work in the house and in the garden. During the summer they each had to weed a certain number of rows a day. They would run into the house announcing, "I have wed my rows!"

Darlene often "wed" her rows when the kids were working on theirs. One day, she noticed someone was missing. "Where's your sister?"

Jimmy said, "She didn't come out today. She said. . .I think she said she felt impaled to read the Bible."

"Do you mean she said she felt compelled? Go in the house, and tell her to get out here right now."

Darlene had little patience with children who felt "impaled" to communicate with God when work needed doing. She explained to April some really good praying can happen in a garden.

∽

DARLENE THINKS of what good workers all the kids grew up to be, and then she wipes away a few tears as she remembers the heartaches each of them had faced. It was hard for her, as a mother, to remember that God gives some of His best gifts wrapped in the rough, ugly cloth of sorrow and suffering.

~

LOSS CAME to the Corners many times through the years. Corners Church prayed for a two-year-old girl with cancer, but the tiny child died. They prayed for many years for a young man with leukemia who lived a few houses from Jim and Darlene. When he was just seventeen, he died.

Death, pain, loss—Jim and Darlene couldn't fully understand these mysteries, but they didn't expect to.

"I might want to explain to my goldfish that we're going on vacation, but we're coming back," Jim preached one Sunday. "But I can't do that because their brains aren't big enough to understand. Maybe God would explain more about suffering to us if our brains were big enough to understand Him."

Darlene knew Jim was right. We can't hope to understand God, and He can't explain everything to us. We just have to choose to trust Him. If we can't look the darkest fact on earth right in the face without doubting God's love, we don't know Him.

These words by Francis Thompson often comforted her:

> All which I took from thee, I did'st but take,
>   Not for thy harms,
>   But just that thou might'st seek it in my arms.
> All which thy child's mistake fancies as lost,
> I have stored for thee at Home.
> Rise, clasp my hand, and come.

> Halts by me that Footfall.
> Is my gloom, after all,
> Shade of His hand, outstretched caressingly.

The small heartaches their children faced grew into huge ones in their teens and young adult years. Broken hearts replaced broken toys. Broken bones and serious health needs challenged faith.

∽

THINKING of their four children now, Darlene thanks God their kids grew up to love the Lord. She's grateful for the people they've married and for the twelve wonderful grandchildren who are now part of the family.

*Should I call the kids? Will they ever forgive me if Jim goes Home tonight, and they aren't here to say goodbye?*

Jim had said not to call. She'd honor that request. It might be his last.

## 39

## THE INTRUDER

It was 2:00 a.m. one silent October morning. How quiet October nights seem after the killing frost mutes summer sounds. The world slept, but Jim and Darlene were wide awake and terrified. What was that noise that had shattered the silence?

"You stay here," Jim ordered. He grabbed his gun, his famous gun that never had any bullets, and snuck downstairs, determined to bravely defend his wife and children against whatever dangerous intruder lurked in the shadows.

He didn't come back. Everything was quiet, too quiet. Darlene jumped out of bed and tiptoed downstairs. What would she find? Would Jim be lying in a pool of blood? Would the psycho-killer be waiting to attack her next?

She got to the kitchen, and her heart skipped several beats. Jim was lying in the middle of the floor, his gun across his chest. What was that sound? Was he moaning?

Psycho-killer or no psycho-killer, she had to see how bad Jim's wounds were. She flicked the kitchen light switch. Jim lay there, trying to smother his laughter.

"This isn't funny! If you're trying to scare me, it worked!"

"Shhh. Don't wake the kids. I'm not trying to scare you. I got down here and didn't find anyone. Then I got thinking how silly I must look, sneaking through the house in my underwear, with this old gun."

Darlene didn't find it nearly as funny as he did.

The next morning, they looked outside for the source of the noise and found several chimney bricks on the ground. The next several nights, between 1:00 a.m. and 3:00 a.m. they woke to hear the same thudding noise, and every morning they found more bricks on the ground.

A chimney repairman solved the mystery. A coon had been building a nest in the chimney and had dislodged bricks. The nest of twigs and hay filled the chimney so tightly that it took the repairman a half-hour to dislodge it by ramming it with a pipe and a chain.

"Good thing you haven't used your furnace yet this fall," he said. "The fumes would have killed you."

## THE NOT SO QUIET TIMES

Darlene was hanging laundry on a beautiful October day. *This will be one of the last Indian summer days.* The lonely sound of wild geese honking broke the silence. Darlene looked up and watched them fly south in unbroken V precision.

Darlene paused with clothespins in her hand, watching the geese, thinking about how quickly the seasons pass. *How often do we even pause long enough to enjoy life?* She wanted to teach the children that life is far more than running from one appointment or obligation to the next. She remembered how she'd held them in her arms as babies, standing at the west door, showing them the sunset over the open fields. Holding them and worshipping the Creator in silence, she'd prayed the babies would grow up to love nature and to worship God.

*Find joy in the journey; look for the shine. It's only in quietness that we really appreciate life.* Life had been unusually hectic, so Darlene decided to create a storybook style evening of quietness. The whole family needed to unwind.

Out came the prettiest placemats and cloth napkins.

Darlene set the table with the best china and candles. Supper cooked perfectly, one of Jim's favorites. He liked anything that wasn't burned.

The evening began perfectly. The children's faces, clean for once, glowed in the soft candlelight. Quiet music played on the stereo. Jim's face began to lose its tense, tired look, and even the children seemed relaxed.

Then Davey said, "Mommy, I don't feel so good."

The supper he'd eaten reappeared.

"Yuk! Gross!" April yelled, jumping up and knocking over her iced tea.

Right then the phone rang. Someone from church needed Jim.

Darlene sighed. "You go," she said to Jim. "I'll clean up here."

In Ecclesiastes 4:6, Solomon, the wisest of men had written, "Better is an handful with quietness, than both the hands full with travail and vexation of spirit."

*God,* Darlene prayed, as she surveyed the wreckage of her planned quietness, *please teach me to stay serene and calm in life's chaos. I want to be a haven of inward quietness so I can give my husband and children handfuls of quietness to carry to school and work, and quiet to come home to.*

"Mom," Jimmy moaned, holding his stomach, "I don't feel so good."

Darlene grabbed Jimmy's hand and made a run for the bathroom. They didn't make it.

## 41

## MANY GIFTS

Darlene and Jim's kids had grown up surrounded by the love of their church family. Corners Church people were the most generous in the world; they didn't have much, but they shared what they had. One farm family regularly gave them milk. When visiting family members worried about the milk being unpasteurized, Jim suggested they fill a glass and pass it in front of their eyes, and that would pasteurize it. They'd frowned, puzzled.

"Past-your-eyes, get it?" Jim laughed

In Darlene's opinion, no milk was better than fresh milk from Jersey cows. The cream rose to the top, and she scooped it off to make whipped cream, butter, or cheese.

Corners Church farmers occasionally gave the young family meat from a half a steer or a whole hog. Almost every Sunday, someone left something in their car, cookies, a pie, a dozen farm fresh eggs; they never knew what they might find waiting for them.

It was a warm Sunday, and the church had no air conditioning yet, so people visited out on the lawn after church. It was too hot inside. Whenever a car or truck drove by, dust drifted over the churchyard, but a little dust couldn't disperse the happy congregation. They lingered until Davey couldn't wait any longer.

"What do you think's in our car today?" he whispered to Darlene. "Can I go look?"

She nodded and smiled. He ran to the car, looked in the front seat, looked in the back seat, and slammed the car door.

"Mom!" he yelled, "Nobody didn't leave nothing in our car!"

Darlene was horrified. Conversation on the lawn stilled, and a few people chuckled. For a long time after that, someone left something in the car.

The kids had grown up without much and had been happy with the little they had. They wore hand-me-down clothes and never had any store-bought treats to take in their school lunches. They didn't tell Darlene until after they were grown that they often traded her homemade cookies with their classmates for anything they could get that had come from a store.

Their Christmas trees were cedars, sometimes more brown than green, cut each year from Deacon Pete's field.

The kids gathered around the tree and sang, "Oh Christmas bush, oh Christmas bush, how scrawny are thy branches!"

One year, Darlene scrimped and saved a little each week until she had $10.00, exactly what she needed to buy a lovely, real Christmas tree.

"The kids are going to be so surprised and happy when they get home from school and see a real tree!"

Jim grinned at Darlene. Sometimes, she still acted like a kid. He only hoped he wouldn't hurt Deacon Pete's feelings when Pete told him it was time to come cut the cedar.

"Look at all those cars ahead of us!" Darlene exclaimed

when they were almost to the Christmas tree farm. "It looks like they're all in the ditch!"

"And now, so are we." Jim sighed.

They sat there watching as a truck with snow tires pulled out each car. The truck driver stopped next to them.

Jim rolled down his window. "How much?"

"Ten bucks."

Jim had no money. He held out his hand. Darlene put her beautiful Christmas tree into it. They cut another cedar tree that year and were grateful for it.

They kids were happy with their gifts of a homemade barn and a homemade doll cradle and a little hand-sewn doll blanket. One year, Darlene made them and their friends craft boxes. She filled them with scraps of cloth, paper, glue, glitter, and crayons. They acted like they'd been given the national treasure.

Jim and Darlene didn't feel poor, and the kids didn't either. They were rich in faith; they knew prayer worked.

It did hurt when the kids came home from school one day looking dejected. They'd been so excited to wear their new shoes to school.

"Your mom take you shopping at Goodwill again?" a classmate had jeered.

That's exactly where they had gotten their shoes.

One summer, Jim and Darlene had saved enough money to buy the kids' school uniforms, but an unexpected bill had devoured all available cash. The uniform pants had already been ordered and were in town, waiting to be picked up, but the boys started school with last year's too short and multi-patched pants.

A few days later Jim reached into the pocket of his sport coat and pulled out an envelope given to him two months earlier. *I forgot someone's thank you note.* In the envelope he found exactly the amount needed to pay for the school pants.

Jim and Darlene laid the new pants over the boys' homemade toy box, so they'd see them and waited for their reaction.

"How did God give you the money?" the boys asked.

Darlene loved that. *How did God give you the money? I'd rather be poor and have God be real to you kids than to be a millionaire and have you not know His power.*

There were so many other gifts. Someone from Corners Church—they never found out who—left a new stove on the porch.

Darlene had many adventures with old stoves; until that new one arrived, she'd never had one where all the burners and the oven worked. Her nemesis was the oven that sometimes spit black carbon on her homemade dinner rolls. She knew she was too proud of those rolls, so maybe that was God's way of teaching her humility, but she preferred to think it was the devil trying to see what it would take to get her to say a bad word. Or two.

As the kids grew, they gave gifts of their own: a gas fireplace, a water heater, a new stove, a chest freezer, a vacuum, a bed, and many beef quarters. If you haven't filled a chest freezer with hamburger, steaks, and roasts from a quarter of a beef, you don't know the satisfaction a squirrel feels when it's prepared for winter! It was a good life, the best life, and they had wonderful kids who'd grown up to be givers.

As Jim and Darlene grew older, the church people gave them many raises and more vacation time, but they continued to bless them with beef, pork, eggs, and best of all, love and prayers.

## 42

## SCARED AND BLESSED

The same little boy who'd been indignant about nothing being left in the car at church was upstairs making his bed one Saturday morning when his brother ran downstairs.

"Come quick!" Jimmy yelled. "Something's wrong with Davey!"

At first Jim and Darlene thought Davey, who loved to have fun, was trying to play another joke on them with his jerking and shaking.

"Davey, stop that," Jim ordered.

Davey looked up and smiled, but the jerking continued. Darlene saw the fear in his eyes. "He's not joking!"

The following hours were a nightmare; the hospital put three different anti-seizure medications in his IV at increasing strength before the jerking stopped. When it quit, Davey couldn't move his right arm or leg, and he couldn't speak. The small hospital sent him by ambulance to a large hospital.

Jim and Darlene's good friends, Pastor Michael and

Andrea, met them at the hospital. They waited in the hall with them as Davey had a brain scan.

The four of them sat outside the test room on a backless wooden bench, heads leaned against a concrete wall. Andrea gripped Darlene's hand. Darlene thought back to when they'd met, the week after Jim and Darlene had come to Corners Church.

"Pastor, we scheduled special meetings for next week," Deacon Pete had told Jim the Wednesday they'd moved in.

"Wonderful! Have you sent out flyers, contacted the radio station, put an ad in the newspaper?"

"I don't rightly think any of that's been done."

Jim and Darlene had scrambled to get the word out. For the first time, they'd delivered flyers to the homes in a three-mile radius of Corners Church. They'd been surprised by how many farmhouses there had been and how long it had taken.

A handful of visitors had attended the meetings. The first ones they'd met had been Pastor Michael and Andrea.

Darlene had hugged Andrea, several years her senior, who looked dignified and beautiful, exactly as a pastor's wife should look.

"I'm so happy to meet you! I think you're the answer to my prayers! I don't know a thing about being a pastor's wife. Can you teach me?"

"I've only been a pastor's wife for two weeks. I don't know much about it myself. Did you go to Bible college?"

"Yes, but that didn't help me a bit!"

"I'm sure it will help you. I didn't go to Bible college, and I don't even have a lace tablecloth. I thought every pastor's wife needed one of those."

Darlene had laughed. "I don't have a lace tablecloth. And I don't know how to play the piano either!"

Andrea did know how to play the piano, quite well. They'd

agreed they'd help each other learn to be pastor's wives, and they'd become good friends.

Darlene was glad to have Andrea with her now. She tightened her grip on Andrea's hand.

Two nurses walked by talking. One said to the other, "That's so sad. An inoperable brain tumor, and he's so young."

Darlene leaned back against the wall and struggled to breathe.

"Darlene!" Andrea said. "They aren't talking about Davey. They can't be. They just took him in for the scan; they can't know anything yet."

Jim left late that night to go home and stay with the other children, but Darlene slept in a chair next to Davey's bed. He still couldn't speak or move his right side. The nurses raised both side rails to keep him from falling out of bed. Darlene woke around 2:00 a.m. Half-awake, she saw Davey standing on the end of the bed.

"What are you doing?"

"I have to go to the bathroom."

Davey, who'd fallen asleep unable to talk or move, was now perched at the end of the bed. He jumped off, landed perfectly on his feet, and ran to the bathroom.

Davey had to stay at the hospital several more days while the doctors ran tests, but Darlene knew he'd be fine. God had healed their son. His progress amazed the doctors.

"We call the kind of seizure your son had a childhood stroke," a neurologist explained. "Fifty percent of the time it ends with permanent neurological damage, and twenty-five percent of the time the result is death. You have a lucky little boy."

*Luck*, Darlene thought, *has nothing to do with it.*

There were a hungry few days for Darlene in the hospital. Jim had to use every cent for gas money to travel the hour and a half between the hospital and home, so there was no money to buy hospital food. When he came to visit, he brought Darlene something to eat from home that wouldn't spoil, usually a peanut butter and jelly sandwich, and that's all she had to eat until he returned the next day.

One day Jim arrived with a huge smile. "I'll stay with Davey. You go to the cafeteria and buy anything you want."

"Where'd you get money?"

"Your sister and your brother-in-law! They drove two-and-a-half hours to the house, handed me a hundred-dollar bill, and said they needed to go right back home because they had to work."

Darlene thanked God all the way to the cafeteria and came back laughing. "The cafeteria's closed. That's okay; I'll dream about food and eat tomorrow."

Going-home day arrived at last. They still had most of the wonderful one-hundred dollars. Jim grinned broadly and pulled into a McDonald's.

"We're celebrating today," he told April, Jimmy, and Davey. "You kids can order anything you want."

They looked at him, wide-eyed and unbelieving. "Anything?"

"Anything!"

Laughing, the kids ran into McDonald's to look at the menu. Darlene and Jim got out of the car and smiled at each other. Their kids were so precious.

Darlene's knees felt funny. She grabbed the car. *What if. . .?* She couldn't stop the flood of tears or the sobs.

"Honey! What is it?" Jim asked anxiously as he hugged her.

She couldn't answer, but he knew. His eyes were wet too. "You pick a fine time to cry," he said, teasing her, "after it's all over and everything's okay."

The hospital bill was an elephant, but they'd eaten many

elephants before, one bite a time. They struggled to make the monthly payments, but they made them.

One day Phil, a farmer friend, stopped by the house. "How you doing with those hospital bills?"

"Oh, we may have them paid off by the time Davey graduates from college." Jim joked.

Phil told them about a fund the hospital had that had helped him pay his son's bills. Jim applied; the hospital approved them, and the bill was paid in full.

## 43

## THE PASTOR TAKES A DIVE

Darlene was vacuuming the church. In the early years, Jim and Darlene did all the cleaning, lawn mowing, and snow shoveling. Jim was on the church roof, touching up the steeple with white paint. He had on his cowboy boots, and Darlene had begged him to be careful because there was a dusting of snow on the roof.

April was in school, but Jimmy and Davey weren't old enough to go yet. They'd wanted to play outside and watch Daddy paint. Above the roar of the ancient vacuum, Darlene thought she heard one of the boys scream. She shut off the vacuum and heard small fists pounding on the heavy wooden door. She opened the door, and there stood her two small, sobbing boys.

"We couldn't open the door," Jimmy cried, "and Daddy's hurt. He's on the ground!"

Darlene ran around the church and saw Jim sprawled, face first on the ground, covered in white paint. There was no phone at the church, and no one close enough to call for help. Somehow, she got Jim into the car and sped down the road.

Darlene drove as fast as possible to the emergency room. Miraculously, Jim had broken no bones, but the twenty-foot fall had pulled and torn the ligaments in his chest. The healing was long and slow, and chest muscle spasms would plague him the rest of his life.

Friends came with love, prayers, and meals. Pastor Landon and Katrina brought a portable whirlpool that fit in the tub and eased Jim's sore muscles. Pastor Michael and Andrea brought food, laugher, and a Bible verse for the occasion.

In his most pastoral voice, Pastor Michael read Proverbs 24:16, "For a just man falleth seven times, and riseth up again."

The laugher made Jim's chest hurt, but it did his heart good. Pastor Michael and Andrea seemed to have a verse for every occasion. Years down the road, an unexpected loss plunged the usually optimistic Darlene into a deep depression she struggled with for a long time. She fell with a thud from her Pollyanna tree, and it took her years to climb it again. She went to church and fulfilled her obligations as a pastor's wife but hid at home whenever possible. Most of those closest to her didn't know about her shattered heart, but Andrea did. She offered prayers, encouraging words, and comforting hugs.

When Darlene's habit of hibernation seemed to be becoming permanent, Andrea called her on the phone.

"I have a verse for you," she said.

Darlene almost groaned. She knew the verses. She knew she needed to give thanks; she knew she should reach out to others suffering more than she was, and she'd been doing that. She really didn't want another sermon, but this was Andrea. She couldn't hurt her faithful friend, so she listened patiently; although, it was probably good Andrea couldn't see her face.

"You know how I've been talking to you for months about getting out more? Well, God has something to say about it too! I'm telling you what David's good friend Jonathan said to him,

'Come, and let us go out into the field.' Go out, Darlene; go out!"

Darlene was quiet for a minute, and then she laughed. "You're really stretching it, Andrea. Your biblical exposition is terrible."

"I know." Andrea laughed too.

Darlene's dark cloud didn't magically dissipate that day, but she did smile every time she thought about those words, "Go out." And eventually she did.

Jim and Darlene put ten dollars a month on Jim's hospital bill. The hospital knew they were good for it. They'd paid off the expense of their babies a little every month. This bill was bigger than the ones for the babies, though. Darlene didn't ask how they would ever finish paying the huge bill. She knew what Jim would say, "Go ahead and worry. God has let us down so many times before."

One Sunday, long after church ended, they walked out to their car. Theirs was the last car to leave the parking lot, because they stayed until the last person left.

Darlene shivered. "Hurry and start the car, honey. I'm freezing."

Jim was staring at a piece of paper stapled around the steering wheel.

"What is it?"

Carefully he detached the paper and handed it to her. It read, "Hospital bill paid in full. From a friend."

Tears spilled down their cheeks. There wasn't one person in the church with money to spare. Someone had sacrificed to pay that bill; that's what love does. How could they ever love their people enough?

There was only one way, the way Amy Carmichael had prayed long ago, and the way they prayed too:

"Love through me, Love of God;

Make me like thy clear air
Through which, unhindered, colors pass
As though it were not there."

∼

SITTING NEXT TO JIM, Darlene laughs, remembering their happiness when they'd read that note. "Paid in full." Three sweet words. She can't believe there's an ounce of joy left when the love of her life is fading before her eyes, but there it is, laughter bubbling under tears. *Truly, God's joy is eternal. Heaven is eternal too.* She leans forward, studying Jim's face. She loves every wrinkle, but the pain lines she sees hurt her heart.

*Yes, heaven is eternal, but am I wicked to wish we had a little more time together here?*

*Stay in your own lane.* That thought is a familiar companion and has helped her more times than she can count in this last decade of life. It's God telling her to let Him be God and to let Him handle the God things.

She takes a mental swerve and jerks back into her own lane.

"Sorry, Lord. I never was a very good driver. I always did have trouble staying in my own lane."

Jim's eyes crinkle. "That's the truth."

*His voice is so strong! Could the nurses and doctors be wrong?*

## 44

## THE FIRST TO LEAVE

Daniel Kamp, his wife Felicity, and their five lovely teenage daughters were a welcome addition to the Corners Church family, and they brought joy and laughter to the tiny church. After they'd been members a few years, the congregation voted to make Daniel a deacon, and he was a good one.

The church had grown enough to have a youth group, and the Kamp girls were a vital part. Jim was youth leader as well as pastor and took the youth to conferences and outings. He filled his old Chevy station wagon with kids and set off on many adventures. The Chevy was a sturdy old car, reliable unless it was cold. If it was cold, the engine wouldn't start unless Jim poured hot water over it.

"What made you think to pour hot water over the engine?" Darlene asked Jim.

"Figured a baptism couldn't hurt." He laughed.

Jim took the youth group kids to McDonalds, and the car wouldn't start when they left. He went back in, asked the manager for a gallon of hot water, and explained why he wanted it.

The manager complied but went outside with Jim. "This I gotta see," he said. He watched, amazed, as Jim poured the water over the engine while one of the Kamp girls started the car.

Jim and Darlene loved the Kamps. When Darlene sat in the back of the church with her children, she often looked at the beautiful Kamp family sitting three rows from the front, smiled, and thanked God for them.

One Sunday, Darlene felt uneasy when she looked at the Kamp's pew. Felicity's warm smile was missing; she wasn't singing, and she sat with her arms crossed over her chest. She looked angry.

Darlene tried to shrug it off. *Felicity must not be feeling well today.* But as Felicity sat week after week, wearing the angry face, not only through the song service, but all through the sermon, and hurrying out after church without a word, Darlene knew something was wrong.

"Do you think you should talk to Daniel and Felicity?" she asked Jim.

"I noticed it too." He sighed. "I'll talk to them this week."

Felicity felt Jim was showing favoritism to some of the church families. Daniel and the girls didn't feel the same way Felicity did, and Jim tried his best to smooth out the misunderstanding, but to no avail. The Kamp family left a giant hole in the heart of Corners Church. The pew looked sad, sitting there so empty.

After Kamp's left the church, Darlene couldn't sleep. She tossed and turned, plagued by thoughts of what they could have done differently and whether being in the ministry was even worth it if they were going to get their hearts broken like this.

It took a while, but eventually Darlene felt like God was saying, "Can you still love people for Me?"

"Yes, Lord, but only if You love through me. It hurts."

"Remember, child, what it cost Me to love you."

Jim didn't say much, but Darlene knew he was still hurting too.

Out of nowhere one day, Jim's college friend, Todd Pritchard stopped by the house when Jim and Darlene were feeling at their lowest.

"What's wrong with you two?" Todd asked. "You look like you lost your best friend."

"Well, we did lose some friends," Jim said. He explained about the Kamps leaving Corners Church as Darlene wiped away a few tears.

Todd stared at them for a few minutes. "I don't know what's wrong with the two of you. This isn't what the ministry is supposed to be like. When people leave my church, I don't even care. It doesn't bother me. It's God's church, not mine. I don't get emotionally involved with my people. Pastors and wives aren't supposed to, and if you think I'm wrong, just call Nick. I know he'd agree with me."

After Todd left, Darlene said to Jim, "Maybe God never meant for me to be a pastor's wife. I can't help getting emotionally involved with people."

Jim hugged her. "Ignore Todd. We're supposed to love like Jesus did, and He sure got emotionally involved with people. Remember He cried at Lazarus's grave. I'm pretty sure Todd is wrong about this. And I don't think Professor Nick Machiavelli would agree with him."

*But would he?* Jim wasn't sure.

Darlene's sadness lingered. Then one Sunday, Deacon Pete handed her a worn, creased piece of paper.

"Keep this," he said. "Me and Janet thought you could use it."

Darlene glanced at the words. No author's name was listed, but the paper read:

### Ministry Is:

Giving when you feel like keeping,
    Praying for others when you need to be prayed for,
    Feeding others when your own soul is hungry,
    Living truth before people when you can't see results,
    Hurting with other people even when your own hurt can't be spoken,
    Keeping your word even when it is not convenient,
    Being faithful when your flesh wants to run away.

"Was it that obvious that I wanted to run away?" Darlene asked Pete.

"Maybe." He grinned and patted her shoulder.

Darlene kept that paper in her Bible. She needed it, because sometimes that feeling of wanting to run away returned.

Late in their ministry, when Jim and Darlene foolishly thought their days of losing beloved families were over, another family who'd sat for years in the Kamp's forsaken pew also got upset and left. It never got any easier, losing cherished friends. Jim and Darlene's hearts broke every time.

Someone said the secret to success in ministry is to get the tough hide of a rhinoceros but keep the tender heart of a child; the trick is to get the one without losing the other. Jim and Darlene didn't lose their tender hearts, but they didn't get the tough hides.

"I'm going to make a sign for that pew," Darlene said to Jim as they lay awake one night.

He didn't ask what pew. He knew. "What's the sign going to say?"

"It's going to say, 'Don't sit here. This pew is cursed.'"

Jim laughed and fell asleep. Darlene lay awake for a few more hours, wiping away tears and praying.

## 45

## THE RESTLESS YEARS

The sorrow over families leaving the church diminished but didn't totally dissipate; still, Darlene felt contented. She loved being a wife and mother; she loved her ministry at Corners Church, and she loved writing.

Darlene's writing took on a life of its own. In addition to writing Sunday school curriculum on assignment, she wrote short stories and articles. A state magazine published her writing in a column for women called, "Rainbows and Dust Mops." After a few years, a national church magazine asked her to write a column for them. She did that for twenty-two years.

Because many people read the column, they felt like they knew Jim, Darlene, and their family. When a church needed a pastor, congregations often thought of the Pastor Jim they'd read about. Churches sometimes requested him to pulpit supply and candidate.

Those were restless years for Jim at Corners Church. He occasionally expressed frustration. "I sure understand Pastor Kole better now," he said one day.

Darlene was confused.

"You've heard the rocking chair story," Jim said.

Darlene laughed. Everyone in their home church had heard the rocking chair story. When Pastor Kole, father of the infamous Judi who'd undressed on the church pew, had been a young, fiery preacher, he'd grown tired of the people's spotty attendance and lack of commitment. He'd called them pew sitters.

One Sunday he'd shouted, pounding the pulpit with each word, "You people are nothing but a bunch of rocking chair Christians!"

Months later, on Christmas morning, Pastor Kole heard his doorbell chime. He opened the door, and snow blew in. He saw footprints on the porch, but no one was in sight. Next to the door sat a beautiful, apple-wood rocking chair topped with a big red bow. The tag read, "Merry Christmas to Pastor Kole from his rocking chair Christians."

Jim's parents had bought Pastor Kole's chair when he'd retired. They'd used it for many years and had recently given it to Jim and Darlene.

Jim loved the people at Corners Church, but no amount of preaching seemed to convince some of them to attend any service but Sunday morning. Some of them also ignored all pleas to help in any of the church programs or ministries.

"I guess I have my own rocking chair Christians now." Jim sighed.

"It's the same everywhere, honey." Darlene reassured him.

Jim thought he was the problem. Perhaps he should preach harder. Professor Nick Machiavelli and Todd Pritchard had both suggested he was too mild in his approach to pastoring. Soon, Jim was loudly mentioning the lack of faithfulness and commitment in every service.

Deacon Pete and Janet invited Jim and Darlene for lunch.

After lunch, Pete cleared his throat. "Now, Pastor," he said mildly, "me and Janet have noticed you seem to be angry a lot lately when you're preaching. Anger won't get you anywhere. You know, you can say anything to us as long as you say it with love." Pete then changed the subject and talked about the fish in his pond and the beautiful elephant grass growing on the side of the road.

Jim was quiet on the drive home. After a while, he asked Darlene, "Do I seem angry to you when I preach?"

"Maybe," she said softly.

"Do you think I'm acting unloving?"

"A little."

The next Sunday began a lasting change. Jim didn't stop preaching about faithfulness and commitment, but he did it with more love and no anger.

Still, when attendance at evening services continued dwindling, Jim couldn't help but feel discouraged at times. Maybe it was time to move on and begin climbing that ladder. He'd never forgotten what Professor Nick Machiavelli had said at that pastor's conference: "Nothing ever happens where two dirt roads meet."

So, when he got many invitations to pulpit supply and candidate at other churches, he accepted them all. He had several favorable votes and was asked to pastor churches five times larger than Corners Church. But, when it came right down to it, he couldn't leave his small congregation, and he didn't really understand why.

He didn't stop pulpit supplying and candidating, though. It was almost an obsession; he couldn't forget Professor Nick Machiavelli's words, "If your first church is small, don't despise the day of small things, but don't stay there either. Think of it as the first rung on a ladder, and aim always to climb to a place of greater usefulness. Climb higher!"

Why couldn't he make himself leave this first rung on the ladder? Todd Pritchard pastored a large church, and when Jim told him about how he was feeling, Todd accused him of fear and of being too comfortable where he was. But Jim knew that wasn't true.

Eventually, the Corners Church board called a meeting and requested Jim's attendance. "Pastor," Deacon Pete said firmly, "we don't want you to ever leave Corners Church. We all love you. But you gotta make up your mind. Go or stay. This constant not knowing what you're going to do is driving us crazy, and we don't think it's good for the church!"

Jim promised to pray about it. At the time, he was considering two other offers. A larger church had a 100 percent vote asking him to come as pastor. A small, local Bible college had asked him to come teach full time and had offered to build him a house. What should he do? If he left Corners Church, which of the two offers was right? Most importantly, what did God want him to do?

Darlene and Jim often passed each other on their way in and out of their praying place, a small rock garden in their backyard. They'd agreed the decision to go or stay had to be mutual.

Finally, they decided. Neither of them felt this was the right time to leave. They were staying at Corners Church, for now. Jim passed the news along to the board. Strangely, after that, he didn't receive another request to candidate anywhere else until he was almost seventy years old. That didn't stop him from wondering about climbing the ladder; he knew he could always contact his professor if he felt it was time to move up to that next rung.

It wasn't the end of Jim's restlessness; though, he stopped blaming the congregation and started blaming himself. As faithfulness and commitment declined more as years went by, he often wondered if he was doing the church a disservice.

"Do you think the evening service attendance would be better if the church had a different pastor?" he asked Darlene. "Maybe I've stayed here too long. People get tired of the same old thing. It's only human."

"Evening service attendance might pick up for a while," she answered. "But I don't think it would solve anything long term. Once they got used to the new guy, things would go back to normal. It's the same everywhere, Jim. I'm not saying it's right or wrong, but people are just so busy. Try putting yourself in their place."

Jim did understand how busy people were, but some nearby churches had great attendance on Sunday and Wednesday nights. What did they do that he wasn't doing? The discouragement was real and reoccurring, but Jim took it to the Lord. He often said that discouragement is the sharpest tool in the devil's toolbox.

Jim told Darlene about an old pastor who when asked the secret of his long-time faithfulness replied, "I know how to plod."

"You do, honey; we both do. We know how to plod."

Plodding was okay, but when was it time to climb? That was still the question, wasn't it?

## 46

## FRIENDS

Darlene had sometimes felt restless too, especially when she was lonely. One day, early in their ministry, the normally talkative Darlene was quiet.

Jim noticed. "What's wrong, honey?"

"I need a friend."

Jim listened patiently while Darlene detailed the qualities she wanted in a good friend.

"And you can't find that kind of friend?" he asked sympathetically.

She shook her head a miserable no. He put his face close to hers, grinned, gave a quick tug on her braid, and said, "If you can't find that kind of friend, be that kind of friend."

And then, as husbands are prone to do when they think they've solved a problem, he walked away.

After several similar conversations Jim said, "Let's pray about this."

They sat on the couch, held hands, and prayed God would give them some good friends. And God answered.

God gave them friends; the first from the church were Ken and Ellen. Next, God sent wonderful pastor and wife friends. The Rosehearts were precious friends too. Jim and Darlene thanked God for the day the Rosehearts came to church. They later learned they almost hadn't come at all.

Dale and Jenna Roseheart pulled into the parking lot late. Church had already started.

"Let's just leave," Jenna said.

"Let's go in," Dale said. "If you don't want to come, I'll go in by myself. I want to get a bulletin."

"Look at that place!" Jenna gestured toward the tiny white frame church. "Does it look to you like they'd have a bulletin?"

The Rosehearts did go inside, and they attended for many years until they moved south. Dale became a deacon. At the first potluck after he became a deacon, he told Darlene, "The first thing I'm going to do as deacon is get running water over here." The schoolhouse fellowship hall had no running water or indoor plumbing.

Darlene was ecstatic. "Really?"

Dale nodded. "Yep. Next potluck, I'll bring a bucket. You can run for the water."

When Dale suggested a choir, he was serious. It was Jim and Darlene who laughed then.

"Why not?" Dale asked. "We can start practicing now for Christmas. Almost everyone in this church can sing."

"But if we all sing in a choir, who will listen to us?" Jim asked.

"I hadn't thought of that. Well, we'll pray for visitors."

The church really started to grow that Sunday the Rosehearts pulled into the parking lot and almost didn't come inside.

Tears flowed the Sunday the Rosehearts said goodbye and moved, but whenever they came back to visit family, they attended Corners Church, and it was as though they'd never left. They were more than friends; they were family.

Todd and Professor Nick Machiavelli kept telling Jim and Darlene not to get too close to their church people, but that advice didn't stick. Jim and Darlene loved their friends; they especially loved praying for them and with them.

Corners Church adopted a tradition they called "circling the wagons." The early pioneers circled their wagons for protection. Often, when someone in the church family had a need, the church family stood around the edges of the auditorium, joined hands, and prayed. Darlene looked around the circle with her heart full of gratitude, remembering that long-ago prayer for friends. God had answered abundantly.

## THE BANK ROBBER MISSIONARY

That's strange. There's no breeze in here, but those wind chimes are ringing. The soft, melodic sound wakes Jim. He looks at the ceiling where the wind chimes are hanging; then he smiles at Darlene. Those glass music note wind chimes are a sweet memory, a gift from Harvey and Anna, missionary evangelists extraordinaire!

"Don't stop talking," Jim says. "Keep telling our story. Tell me about Harvey and Anna."

~

HARVEY WAS a convicted Canadian bank robber, out of jail, and on his way to rob another bank. He had a bit of time before his scheduled meeting with his partner in crime and was looking to establish an alibi. He was curious when he heard singing coming from a storefront. Popping his head in, he saw people sitting in chairs, and a beautiful young woman enthusiastically leading the singing, putting all tiny five feet of herself into the song. Intrigued, Harvey took a seat. Not only did this look interesting, it would make a good alibi.

When it was time to go rob the bank, the lovely lady was preaching, and Harvey was squirming. He felt like she was talking to him. Sinner? She didn't have to convince him; he knew he was that. Headed to hell? Probably. He had joked about hell more than a time or two, but suddenly it seemed real and not so funny. A way to escape hell and go to heaven? Harvey almost left then, sure she was going to ask for money. In his mind, you didn't get anything for nothing.

But wait. She was saying Jesus, God the Son, had taken his punishment for sin, paid his price. Eternal life was a gift. Free! To go to heaven, all Harvey had to do was admit he was a sinner and believe Jesus Christ had died on the cross for him.

The pretty lady said, "Ephesians 2:8 says, 'For by grace are ye saved, through faith, and that not of yourselves, not of works, lest any man should boast.'"

Harvey almost forgot how lovely the lady was. All he saw was the beauty of hope. When she asked for anyone to come forward who wanted to accept God's free gift of salvation, Harvey was on his feet and down the aisle.

That was one bank that didn't get robbed.

Harvey later married Anna, that lovely lady. They became missionary evangelists, traveling to small churches, first in Canada, and then in the United States. They served God together for many years, well past retirement age.

Harvey and Anna were in their seventies when they first visited Corners Church. Harvey did the preaching, and Anna kept him in line. Corners Church loved them both. Harvey was rather soft-spoken for an evangelist, and, a great plus, he let the congregation out on time. He didn't preach at people so much as he talked with them.

Harvey and Anna proclaimed Corners Church their

favorite. They stayed with Jim and Darlene, not only when they ministered at Corners Church, but whenever they were speaking at a church within 100 miles of it. Darlene and Anna talked late into the night on those visits. Darlene loved listening to Anna's many stories.

"I was teaching a group of older kids once," Anna said. "I didn't want to read the verse that says 'out of his belly flowed rivers of living water.' You know how kids are. They would have laughed the minute I said 'belly.' So, I reworded the verse, and in my most enthusiastic voice I said, 'Out of his innermost being flowed livers of riving water.'"

Darlene and Anna laughed until Harvey knocked on the bedroom wall, his signal for Anna to please be quiet and come to bed.

"Yes, my lord!" Anna yelled. Then she winked at Darlene and said goodnight.

On one visit, Harvey came out of the bedroom, in his pajamas, and without his teeth.

Davey looked at him wide-eyed. "Mom," he whispered, "can all missionaries take their teeth out?"

Harvey and Anna gave Jim and Darlene the glass music note wind chimes. Darlene hugged Anna. "They're beautiful! I'll think of you every time I look at them."

Anna sighed. "I'm glad you like them. My cousin didn't."

"Why not?"

"Well, in all the years I've known her, I've never been able to buy her something she likes. She always makes negative comments. I thought for sure she couldn't find anything to criticize about these wind chimes, but she did. She looked at the box, read the fine print, and said, 'Humph. Made from recycled beer bottles. I'd never give anyone something made from recycled beer bottles.'"

∽

JIM IS STILL AWAKE and listening.
"You remember how Harvey died?"
Jim nods and smiles. His eyes say he knows he'll see Harvey and Anna soon.
Darlene swallows a lump in her throat. She hopes, she prays, she won't be left on earth too long after Jim leaves.

∽

HARVEY AND ANNA were in their eighties, still ministering, when they decided to buy a camper to stay in on their mission road trips. They spent the morning looking at campers, and then went home for lunch. As they ate, they enthusiastically discussed the merits of different campers.
"Do you want more soup?" Anna asked. Harvey did.
Anna went to the stove and refilled Harvey's bowl. She asked him a question, and he didn't respond. "Harvey?" She turned to look at him.
Harvey was slumped foreword, his head on the table, a smile on his face. He'd gone, that quickly, to meet the Jesus Anna had introduced him to some sixty years before. Anna followed him a few months later. She died of brain cancer.

∽

DARLENE TAKES Jim's cold hand. "Harvey and Anna were lucky," she says. "They got to go to heaven only a few months apart."
Once again the wind chimes ring. *Is it an angel, come to take Jim Home?* Darlene holds his hand a little tighter.

## 48
## DOWN A COAL CHUTE

The phone rang early one morning. "Pastor, please come help me, and hurry! I'm calling from the barn. I ran out to get the mail and left the kids inside. The door locked, and I can't get back in!"

It took a half hour to get to Gladys's house, and all the way there Darlene imagined the horrible things that might have happened to the unsupervised toddlers and the baby.

"Can't you drive any faster?"

"Not unless you want to see my name in the paper for speeding."

"With one policeman patrolling the whole county? That isn't likely to happen!"

Jim drove faster.

They found Gladys, shivering in the cold in her bathrobe and nightgown, worried sick about her kids.

"I thought of how you can get inside, Pastor. You can go down the coal chute."

Jim felt a little uncertain about her plan. "How big of a drop is it?"

"How would I know?" Gladys was crying now. "I never went down the coal chute!"

It's a good thing the Gladys incident didn't occur twenty years later when Jim was fifty pounds heavier. He said a prayer and barely squeezed himself through the coal chute. He landed in coal dust and dropped to his knees. Black dust flew up around him, making him cough. Something told him to hurry. He raced upstairs just in time to see one of the toddlers pull the baby's infant seat off the kitchen table.

Jim caught the baby on her way down. Heart pounding, he went to the door, carrying the baby, and let Darlene and Gladys inside. The baby and the preacher both needed a bath, but all's well that ends well, or so they say.

## BEAUTY AND THE BEAST

Second Baptist Church sat in a cornfield about ten miles south of Corners Church. When a visitor from there attended Corners Church, Jim and Darlene invited her home for lunch. That lunch was the first time Jim and Darlene heard the stories about Second Baptist, but it wouldn't be the last time. The many tales about Second Baptist's long and colorful history made Darlene chuckle.

"So, you're from Second Baptist. Where's First Baptist?" Darlene asked the visitor.

"Oh, there's no First Baptist. Our founding fathers chose the name Second Baptist because they didn't want to look prideful, don't you know."

The visitor told about legendary Pastor Willis North, a soft-spoken, gentle man who'd spent sixty years as pastor at Second Baptist. One Sunday, with no notice, he up and retired. He said he wanted to go back to the family farm and sit on a tractor. Six months later, his wife found him dead; he looked happy and peaceful with his head resting on the steering wheel of his tractor.

After Pastor North left Second Baptist, the congregation hired Pastor Green, a young man right out of seminary. He often referred to the Greek, Hebrew, Aramaic, and sometimes read entire paragraphs in Latin—without translating them.

At the first business meeting of the New Year, Second Baptist voted on whether to keep the preacher for another year. For the first time in sixty-one-years, the vote came back no. They sent Pastor Green packing.

Pastor McCoy was Second Baptist's most famous preacher. He was a single man, and his most treasured possession was his 1920 Harley-Davidson motorcycle named The Beast. Pastor McCoy rode The Beast to church in all seasons, unless the snow got too deep, and then he rode his work horse, inappropriately named Beauty. Whether Pastor McCoy went to church on Beast or Beauty, his ancient 1903 Springfield rifle went with him, propped across the handlebars of The Beast or angled in front of him on Beauty's saddle. When he got to church, he put the rifle on the pulpit with his Bible behind it and let loose with a hellfire and brimstone message even an atheist would admire for its sheer volume.

Visitors to the church, seeing the rifle, jokingly asked if Pastor McCoy brought his rifle to church because he feared some Hatfields might attend. Church members assured the visitors there were no Hatfields around, but there were rabble-rousers who'd been terrorizing families in the area. Everyone knew Pastor McCoy could hit a squirrel between the eyes at 500 yards. The rabble-rousers didn't bother Second Baptist Church.

Pastor McCoy stayed on at Second Baptist for many years. The Beast gave up the ghost long before he did, and he laid Beauty to rest with many a tear and a solemn eulogy, but the rifle stayed with him until the end. By the time he was eighty, his rifle was his trusty cane. He was a bit forgetful by then, and when he hobbled to the pulpit, leaning on his rifle for support, the congregation hoped he'd remembered to unload it. When Pastor McCoy died, they buried him in the churchyard. The church members paid for the headstone. It read: *Here lies a good man. He had all he needed, the good Lord, a good horse, and a good rifle.* Some members thought they should mention The Beast in the engraving on the tombstone, but the trustees objected.

"You have to pay by the word for those things, don't you know."

## 50
## BAPTISM BY FIRE

Jim and Darlene knew some of the pastors and wives from Second Baptist, including Pastor Johns. He was a quiet man, and his congregation found his preaching style soothing; they could nap through Pastor Johns' sermons.

Pastor Johns had a spitfire of a little girl. His wife was as quiet and reserved as he was, so the congregation wondered where little Annie got her personality. She spoke her four-year-old mind with all the firmness her parents lacked.

Once, Annie shocked the deacons. "You better behave," she said, shaking her finger at them. "My daddy owns this church you know."

During a prayer meeting, little Annie raised her hand. "You people need to pray for my daddy to get another job," she said, "because this one gives him a headache."

Although he was soft-spoken, Pastor Johns was the first to admit he had a problem with pride, and he implored the Lord to give him humility. Second Baptist was a humble building and a small congregation, but they had one pride and joy, an elevated baptistery with a glass front.

One Sunday, Pastor Johns was surprised to see a pulpit committee sitting in the back. Pulpit committees think they're secret agents, but if they're from the city, they're easy to spot in a country church. They're usually more dressed up than country people are. Pastor Johns knew they were from a church looking for a new pastor. He wouldn't mind moving. In his opinion, Second Baptist was going nowhere fast. He'd even talked to Jim about it.

"Have you ever thought small churches are a rung on a ladder, and God means to give us something bigger and better?" Pastor Johns asked Jim.

"I've heard others say it plenty of times; that's for sure. I don't know, though. I've started to wonder; is bigger always better?"

"Well, sure it is. How many people come to your Wednesday night prayer meetings or your Sunday evening services?"

Jim sighed. This was something that deeply troubled him. "Sometimes there's only four of us."

"Same here. Last Wednesday night we had three. If I went to a larger church, more people would hear the sermons I work so hard on."

Pastor Johns eyed that pulpit committee. Maybe this was his chance for bigger and better.

*They couldn't have come on a better Sunday. I worked extra hard on my sermon this week, and I'm baptizing someone. That should impress them!*

After his sermon, Pastor Johns began the baptism. He descended the stairs on one side, and the man he was baptizing walked down the stairs on the opposite side. Pastor Johns held his 1611 King James Bible in his left hand, intending to read from it.

Without warning, Pastor Johns' foot slipped out from under him on the second step. He bounced down all the stairs and lay, with King James, on the floor of the baptistery, completely submerged, in full view of the congregation and the pulpit committee. If King James hadn't been baptized by immersion in the 1600s, he was dunked that day.

"I wanted to lie there and pray for the rapture," he later told Jim. "God has some sense of humor. When I prayed for humility, I didn't expect such a hard lesson."

The pulpit committee went home and never contacted him. Pastor Johns wasn't surprised.

A few months later, Pastor Johns needed surgery. The doctor released him from the hospital with heavy duty pain medication and warned him not to preach while on narcotics. Pastor Johns was proud of his church attendance record. Except for vacations, he hadn't missed a Sunday at Second Baptist in five years and didn't intend to start now. He wanted to give no excuse to those members he secretly thought of as lazy, no-good pew warmers.

Against doctor's orders, Pastor Johns preached his most memorable and his final sermon at Second Baptist. Under the influence of the narcotics, he raised his voice in a tone somewhat reminiscent of Pastor McCoy and called out church members by name from the pulpit. He told the members exactly what he thought of them. Phrases like "get off your butt" were used. People in the pews looked at each other. Maybe Annie's spitfire personality wasn't so much of a mystery after all.

Immediately after the service, the board fired Pastor Johns.

"Please, give me another chance," he begged. "That was just the medicine talking."

The board was firm. "No second chance," they said. "If it wasn't in your heart, it couldn't have come out of your mouth."

Pastor Johns moved from the community and became a used car salesman. He didn't do well at that because of his meek, mild personality. The members at Second Baptist talked about it.

"Maybe if he had surgery again and got more medicine, he might sell more cars."

## 51

## THE $10,000 GIFT

Sometimes things happen that are too good or too funny to seem true, and both happened when Pastor Roman was at Second Baptist.

He and Jim enjoyed swapping stories. When Jim came home from having coffee with Pastor Roman, he usually had a story or two to tell Darlene.

"Pastor Roman had a visitor at church Sunday," Jim said.

"Oh good! I've been praying about their attendance."

Second Baptist was even smaller than Corners Church.

"The visitor stood during their meet and greet time and asked to say a few words. He said he'd recently become a Christian and started reading his Bible. He suddenly realized he'd sinned when he'd divorced his first wife and married his second wife. He told everyone he'd made it right, though."

"How do you make something like that right?"

Jim laughed. "He was pretty proud of how he'd fixed it. He divorced his second wife and remarried his first wife."

"What did Pastor Roman say?"

"Not a word. What could he say? The man came to church alone. His wife didn't come with him. Neither of them."

Darlene sighed. Jim thought this story was entirely too funny.

Like all country churches, Second Baptist had ups and downs in attendance and offerings, but Pastor Roman and the people became seriously concerned when the tiny congregation couldn't scrape together even enough money to pay their missionaries. For three weeks, Pastor Roman refused his own salary so the church could pay the bills. The congregation's spirits were as low as their finances.

Pastor Roman called a special praise and prayer meeting. "We won't complain about what we don't have. We'll praise God for our many blessings. Then we'll ask Him to supply our needs. We need money. It's only money, and God's got a lot of it. He can bring that money in from anywhere."

The people were skeptical. Anywhere, USA hadn't sent them money before, but they praised and prayed as Pastor Roman requested.

A few days later, Mrs. Roman had a garage sale. Surely, she could part with a few things to make ends meet. She was setting out items when a truck pulled in the driveway. *Good, a customer already.*

The driver got out and asked for the pastor.

"Well," he said, after learning Pastor Roman wasn't home, "I think God wants me to give him this for the church. I'll leave this bag here with you."

When Pastor Roman got home, he and his wife dumped the contents of the bag. It was full of money. When they finished counting it, they looked at each other in astonishment. What a gift, and from someone they didn't even know! The total came to a little over $10,000.

Pastor Roman could hardly wait for Sunday testimony time

to share the good news, but when the time came, Mrs. Iris struggled to her feet, waving one hand in the air, and tipping left and right. Alarmed, people on both sides and behind her jumped to their feet to steady her.

Once she was sufficiently propped, Mrs. Iris said, "My knees remind me I will be one hundred and two next Friday; if anyone wants to remember my birthday, chocolate chip cookies are my favorite. Anyway, I may be one hundred and two, but I remember being a child like it was yesterday. My mother was a strict woman. She didn't allow us to use cuss words. We had to go to bed early if we said words like. . ." and she proceeded to list an amazing variety of swear words.

Parents shushed giggling kids as Pastor Roman tried to get a word in edgewise.

In desperation, he interrupted her. "Before we continue with testimony time, we have a special. The cherub choir will sing for us."

The cherub choir, all three of them, went to the platform wearing their tiny white robes. With angelic faces they sang, "Oh, be careful little mouth what you say. Oh, be careful little mouth what you say. For the Father up above is looking down in love, so be careful little mouth what you say."

As they finished to a round of applause, Mrs. Iris struggled to her feet again.

"That sweet song reminded me of more words Mother didn't allow us to say." She began another list.

The cherub choir still stood on the platform, eyes wide, little hands over their mouths as they listened to the swear words.

Pastor Roman groaned. He later told Jim the whole story.

"What did you do?" Jim asked.

"I let her finish. What else could I do? Then I gave my testimony about the $10,000 gift. I don't think it impressed the people as much as it would have if their minds weren't full of Mrs. Iris's 10,000 cuss words."

Darlene chuckled. She loved Pastor and Mrs. Roman. Mrs. Roman was one of those who'd definitely been called to be a pastor's wife. Darlene sighed. She wished she knew for sure she was doing a job God had called her to do. Maybe knowing for sure God had called her wasn't all that important.

Years before, a friend had come to dinner and gladly helped pitch in with the cleanup. As they'd washed and dried the dishes, Darlene had smiled at Lily. "I think I know your spiritual gift. I think it's serving."

"Ha!" Lily had grinned. "Who would know? I didn't have time to find out. Whenever there was anything to do, Mom always told me to get up and do it."

*If God gives you a job to do,* Darlene thought, *you don't worry about whether you've been called. You get up and do it.*

Still, even after all these years, Darlene wasn't sure she was cut out to be a pastor's wife. She loved being Jim's wife, but the poor guy sure hadn't married anyone like the ideal Mrs. Kole or Mrs. Roman.

## 52

## CAMPING WITH FRIENDS

Darlene yawns and rubs her eyes. *What time is it? This feels like the longest night ever, but I don't want it to end.*

"We have so many good memories that the smiles have crowded out the tears," she says to Jim. But he's sleeping soundly. Her mind drifts to friends, and warm tears flood her cheeks.

"I think it was Erasmus who said, 'We had one soul between us,'" she said. Darlene knows she's a tapestry of all the words she's ever loved and all the people she's cherished. She's thinking about their good friends, Katrina and Landon, the ones they'd spent so much time camping with. Even now, in their old age, she and Jim are still grateful for the memories of those times of swimming, laughing, eating, and talking around the campfire as darkness deepened.

Darlene loves every friend God has ever given her, especially those camping friends. They were a definite answer to the prayer she and Jim had prayed on the couch.

∽

PLANNING, cooking, packing—and they were off! Nothing was more fun than a camping vacation with good friends, and Jim and Darlene cherished the six summers they spent camping with Katrina, Landon, and their kids.

Katrina and Landon had four children, and Jim and Darlene had three. Darlene and Katrina prepared meals and cooked ahead as much as possible. Both families were enthusiastically grateful for all the food, with one notable exception.

One year, Darlene canned Brunswick stew. One taste, and everyone but Landon said it was disgusting and refused to eat it. Gentle, loving Landon really tried.

"It's pretty good; it really is. This isn't too bad. He ate a few more bites, put down his spoon, and apologized.

"I can't. I'm sorry, but I just can't."

The weather was cool one summer, so the two families spent a lot of time near the fire, feet stretched out to the flames.

Landon and Jim discussed how they were going to butcher the 100 chickens, Phil, their farmer friend had offered them.

"They run wild," Phil had said. "You two can have them, but you'll have to catch them first."

Where should they butcher the chickens? Whose house would work better for cleaning and freezing the meat?

"I smell something burning, Jim," Landon said. "Do you smell anything?"

Suddenly Landon jumped to his feet and did what looked like a strange version of a rain dance. The rest of them looked at him, wondering, until Jim figured it out.

"I think he got his tennis shoes too close to the fire!"

The seven kids often wandered off, hiking, riding bikes, or looking for dead wood for the fire. One day they ran back to camp.

"Someone tried to kidnap us!" they shouted.

The parents looked at each other and smiled. They were used to dramatic tall tales.

"It's true," one child insisted. "A man told us to get in his car!"

"All seven of you?" a disbelieving parent asked.

"Yes!" they insisted. "He tried to kidnap all seven of us."

The parents later agreed privately if the story was true, the man must be crazy, trying to kidnap their combined brood of wild, noisy kids.

When the story persisted year after year, the parents started to believe it, and they kept a better eye on their children. And after all the talk about catching, killing, cleaning, and freezing the chickens, Jim and Landon never did it. It made for a lot of good campfire conversation, though.

## 53

## FAMILY FRIENDS

When Darlene thinks about friends, she wonders with Amy Carmichael, "What is it that causes some minutes to be preserved as though they were of singular preciousness? The years make no difference.... They are imperishable."

∽

JIM AND DARLENE tried to teach their children a friend can be any age. One of their favorite friends, Kenyon, was in his eighties. They cherished him for his kindness, gentleness, sense of humor, and cheerful optimism.

Jim and Darlene returned from an errand to see Jimmy and Davey next door, outside with Kenyon. They balanced on their bikes, laughing and talking to Kenyon who sat on his lawn mower. Darlene smiled. What could be more lovely to the Lord than seeing His children enjoying each other—one age nine, one twelve, and one eighty-three?

Age is an artificial division. True friendship isn't based on what you can get, but on what you can give, and you can give at any age.

Emily Dickinson wrote one of Darlene's favorite friendship quotes: "They might not need me; but they might. I'll let my head be just in sight; a smile as small as mine might be precisely their necessity."

The boys and Kenyon needed each other's smiles.

## 54

## HARD WORK

In July and August, Darlene began a marathon endurance race that lasted until October's killing freeze. The children ran with her, sometimes willingly, sometimes not so willingly. The race was called canning and freezing time.

Darlene loved the poem about canning Betty gave her after church one day.

"I don't know who wrote this," Betty said, "but I thought you might like it. You've come a long way from that girl who didn't know how to can a bushel of tomatoes."

"I hardly remember that girl! Sometimes I feel like canning and freezing are about all I do." Darlene laughed and held out berry-stained hands.

"Been making more jam? I'll tell you a trick. Lemon juice will take those stains right off."

"I guess I still have a few things to learn."

"I guess we all do." Betty hugged her. "Hope you like the poem."

## A Country Mouse to a City Mouse

A garden's a wonderful thing to have,
    I realize this is so,
    But before you get too carried away
    There are some things you ought to know.

When summer time comes, and the broiling sun
    Sends the city gals off to the beaches,
    Where do you s'pose the country gals are?
    We're at home—canning peaches!

When we're tired and hot, and weary of work
    And would like to do as we please
    Can we sit down and put our feet up?
    No—the string beans are ready to freeze!

Our hands become stained, our fingernails break,
    Our hair gets scraggly and wild—
    If you think that I exaggerate some,
    I assure you, I'm putting it mild!

So before you envy the table we set
    And the food we have on the shelf,
    Just let me remind you again, my friend,
    It didn't get there by itself!

ONE LONG, hot summer day, the kids helped Darlene freeze eighty quarts of corn. Five-year-old Davey said, as Darlene tucked him into bed, "Today was a funny, funny day. I didn't get to play, not even one time."

Darlene felt bad. She didn't want to make the kids work too hard, and she usually gave them plenty of time to play.

"I'm sorry, honey."

But Davey was already asleep.

During the long winter months that followed, Darlene often reminded Davey of his helpfulness when she cooked some of "his" corn. Come December, he grudgingly conceded garden work was worth it. Maybe.

When Darlene looked back on all the hard work the kids had helped her do in the garden and the kitchen, she realized she'd accomplished two things. First, she hadn't raised any lazy children. Second, all the kids had grown up to hate vegetables. Wait. One child did like vegetables, but she'd developed a severe allergy to them.

When they were grown, Jimmy and Davey said to Darlene, "Hey, Mom, you should be proud of us. We went out to eat today, and we ordered a double helping of vegetables."

"Really? What vegetable?"

"French fries!"

The children worked hard and played hard. Darlene wrote:

> Three barefoot children
> > Romping in the grass,
> > Lovely, tanned, and laughing—
> > How I wish these days could last.

~

DARLENE LOOKS AT JIM. She thinks, if she listens hard enough, she may hear God calling his name. Too soon, he'll be where the good days do last.

*I wish I could go too.* Her work isn't finished. Someone has to comfort the children and grandchildren and help them through sad days ahead. Darlene will do that. Perhaps that will be the last job the Lord gives her to do. She hopes so, because it will be hard work, the hardest work she's ever had to do.

## 55

## VACATION ADVENTURES AND MISADVENTURES

When someone in the family said the word "vacation," someone else in the family snickered or sighed. Jim and Darlene didn't have a very good time-off track record. There were many aborted attempts to go to a parade, the fireworks, the zoo, or a park. Plans had often been sidetracked because someone had needed them.

Camping was their favorite way to spend a vacation. The first week of August usually found them airing out the tent, checking lantern wicks, rolling sleeping bags, and packing marshmallows. As Darlene packed, she grinned, thinking of something she'd read.

An old woman worked circles around her younger neighbors. They asked her secret, and she replied, "When I works, I works hard; when I sits, I sits loose."

Vacation was a time to sit loose. Jim and Darlene's favorite vacation spot was a primitive campground in a Michigan state forest. Whenever Darlene left that campground, she determined to simplify life at home. There's beauty in simplicity.

One year a camping vacation became a staycation instead.

They made day trips instead of going camping because a young woman was in the hospital with complications as she waited the birth of her first child. Her mother asked Jim and Darlene to please stay within shouting distance.

Another August, their elderly neighbor and friend, Kenyon, asked Jim and Darlene to delay a camping trip because his health was so precarious. When they did get to go, the kids were ecstatic. They spent an entire day hunting for dead wood in the state forest, splitting it, and stacking it between two trees. They were excited and proud about the large woodpile and planned huge campfires every night the rest of the week.

Later that same day, a state trooper found Jim and Darlene on the beach. He gave them a too familiar message, "Call home."

Mabel Hall had been fine when they'd left home, but now she was in the hospital, dying. They got home barely in time to say goodbye, to mingle their tears with Kenyon's, and to officiate her funeral. Mabel had been like family, and she left a hole in their hearts when she went Home to heaven.

Darlene would always remember seeing Kenyon bending over Mabel's hospital bed. His tears dripped down over their gnarled, entwined hands.

"What will I do without you? You've always been the strong one."

Mabel looked at him tenderly, as she struggled to breathe and talk at the same time. "Fifty-fifty," she said.

*I think you both give one-hundred and fifty percent to each other and to everyone around you,* Darlene thought. That's how she wanted to be. She knew what Jim would say about it.

"Better get a move on then."

They didn't mind coming home from vacation for Kenyon and Mabel, and none of the kids complained about it either. The children learned young that love means giving, and giving often comes at a cost. It wasn't their first interrupted vacation, and it wouldn't be the last.

The kids balanced vacation disappointments with genuine compassion and all grew up to have a deep concern for others. For that, Jim and Darlene were grateful.

## TEA WITH FRIENDS

*Why is it,* Darlene wondered, *that celebrations so often involve something to eat or drink?* She and Jim had fond memories of the hot spiced cider Dad Peters had served at his Christmas parties, of drinking hot chocolate with their kids on cold winter nights, and of huddling with friends around campfires, warming their hands with steaming cups of coffee and warming their hearts with love and laughter.

Even in fiction, the simple act of sharing a cup of tea means more than the words actually say. As they hurried to Thad and Caroline Nowling's house, Darlene thought about how she loved hearing Caroline read *A Cup of Christmas Tea* at the candlelight service at church every year. Now they were on their way to Nowling's for a cup of tea, and they were very late, because they'd forgotten the invitation. They were supposed to be at Nowlings at 10:00 a.m. At 10:45 a.m., Thad had called to see if anything was wrong.

"Help me write an apology poem?" Darlene asked Jim as he drove to the forgotten appointment. He laughed but agreed.

Darlene and Jim knocked on Nowling's door and dropped to their knees. When Thad and Caroline opened the door, Jim and Darlene greeted them with this poem:

> We repent in ashes and dust!
> We fear our brains are filled with rust!
> Can you forgive this social blunder, and
> Overlook two brains that slumber?
> Oh, do forgive; we beg you, please!
> We even ask on bended knees.

Nowlings laughed, invited in their forgetful pastor and wife, and served them cookies, brownies, coffee, and their home-brewed lemon balm tea.

Caroline and Thad's fascinating herb cupboard held many glass jars of dried herbs: lemon balm, tansy, yarrow, mullein, and many others. Darlene laughed when she saw a jar labeled "boneset."

"I had the flu one Sunday and missed church," Darlene told Thad and Caroline. "Marsha sent me a jar of boneset and said I should use it to make tea and drink it to the last drop. I'd never made tea with anything but a tea bag. I didn't know enough to strain the boneset leaves before drinking the tea. There's nothing like being sick to your stomach and then having to gag down half a hay field! You don't want to know the rest of the story!"

Nowlings laughed, and so did Jim. He knew the rest of the story.

"I swear," Darlene had told him, "that's the last time I ever miss church. I don't care how sick I am; I'm going. I can't stand anymore of this country kindness. It's killing me!"

Thad said boneset had been used as long ago as the Civil War and really does help promote healing.

After Darlene's boneset blunder, Jim had preached that life is called a "cup" in Scripture and is a figure of speech for a divine appointment. Jesus took the cup His Father gave Him and willingly drank it all, and we need to do the same.

"The will of God must be very important," Jim said, "because the New Testament mentions that phrase twenty-three times. When we pray for God's will, we're really saying, 'Thy kingdom come; my kingdom be gone. Thy will come; my will be gone.'"

Darlene had listened to that sermon, and she'd agreed with what Jim had said, but she'd also thought that it's sometimes easier to accept God's will in life's giant troubles than it is to remain cheerful when a groundhog eats half of the garden. *Had it been easier*, she wondered, *for Daniel to face the lion's den with grace than it was for him to be chewed by the millions of mosquitos that must have bitten him when he prayed at his open window three times a day? Probably the mosquitos in life give us the courage to face the lions.*

Jim had closed the sermon by praying, "Lord, help us take with both hands the cup of life, drink it fully, and find Your joy even in pain. I pray we will accept every circumstance You send."

"Good sermon, honey," Darlene had said. "I really want to drink fully whatever cup God gives me, as long as it doesn't have boneset in it!"

~

JIM STIRS in his hospital bed, and Darlene tucks the sheet around him.

"Jim, do you remember that awful boneset tea I had to drink? Do you think I'll get a crown in heaven for doing that?"

She leans in close to hear his answer. "Doubt it," he whispers. "You had a bad attitude."

"Easy for you to say. You didn't have to drink it."

But he's sleeping again. *The cup he's drinking now is far more bitter than boneset. Soon, it will be over for him. He'll be forever with God, family, and the many friends from Corners Church who are already in heaven. But I'll still be here saying,* "Thy kingdom come; my kingdom be gone. Thy will come; my will be gone."

She wipes away tears. They aren't the first tears she's cried that long night, and they won't be the last.

## A SNOWY VALENTINE'S DAY

They called Valentine's Day 1985 the worst storm of the season. The kids were out of school long enough to build a two-story snow fort, complete with steps. They coaxed Darlene to come sit in it and rewarded her with a soggy valentine candy heart. Darlene admired the animals they'd made from snow and put around the fort. They'd created a bear, a duck with ducklings, an elephant with a curved trunk, a bunny with a cute tail, and a lion with a straw mane.

The school canceled every day that week. Seven-year old Davey fell on Tuesday and cut his eye. Next, he tumbled from the top of his toy box. Darlene hoped no one asked her what he was doing up there; a good mother might know, but she did not. Then he scraped his arm on his bunkbed and bruised his hand doing some gymnastic trick. He also ran around a corner, misjudged the tricky manipulations involved in waiting until the last minute to swerve, because no true boy swerves a second before necessary, and crunched his toe on a chair.

It had been a long week, but Jim and Darlene admitted to

each other they'd enjoyed the week spent in forced isolation. On Tuesday, the lights went out. They ate supper by kerosene lamps and candles. Jim studied at one end of the table as Darlene tried to see well enough to cut cloth flowers at the other end.

The children played their favorite game, UNO, on the floor. The dim light caused many disagreements about whether a card was blue or green.

Jim sighed and suggested they all gather around the kerosene heater, the only source of heat. He read aloud from *Little House in the Big Woods*.

Electricity returned the next day, but the snow kept falling. Darlene had a spring article due for a magazine. She tried to think spring as the wind howled. April asked if her molasses cookies looked done; Jimmy and Davey giggled in the living room and asked when she was going to make snow ice cream. Darlene turned off the electric typewriter, looked at the boys, and sighed.

With a sudden idea of how to improve her writing environment she asked, "Wouldn't you boys like to play upstairs?"

Too late she remembered a maxim she'd learned in child psychology: Don't give a command in the form of a request.

"We want to play here," Jimmy said. "We've played upstairs tons of times lately."

"Oh." Darlene groaned. "It doesn't feel like it."

Jim, studying at the other end of the table, smiled at her with the look of a conspirator. It didn't feel like it to him either. Still, the boys had a valid point. Jim and Darlene weren't working upstairs either. It was cold up there. Some of the inside walls were made from refrigerator boxes, the logos still visible. One winter, Jim's books had frozen to the wall.

Better Jimmy and Davey played downstairs anyway. They

would be closer when someone acquired the next bruise, likely to happen any minute.

"Please, come look at my cookies," April begged.

*Whose idea was it for a twelve-year-old to bake cookies when I have a column due?* Then she remembered. It had been her idea.

Darlene checked the cookies. She'd finish the writing the way she always did, in bits and pieces, when she could fit it in around family and church family who needed her. She'd never be an Emily Brontë or even an Edgar Allen Poe, but that was okay. She hoped someday people would say of her as the Lord had said of Mary, "She did what she could."

Right then the phone rang. "Darlene, do you have time to talk today?" a church lady asked.

And that was the end of writing for that day.

# CHRISTMAS 1986—THE GLITZY LADDER

The glowing lights of the tree in the corner captured the eyes of the children sitting on the short, wooden pews. Candy bags packed with homemade fudge and other goodies sat ready to give to kids of all ages, and the ornaments Jim and Darlene had made for their beloved church family waited in a box in the entryway.

In a small church, children and adults participate together in the musical programs. Jim and Darlene stood on the platform with the children and sang, "It's true we're growing older. . .but when it comes to Christmas, I will always be a child."

April, Jimmy, and Davey sang with them. For years, Darlene had hoped and prayed for one more child, but now she doubted it would ever happen. Little did anyone guess that when Darlene stood on the platform for the 1988 Christmas program she would be like Mary in the Bible, "great with child" expecting a little girl, Becky Joy.

April, Jimmy, and Davey loved everything about Christmas, the church programs, putting up the cedar tree, and running to the mailbox to look for Christmas cards. There were a great many cards that year.

"Look, Mom," April said. "Dad got a package from his old college professor. I wonder what's in it?"

Darlene wondered too. Professor Nick Machiavelli sent a card every year, usually telling Jim what great things he and his other past students were doing, and always signing it, "Climb higher! N.M." But he'd never sent a package before.

Jim laughed when he opened the package. Inside was an elaborate glass ornament, a glitzy, heavy, glass ladder with Santa Claus on it. Santa wore a necklace engraved with the letters N.M. There was no mistaking the not so subtle message of the ladder: Climb higher!

"Do you want me to hang the ladder on the tree?" Davey asked.

"Sure, go ahead."

The heavy ornament pulled the fragile cedar branch to the floor.

"I don't think it looks very good," Jimmy said.

"I don't think it looks good at all." Darlene snatched it off the tree and glared at it the way she'd like to give the evil eye to Professor Nick Machiavelli. She was getting more than a little tired of him. Jim had a hard time sleeping for a few nights every time he heard from old N.M.

"What are you going to do with that ornament?" Jim asked suspiciously.

"Goodwill Industries has helped us enough in the past; I'm going to donate this ornament to them."

No one objected. Not even Jim. Glitz did not belong in their house.

*But was the climb higher philosophy right?* Jim could forget about that question for months at a time, but it always came back to haunt him, and he still wasn't sure of the answer.

## "I LIED."

Jim went to the hospital to visit Harry, an older man who was very sick.

"Harry says he has asked the Lord Jesus to save him," Jim told Darlene, when he got home.

"That's wonderful!"

Jim shook his head. "I don't know why, but I don't believe him. I think he was just saying that to get rid of me!"

The next Sunday, halfway through Jim's sermon, the door flew open, and Harry's son-in-law hurried in. "Pastor, please come quick. Harry's dying, and he's asking for you."

Jim left Deacon Pete in charge and hurried to the hospital.

Harry looked at him with fear in his eyes. He only had strength enough left for two words. "I lied."

"You lied to me about accepting Jesus as your Savior, didn't you?"

Harry could no longer talk, but he nodded.

"Do you know you're a sinner?"

A miserable look and a tearful nod.

"Do you believe that Jesus, God's son, died on the cross to take your punishment for sin, was buried, and rose again?"

A weak nod.

Jim took Harry's hand. "Squeeze my hand once if you want to ask Jesus to save you from sin's punishment and give you eternal life in heaven."

Harry squeezed once.

"Pray with me silently, Harry," Jim said. "Lord, I know I'm a sinner, and I deserve hell. I believe you love me and suffered and died to take my punishment for sin. I accept your death in place of mine. Please, forgive my sin and give me eternal life."

Jim looked into Harry's eyes. All fear was gone, and Harry smiled weakly.

"Squeeze my hand if you prayed that prayer."

Harry squeezed.

"What happened to him?" a nurse later asked his family. "He was so terrified and restless earlier today. Now, he's so peaceful."

Harry lived only a few more hours before he went home to heaven to enjoy the eternal life and love he'd found just a short time before.

## THE MACDONALD THANKSGIVING

It was almost time. Penelope and Gertrude felt a mixture of sadness and relief as they reflected on the Thanksgiving meal notebook.

"Pastor Jim had a good Thanksgiving sermon, but it was hard to pay attention. We kept thinking about our notebook," Gertrude told Darlene.

"What notebook is that?"

The sisters explained. The MacDonald Thanksgiving notebook had been passed down for generations. As each generation of sisters turned sixty, they passed the notebook to daughters and nieces. From then on, it was the younger generation's job to prepare Thanksgiving dinner for the huge MacDonald family. This was Penelope and Gertrude's last year to be in charge. They would turn the notebook over to their daughters and granddaughters after this year. They had already stubbornly hung onto the notebook twenty years too long.

The notebook was a huge help with planning the Thanksgiving menu. It listed how much food had been prepared each year and how many had come.

The notebook also cataloged any mistakes. Younger generations snickered when they read notations from great grandmothers and great aunts.

"Sophie and her clan did not come, even though they promised three times. They were supposed to bring the sweet potatoes, so no sweet potatoes were had this year. Everyone missed the potatoes."

No mention was made of missing Sophie or her clan.

"Don't let Matilda bring food next year. That woman's burned everything she's brought for the last five years. Put her in charge of paper napkins. She might bring Halloween ones, but at least we won't have to eat them."

The notebook listed the pounds of potatoes, numbers of turkeys, bags of stuffing, and amounts of corn, squash, and cranberries. It noted what worked, what didn't, and gave suggestions on how to do better next year.

One year, someone wrote in tiny print, "Eighty pounds turkey, forty pounds potatoes, fifteen gallon bags frozen corn, ten butternut squash, five acorn squash. We ran out of potatoes. There would have been plenty if some of the youngsters had been taught not to make pigs of themselves."

"We're feeling a bit sad," Gertrude said to Darlene after they finished telling her about the notebook. "How long before this younger generation starts using store-bought frozen squash or instant mashed potatoes?"

"Worse yet, how long before they decide to go to a restaurant for Thanksgiving?" Penelope added. "Someday, someone will probably toss this notebook in the trash along with the Thanksgiving traditions."

"Well, we can hope and pray they don't give up the MacDonald tradition of being grateful. We're known for that, aren't we?"

The two sisters linked arms and helped each other down

the church steps. Darlene watched them limp down the sidewalk. She wondered if she'd still be excited about peeling pounds of potatoes when she was eighty-something years old. She doubted it.

*What will Gertrude and Penelope's last entry in the notebook be? Maybe I'll ask them next Sunday if they wrote anything about youngsters who'd made pigs of themselves.*

## PHONE CALLS

"Someday, I might need surgery to remove this thing from my ear." Darlene slammed the phone back on the receiver. "If this was 1876, I'd feel tempted to shoot Alexander Graham Bell before he could get a patent for this wretched thing."

"Seems you don't mind talking to Andrea or Katrina for an hour," Jim said.

"That's different. They're friends. They don't call me day and night with impossible counseling questions like Candy does. Sometimes she talks to me for more than two hours. What am I going to do?"

Jim looked at her sympathetically. Candy was a child in an adult's body. She called early and late, with problems, questions, or some tall tale to tell. Sometimes Candy trailed off into silence.

When Candy was quiet on the phone and Darlene talked, Candy would reply, "Shh. I'm trying to watch a good part in my TV program."

"Oh, I'll let you go so you can watch it then," Darlene would reply, hoping against hope she could hang up.

"Nope. I've seen what I want to. I have more things I need to talk to you about."

Sometimes, when it got late and Darlene was desperate for rest after a long day, she prayed Candy would hang up. She didn't have the heart to cut her off because Candy was so needy, but she didn't have the energy to keep listening either.

When Candy eventually said goodbye, Darlene would stumble to bed, too tired to say anything to the Lord except, "She's one of Your little ones, Jesus. Love her through me, and please give me strength!"

Once, when Darlene was trapped on the phone, Jim walked past her, grinned, and sang, "I'd like to buy the world a coke." Darlene scowled and Jim laughed.

In later years, Darlene found the invention of the cell phone a blessing and a curse. It didn't have a cord, so she wasn't stuck in one place and could do other things if she had to be on the phone for two hours with Candy. It also had caller ID so she could tell if a telemarketer was on the other end. Before they had caller ID, the phone rang one day. Darlene sighed and answered.

"I'm taking a survey, ma'am," a man said. "May I have a few minutes of your time?"

Just what she wanted to do—answer survey questions, but people expect pastors' wives to be polite, so she stifled a groan and agreed.

First question: "What do you think of the equal rights amendment?"

Darlene answered.

Second question: "Do you support legalized abortion?"

Darlene answered.

Third question: "Do you think we should allow Italian immigrants?"

Darlene hesitated. *What kind of question was that?* Then came laughter from the caller and others in the background. The voice hadn't sounded familiar, but the laugh sounded like Ken's, the deacon who often teased Darlene about her Italian background.

Ken stopped disguising his voice. "Happy April Fool's Day, Darlene."

Darlene laughed. Sometimes, rarely, she was glad for the phone. In later years, when cell phones freed her from the three-foot phone cord, Darlene grew to enjoy phone calls from Corners Church people. It was a family connection she was glad to have.

## OFFERING PLATE MISHAPS

Jim tossed his suit coat over the pulpit chair, pulled his tie down a bit, and preached in a short-sleeved shirt. Women used bulletins for fans, and the men looked miserable and uncomfortable, beads of sweat forming on foreheads and running down faces.

The old wooden windows were propped open, but there was no breeze. When the occasional vehicle drove down the road, the dust drifted lazily to the ground behind it. Everyone wished for a strong west wind. True, it would blow dirt from the road into the auditorium, but at least it would give a little relief from the sweltering heat. The skies grew ominously dark, but still, there was no wind.

Suddenly, as if in an answer to unspoken prayers, a strong west wind kicked up and came through the open windows. People sighed with relief. The breeze played with the children's hair, and then with a giant breath it blew money from the offering plates. Ones, fives, and the occasional ten scattered in every direction. What was that? A thousand-dollar bill? That would have been a record offering, but it was Monopoly money. Everyone was watching the money. No one was looking at Jim.

A wise preacher knows when he's lost his audience. "Do you kids want to come up here and pick up the money?" Jim asked.

The kids had no children's church that day, and they were only too happy to leave the hard pews before the final amen. They rushed up front, picked up the money, and put it back into the offering plates.

Then it started pouring. The wind drove the rain straight through the screens. People yanked down the swollen wooden windows, but by then half the congregation was wet.

Jim sighed. Perhaps he could use point three of his sermon another time. He called the piano player to the front. They closed with an appropriate song, "There Shall Be Showers of Blessings."

~

THE CONGREGATION WAS USED to Candy's behavior at offering time. As soon as the ushers started down the aisle, Candy jumped to her feet, smiled, and waved her dollar bill in the air. Perhaps she feared the ushers would miss her. That would have been hard to do because there were only seven half-size pews on each side of the auditorium.

"Candy's a bit distracting, Pastor Jim," someone remarked. "Do you think you should say something to her?"

"I'd really rather not," Jim responded with a small grin. "The Bible says God loves a cheerful giver."

Candy was nothing if not cheerful. One Sunday, she jumped to her feet waving, not her usual one-dollar bill, but a ten. When the usher stopped next to her, she said loudly, "Just a minute. I have to make change." It took her a long time to count out nine dollars of change. Eventually, the usher helped her. Everyone agreed offering time was unusually entertaining that day.

Candy loved Jim and was eager to contribute whatever she could. In the early years, the Corners Church congregation was so quiet and reserved they would have made their New England ancestors proud. Jim knew better than to hope for a "Hallelujah!" or a "Preach it, brother!" But was it too much to expect a simple, quiet, "amen" now and then?

One Sunday, Jim said, "It would really encourage me if you said 'amen' sometimes when you agree with something I'm saying."

His sermon was on sin that day, and a few sentences later, Jim said, "Please, don't think I'm pointing fingers at any of you. I know I'm the biggest sinner in the room."

"Amen!" Candy enthusiastically yelled. That day, she contributed far more than her dollar.

## A GUEST PREACHER

Jim's college friend, Todd, was coming to visit. "Where will he sleep?" Darlene asked, looking around their tiny house.

"It's not only him." Jim avoided her glance. "He's bringing his wife and eight kids with him. The Bible says to be hospitable. What could I do? He invited himself. Oh, he also offered to preach. He's been asking me for a long time to let him preach at our church."

Darlene was trying to master the art of poise, raising her eyebrows instead of her voice. "Isn't he the one you told me always preaches at least an hour?"

Jim sighed. "At least."

It was a long weekend. Todd talked fast, loud, and long. All eight children took after their father. Demi, Todd's wife, was quiet and shy. She barely spoke the entire weekend, and she wore a perpetually worried frown. Darlene felt sorry for her.

Todd insisted he and Demi have a bedroom to themselves since he needed the quiet to "think about my sermon." That left the other fourteen to squeeze into one small bedroom and overflow onto the living room couch and floor.

On Sunday morning, Todd took a half hour shower in the only bathroom while the others waited for a turn.

"He always takes long showers on Sunday mornings," Demi explained apologetically. "He says it helps clear his mind."

Todd didn't think much of Corners Church's small white frame building. He almost sneered as he stood in the gravel parking lot, looking at the two dirt roads.

"This place is even more pathetic than I imagined. You've been here too long," he said to Jim. "Do like Nick taught us; move up the ladder as soon as you can. This church is going nowhere fast. Do you know the three things most important for church growth?" Before Jim could answer, Todd continued, "Location, location, location." He gestured dismissively at the church building and at the two dirt roads that framed it.

Jim wanted to say something to defend the church he loved, but a nagging part of his mind wondered if Todd was right. Others had said the same thing. They had implied real success was measured in numbers, something Jim knew he would never have at Corners Church. Part of Jim despised the nickels and noses counting philosophy, but part of him wished there were more nickels and noses to count.

The wooden church sign said the worship service started at 11:00 a.m., but at 11:05 a.m., people were still standing around and talking. No one had come into the auditorium. Todd was fuming.

"Why do you let these people get away with this?" he demanded.

Jim grinned, remembering when he'd felt like Todd did. It seemed so long ago.

Todd grew more irritated. It had been announced he was

preaching, and he took it as a personal insult. At 11:20 a.m., after a short song service, Jim welcomed Todd to the pulpit. Right away, Todd lectured the congregation about starting church on time. He told them they were being a bad testimony.

He thundered, hitting the pulpit with each word, "When the service is supposed to start at eleven, the service should start at eleven." People glanced sideways at each other and tried not to grin.

Next, Todd gave the folks a run-down of his degrees, B.A. in religious education, Bachelor of Theology, Master of Divinity, and three doctorates, one in Greek, one in Hebrew, and one in theology.

A man sitting near the front, who was hard of hearing, whispered loudly to his wife, "I hope he don't preach on humility." Someone in the next pew giggled. Todd paused for a minute.

The sermon began. There was much pacing back and forth, multiple references to Greek and Hebrew texts, and a twenty-minute sidebar on the merits of the Authorized King James Bible, 1611 edition. Unlike Jim, Pastor Todd was fond of shouting, pounding the pulpit, and occasionally walking half-way down the aisle. Pastor Todd didn't need a microphone.

Darlene squirmed in the pew, almost wishing for another lightning strike. It was a warm, humid day, like it had been that day, and the windows were opened, facing the beautiful fields of growing corn. On the day lightning had struck, everyone had been a bit drowsy in the pews, wishing for a breeze. Darlene had glanced out the window at the ominous, black sky.

*Strange that the wind isn't blowing yet,* she'd thought. At that moment, thunder had exploded, shaking the church, and Darlene had seen a wide bolt of lightning strike Lickley Road. It had been white with blue stripes on each side.

Becky Joy, a baby, had been sleeping in her arms. She'd

awoken with a terrified scream, throwing her arms out in a baby reflex. She hadn't been the only one who had screamed; an entire row of teens on the other side of the church had screamed too, and Jim had ended the service after one look at the sky.

*If only lightning would strike again. Maybe we could escape Todd's tirade.* It crossed her mind she should feel guilty for thinking that. But she didn't, not even a little bit.

The clock hands inched their way toward noon. People waited anxiously for the words, "in conclusion," but they didn't come. Years later, no one remembered what the sermon topic had been, but everyone remembered Todd Pritchard, B.A. in religious education, Bachelor of Theology, Master of Divinity, and doctorates thrice over had preached until 1:00 p.m.

Everyone also remembered Deacon Pete's closing prayer, each word emphasized by a loud tap on the pew, "And Lord, help this young man to remember that when a service is supposed to end at noon, the service should end at noon."

After Sunday dinner, Todd and his family left for home. An exhausted Darlene put away leftovers and washed dishes, and Jim helped.

"Proud as the proverbial peacock!" she muttered.

"Darlene!" Jim rebuked gently. Then they laughed.

## LOVE, LAUGHTER, AND LONELINESS

Darlene's glad for the big home they live in now and for the generous people who had made it possible for them to live here. Where would they have put this hospital bed in the little house they'd lived for twenty-one years?

~

THOUGH THE LITTLE house had been small, they'd made room for friends, missionaries, cousins, and a multitude of the kids' friends. Love and laughter had filled the rooms.

With the passing of the years, the little house became more and more crowded. Jim and Darlene's bedroom doubled as a study. They'd said goodnight under the shadow of books by Spurgeon, Maclaren, Ironside, Lenski, Morgan, Wiersbe, Tozer, Lloyd-Jones, and Keil and Delitzsch. Who'd dare go to bed in a huff when in such noble company?

Loneliness, however, sometimes snuck in along with the love and laughter. Their two high school sons, Jimmy and

Davey, shared a bedroom as did their high school daughter, April, and their preschool daughter, Becky Joy. Whenever April returned to college, Becky Joy, distressed at being "the only one who has to sleep by myself," suggested creative solutions. She begged to share her room with a dog, cat, fish, horse, or an elephant.

Becky Joy wasn't the only lonely one. Darlene often talked with two miserable women, one lonely because she was single and the other because she was in an unhappy marriage. Longing to share life with someone compatible isn't wrong. God created us to love and be loved, but marriage or singleness, friendship or its lack—these things don't create or cure loneliness. Unfortunately, loneliness is part of being human.

But how do you explain that to a little girl who wants to share her room with an elephant? It's difficult enough to explain it to a grown woman with a hurting heart.

A mom once tried to comfort her little girl who was lonely and afraid of the dark by telling her Jesus was with her. "I know Jesus is here," the little girl said, "but I want someone with skin on."

We all do, don't we? We want someone with skin on.

## SUGAR AND SPICE

"Guess we'll just have to start calling you Abraham and Sarah." Dale Roseheart teased when Jim and Darlene shared their news. God was sending them a new baby, and they were forty-years old.

"You look like you're in love," Jenna Roseheart commented the first Sunday Darlene brought Becky Joy to church.

"That's just how I feel, in love!"

It didn't take Becky Joy long to add her own spice to Corners Church. She talked in complete sentences when she was fifteen-months old; this was not a good thing.

"Grandma Posy," she said one Sunday, as she snuggled into the lap of an adoring admirer, "you have a very nice mustache."

Darlene winced and hoped Grandma Posy hadn't heard, but the dear lady wasn't at all deaf.

Darlene was fond of teaching Becky Joy old sayings and often told her, "If at first you don't succeed, try, try again."

Jim and Darlene were standing at the door in the entryway shaking hands after a service when they kept hearing loud bursts of laughter from the auditorium.

"It's your daughter," Mary Beth told them. "She's going from group to group telling people, 'Mommy say, if at first you don't conceive, try, try again.'"

The Sunday Becky Joy turned two, Darlene sent her to her first Sunday school class.

After class, the Sunday school teacher brought Becky Joy back to Darlene. "I promise not to believe everything she says about you if you promise not to believe everything she says about me," the teacher said.

"What did she say?"

"Well, I didn't believe her for a minute, but she said, 'When I'm bad, my daddy put me on top of the car. And I say, 'Oh, please, my Daddy, let me down.' But he say, 'No! You stay there!'"

Darlene quickly agreed to the proposal. She wouldn't believe everything Becky Joy said about the Sunday school teacher either.

When Becky Joy was about that same age, she watched her dad set up for communion. "Which two demons are going to help you tonight, Daddy?"

None of the deacons were there yet to hear their new nickname.

Becky Joy loved everyone at Corners Church, and they loved her. Darlene often said she was the church baby. When she got a little older, Becky Joy loved the neighbor's barn cats and spent every spare minute with them. She'd sit under the huge shade trees with the cats and kittens curled up on her lap and pet them and talk to them.

"I think she loves those cats as much as she loves people," Darlene said to Jim.

Barn cats don't have very long lives.

*Love anything at all, and it will break your heart*, Darlene thought many times when she wiped tears from Becky Joy's face. *How many cats had died in one year?*

Pretty Boy had died first. How Becky Joy's brothers had hooted at that name. It ranked second in derision only to Little Gray Muffin. Her brothers had nicknamed Little Gray Muffin "Moldy Biscuit." She was dead now too, and so were Simba, Nala, Kiara, and then Angel.

Angel had been Becky Joy's favorite. She'd loved her so much she'd given her to Darlene. "I want to give you my best thing, Mommy."

The day after Becky Joy had given Angel away, she'd found the tiny kitten dead, lying by the door, her white fur still perfect.

When kittens died, Darlene offered hugs, tissues, and reminders that if Jesus sits beside a dying sparrow, He doesn't leave tiny kittens to die alone.

One winter day, when another kitten died, Jim put on his jacket and went outside in a blowing snowstorm to dig yet another grave in the frozen ground, because that's what love does. Carrying the tiny kitten in his gloved hands, Jim laid it gently in its shallow grave under the snow as his little girl cried.

After the tears dwindled to an occasional sob, Darlene said, "Daddy did that because he loves you. Do you want to do something to help him?"

So, Becky Joy sat at the table and stamped 600 pamphlets with the church's name and address. She loved to stamp. Darlene's heart ached as an occasional low moan interrupted the noise of the stamping. How much deep heartache would this child, who loved so much, face as she grew older? And would she remember that it sometimes helps, in our pain, to do something for others?

There were tears over a balloon too, a red helium balloon, a waitress gave Becky Joy.

"It wants to fly." Becky Joy giggled in the parking lot as the wind blew and tugged at the string.

"Do you want Mommy to hold it for you?"

"No! I can hold it, Mommy. I'm a big girl now." This was the same day she'd told a store clerk, "I grew up a long time ago."

When Jim opened the car door, a gust of wind ripped the balloon out of Becky Joy's hand and sent it flying high into the sky. It flew no higher than her wail of sorrow. We can hold our balloons as tightly as we wish, but we will lose some of them.

Darlene hugged her close and sighed, thinking of all the sorrows, large and small, she would face. Sooner or later, she'd lose her mom and dad, or they'd lose her. Loss comes to all, sometimes unexplainable, unavoidable, agonizing loss. But life is full of joy, too, and it is joy and her children who will win in the end.

## 66
## BURDENS AND BLESSINGS

As the size of the congregation increased, the blessings grew, but so did the burdens. A group of people who'd once been good friends and staunch supporters now stood in the back of the auditorium after church and served up roast preacher for a pre-lunch snack. It crushed Darlene to hear people say unkind things about her husband. They didn't even try to lower their voices when they saw her. She hurried by them, trying not to look at them, but she felt so hurt.

> *"If you're not very kind, you're not very Christian."*
>
> — AMY CARMICHAEL

Darlene thought of that quote when she heard people talking about Jim.

Darlene knew exactly when her hatred of unkindness had begun. She'd been the girl who didn't cry, but she'd cried bitter tears when she'd been nine. She'd read *A Girl of the Limberlost* and had decided she wanted to be an entomologist. She'd caught a beautiful dragonfly and had felt so excited to have her first specimen. All the colors of the rainbow reflected in its wings.

Darlene had pinned the dragonfly to a piece of cardboard and had felt immediately sick to see it struggle. That part hadn't been in the book. She'd run to her mother and had begged her to help set the dragonfly free. Her mother had glared at her.

"You pinned it on; you get it off. I don't want you ever to forget what you've done."

Sobbing almost too hard to breathe, Darlene had unpinned the beautiful dragonfly and had prayed it would magically live and fly away. It had died in her hand. She had buried it. She'd never forgotten what she'd done; her childish, thoughtless act had killed one of God's lovely creatures. That's when it had been born, Darlene's revulsion of unkindness.

Whenever she saw a Christian sneer, mock, gossip, or whisper an unkind word about others, she cringed. She thought of how the people would feel if they found out, and sometimes they did.

*Do we have to pin each other to a piece of cardboard with our words, our mocking looks? How does God feel when He sees His children hurting one another? Jesus said all men would know we're His because of our love. Can't we love each other? The world is full of hurt; can't we comfort?*

Deacon Pete noticed the gossipers and Darlene's hurt. He took her by the elbow and steered her away from the gossiping group.

"There's something you need to know," he said. His kind smile made her tears worse. "People need balance more than anything, don't you know. Remember your husband quoting

Martin Luther a few weeks ago? Luther said humanity is like a drunken man on horseback. Prop him up on one side, and he falls off on the other. Well I have another quote for you. Someone said that everyone who has a dog to love 'em needs a cat to hate 'em, just for balance. Not everyone is going to love Jim. They didn't all love Jesus, now did they?"

Darlene smiled at Deacon Pete through her tears.

"And that group of cats there?" Deacon Pete nodded at the people who were still roasting the preacher. "I've seen their kind many times. Leave 'em alone, and sooner or later, they'll go home, dragging their tails behind them."

Darlene laughed. Deacon Pete looked mighty pleased with himself. "And here's another thing," he said. "I call them porcupine people. Anyone who gets too close to them gets poked. They might move on to another church," he said. Darlene looked sad again. "It wouldn't be the worst thing in the world." He assured her. "There's blessed additions and blessed subtractions. If they do move on, I hope they don't all move to the same church, because sooner or later they'll get tired of poking preachers, and they'll start poking each other."

Several families did leave, taking with them Becky Joy's two best friends. She was inconsolable when she found out that their parents would no longer allow their girls to be friends with her. She came downstairs one day, her face streaked with tears. "Mommy, I know right where my heart is," she said.

"You do?" Darlene asked.

Becky Joy nodded, and her bottom lip trembled. "It's right here," she said, putting her hand on her chest. "I know it is, cause I felt it break."

Darlene's heart broke for her little girl. It's not only the preacher who needs a tough hide; his wife and kids do too. But oh, how important it is to keep a tender heart!

It was a hard lesson Jim and Darlene needed to learn; not

everyone would love them or Corners Church. That was okay. They needed to keep loving and praying for the people who left, and that's what they did throughout the years. Though they kept tender hearts, they didn't manage to get that rhinoceros hide.

One disgruntled couple who left didn't live far from Corners Church. Every time Jim and Darlene drove by their home she prayed, "Bless them, Lord; bless them real good." She prayed it aloud and with as much fervency as she could muster. Years passed, and God did bless that couple with a new home and several new barns.

One day as they drove by Jim said, "You forgot to pray for them."

"I didn't forget. It looks to me like God has blessed them just about enough."

Jim looked at her.

Darlene sighed. "Okay, Lord, bless them. Bless them real good."

Jim smiled. Jim and Darlene learned a blessing a day keeps bitterness away.

Jim and Darlene weren't bitter, but how would a deep hurt at such a young age affect Becky Joy? Darlene worried about that. It's one thing to be hurt yourself and pray the bitterness away, but it's another thing entirely to see your gentle, loving child hurt. Darlene prayed her little girl wouldn't lose her tender heart, and she didn't.

## MISS HEART

Becky Joy was a big fan of Cupid. Valentine's Day usually got lost in life's shuffle until Jim and Darlene's sweet daughter started her tradition. Each year, she invited her parents to a party in her room. She got Jimmy to take her shopping and bought treats with money she had saved for months.

"Miss Heart," Becky Joy's construction paper creation, was usually part of the party. Miss Heart, led Jim and Darlene on scavenger hunts through the house. When Becky Joy learned arithmetic, she had Miss Heart deliver math problems for her parents to do. Eventually, the clues led to Becky Joy's room, where she'd covered a card table with a pretty tablecloth and had put out treats and drinks.

What a giver that little girl had been, what givers all four of their children had grown up to be!

Darlene once wrote that Valentine's Day was a time for moonlight and romance, candlelight and roses, and a dash of cold water in the face. The dash of cold water is to remind us that when we want to define love, Scripture does a better job than Shakespeare.

Darlene was a romantic at heart. She loved *Sonnets from the Portuguese* by Elizabeth Barrett Browning, but she was realistic enough not to confuse Cupid with croup and valentines with vacuum cleaners. Romance isn't love. Getting up ten times a night when the baby has croup or running the vacuum cleaner for the third time in a day—now that's love.

Jim and Darlene didn't want to startle Cupid into dropping all his arrows, but though they loved each other, they determined early on that "feeling in love" wasn't a requirement for a successful marriage. They'd seen agonizing divorces like Gary and Mandy's happen because one partner no longer felt "in love."

Jim preached that marriage requires commitment. He once read James Dobson's words in a sermon, "'Did you know that the ideal of marriage based on romantic affection is a very recent development in human affairs? Prior to 1200, weddings were arranged by the families of the bride and groom, and it never occurred to anyone that they were supposed to 'fall in love.' In fact, the concept of romantic love was popularized by William Shakespeare. There are times when I wish the old Englishman was here to help us straighten out the mess that he initiated.'"

Jim read I Corinthians 13 in that same sermon. "Do you want to find out how loving you are? Whenever I read the word 'love' put your name there."

"Well, what did you think of the sermon?" Jim asked Darlene after church when they were on their way home.

"I think you've quit preaching and gone to meddling," Darlene replied, but she smiled.

Jim and Darlene were learning that biblical love is the

essential ingredient not only for marriage and ministry, but for life.

Darlene wrote for one of her columns: "How important is love? Without love, my words are noise pollution. Without love I will fail. Without love my epitaph will read, 'Here Lies Just So Much Noise.' Everything is nothing without love."

> *Love through me, Love of God*
> *Make me like Thy clear air*
> *That Thou dost pour Thy colours through*
> *As though it were not there.*
>
> — AMY CARMICHAEL

Fanny Crosby served God without eyesight; Beethoven served God without hearing; Joni Eareckson Tada served God without the use of her arms and legs. But no one yet has ever served God without love.

Becky Joy knew love involved sacrifice. No one liked candy more than that little girl, but she gave it away on Valentine's Day. Love and sacrifice became a part of who she was.

## ANNETTE

Soft white curls framed the lovely face of Jim and Darlene's neighbor, Annette.

"I can only stay five minutes," she said. Her eyes sparkled, and she smiled as she exclaimed enthusiastically about Darlene's spoon collection, the crewel embroidery on the wall, the children's room, her approaching golden wedding anniversary, and her winter Florida visits.

Annette pointed out with delight some good articles in an old *Capper's Weekly* she'd brought with her. As she laughed, talked, and sparkled, Darlene thought, *you, Annette, could make a person excited over an empty toilet paper roll.*

Annette told about a new quilting secret she'd learned, showed Darlene how to thread a needle with a piece of paper, and looked with interest at one of Darlene's old books.

Annette abruptly stopped talking and laughing and asked, "Is five minutes up yet?" Her eyes twinkled with the certainty that five minutes and many of its cousins were long gone.

"Maybe if I finish talking by the door I'll leave when I'm done."

Leave she did, but not before she said, "I do some just right things and some awful wrong things. My granddaughter asked me if I liked those nice porcelain figures of old people holding cats and dogs and things. I told her I absolutely do not! Those things have too many wrinkles. After I look at them, I don't want to look in the mirror. I think they're perfectly horrible." Annette sighed. "How was I to know she'd already bought two of those figurines for me? I kept them, but I still don't like to look at them."

With a laugh and a hug Annette left Darlene to go visit Kenyon next door. There Mabel, Kenyon's wife, had loved, laughed, and finished living her eighty-two years. Days seemed much longer to Kenyon now without his friend, wife, and companion of fifty-eight years.

When Annette celebrated her ninetieth birthday, she tried to make sure everyone else at the party had as much fun as she did. Under a halo of white hair her eyes sparkled with fun. Every one of the many lines on her face told its story of her undiminished sense of humor.

Annette had packed an amazing amount into life. In high school she'd played the violin, taken art and debating classes, and had graduated third in her class.

"Was there anything you didn't do well?" Darlene asked. Annette replied, "We won't mention gym."

"I sang my first solo at a pauper's funeral," Annette recalled. "Pauper's funerals were held in the furniture store that sold caskets. Only three people came to the funeral, not too many to hear my perfect alto rendition."

Though she was a hardworking farmer's wife, Annette still made time to teach Sunday school for thirty-two years in the Methodist church.

"I trusted Jesus as my Savior seventy-seven years ago," she

told Darlene. "I thank Him every day. It means so much to put all your faith in God."

Three words summed up Annette's life: faith, love, and laughter. The members of the Corners' Grange loved her funny readings and humorous one-act plays.

One day, Annette called Jim. "I'm at the funeral home, and you won't believe how much I paid them. When you preach my funeral, you better be sure I get my money's worth."

When Annette told Jim the exact amount she'd paid, he laughed and assured her he'd do his best to make sure she got her money's worth. When God called her home, Jim tried to keep that promise.

Annette was one of a kind. But then, they all were. And Darlene and Jim loved them, the sweet people, the porcupine people, the hard workers, the pew warmers; they loved every single one.

~

As SHE SITS by Jim's bedside, Darlene's eyes fill with tears as she recalls the many loved ones from Corners Church who are in heaven. *I wonder if they are already lining up, forming a welcome home parade for Jim.* She wants to go too. She's tired, and the road ahead looks bleak and lonely. She has work to do, though. Someone must comfort the rest of the family when Jim goes Home.

Darlene keeps thinking of the many wonderful women who had been part of her life. *Godly older women come in all personality types,* she thinks. *Some are quiet; some are vivacious extroverts, but all are remarkable for the same reasons. They've been grateful to God for such a long time, they've almost forgotten how to complain. They've forgotten self and loved others so long it has become a graceful habit. I want to be like them, but I'm not there yet. Maybe that's why God is leaving me here.*

## 69
## CHRISTMAS 1994—A VERY GIVING YEAR

With Darlene's failing memory, she's happy to have the back issues of her columns to remind her of the past. Jim keeps saying she's the keeper of their story and asking her to tell him more about their years at Corners Church, but she's forgotten so much. She was happy when she found her column from Christmas, 1994; it was something she could read to Jim

She thinks about that Christmas as she sits quietly next to Jim. *Let's see, on Christmas 1994 April would have been twenty-two, Jimmy a few days from twenty, Davey seventeen, and Becky Joy five.*

∼

IT HAD FELT like Christmas many times that year. July had brought a wonderful surprise when church family, relatives, and friends had gathered for a weekend celebration of Jim and Darlene's twenty-fifth wedding anniversary and their twentieth year at Corners Church. Love, laughter, and encouragement had flowed abundantly.

When the weekend had ended and Jim and Darlene had locked the church doors, they'd thanked God and had said to each other, "Nothing could top this!" They'd been right, because in a sense nothing can ever top anything else. Each moment, each friendship, each holiday spent with family is precious, one of a kind.

The whole year had been a gift-giving year. Family and church family had given Jim and Darlene a car, microwave, riding mower, rototiller, and a computer. It hadn't mattered to Jim and Darlene all the gifts had been used, some very used; they'd come with love, and love never grows old.

That year had also been one of great joy and great sorrow. From Memorial Day until August 9, Jim, Darlene, Becky Joy, and the other kids, when they were home, had driven thirty miles several times a week to try to comfort and pray with their dying friend, Kenyon.

The human body, even when old and worn out, can take an agonizingly long time to die. As Jim and Darlene watched their dear neighbor fight his long battle they often thought, *yes, death, you are a conquered enemy, but you are still the enemy.*

Kenyon had been a friend for twenty-one years. Whenever they'd needed a ladder, the tractor and disc, the pick-up truck, or a listening ear, Kenyon had been there. They'd tried to be there for him too, especially when he'd grown older and Mabel had gone to heaven.

Whenever Jim, Darlene, or one of the kids did something for Kenyon: made a meal, did a load of laundry, mowed his lawn, he said, "I'll get even with you." They thought he'd gotten more than "even" with his many years of help and friendship.

They could do little to help Kenyon when he was dying—a sip of water held to trembling lips, a sheet smoothed, a hand held, even the words "I love you"—what do these mean to someone losing the battle with pain? Five-year-old Becky Joy thought chocolate chip cookies would make him feel better. She'd sobbed when she'd learned Kenyon wouldn't be able swallow them.

During those days, Jim and Darlene relearned the power of God's word. When their words could comfort little, or not at all, Scripture soothed Kenyon's restlessness. Hymns seemed to help too. One day that was especially hard for him, the whole family went to visit. Jim, Darlene, and the kids sang "The Haven of Rest" with tears streaming down their cheeks.

Kenyon was a very giving man. When his will was read, Jim and Darlene were stunned to discover he'd been the one to give the last gift. He'd given them the little tenant house, their yard, and their large garden spot. It was a gift too dear for words. Only their tears and prayers could express their gratitude.

The little house was theirs! Before Jim and Darlene grew accustomed to the idea of being homeowners, Dell Russell, a neighbor, stopped by. "How would you like to have Kenyon's big house to live in instead of this little house?" he asked.

"We can't afford that, Dell," Jim replied.

"Well, I've prayed for years God would give you a bigger place to live. Then it was like God said to me, 'You know, you could answer that prayer yourself.' I've talked with my wife and all the kids, and they agree. We want you to have the big house. I'm going to buy it and give it to you."

*Who buys a house and gives it to someone else?* Jim and Darlene didn't recover from the wonder of that as long as they lived. Some people are the hands and feet of Jesus, and Dell was one of those people.

Not long after that, they moved from the little house to the big white one next door. Darlene went from room to room, silently praying, giving the house back to the Lord, and telling Him the house was His to use anyway He wanted.

God took Darlene up on that prayer when Mom Peters moved in with them. Jim and Darlene cared for her as her dementia worsened. They thanked God for the big house then. Of their many married years, Jim and Darlene lived alone very few of them. Darlene joked that maybe they didn't really get along as well as they thought; perhaps having people live with them kept them from fighting!

As years passed the kids grew up, left the big house, and went to college. Darlene sold a magazine article titled, "The Not So Empty Nest," because one by one, the kids returned, some for a few months, some for a few years. April graduated from college, came home to work, and had a serious car accident. She recovered at home and stayed there until she married her wonderful husband.

Their confirmed bachelor son, Jimmy, moved back home after college and stayed until he noticed a girl from church who sent his bachelor ideas packing.

Davey moved back home with his sweet wife and their two adorable girls while he and his wife built their new home five miles down the road.

Jim and Darlene loved having their two granddaughters live with them. They kept forever in their memories the funny things those girls said and did, their songs, and their sticky-sweet hugs and kisses. When moving day came, Jim and Darlene were happy for them; it was as it should be, so they hid their tears from everyone but each other.

Several years later, Becky Joy and her husband moved back home. Jim and Darlene were getting older by then, and they enjoyed having the company and the help.

Jim and Darlene never did rattle around, just the two of them, in empty rooms in the big house. They didn't mind not having an empty nest; from where they stood, an empty nest looked like a pretty lonely place. They never forgot that their house had been a gift, and gifts are meant to be shared.

Yes, Christmas 1994 wrapped up a very giving year, and Jesus Himself was their best gift that year and every year.

~

DARLENE REPEATS the last words a great saint had said when he was dying, "The best of all is, God is with us."

Jim opens his eyes. "John Wesley."

Darlene nods and squeezes his hand. Soon, she knows, she's going to have to let go of that hand when Jesus comes to claim his dying servant. What will Jim's last words be?

## THE BIG TREE

Jim and Darlene used every nook and cranny of the "big house." They converted an upstairs bedroom into a study. Though their desks stood only a few feet apart, they seldom interrupted each other as they worked in their own worlds, Jim writing sermons, and Darlene writing columns and curriculum assignments.

The study windows faced south and west. Jim and Darlene could look up from studying and see the giant maple tree that stood sentry at the corner of their property and towered over all other trees at the Corners. Mabel had said that maple tree had been there when the Potawatomi Indians had lived in the area.

Unlike some of their tribe, the Potawatomi of about 150 who roamed the area near the Corners, were peaceful and generous. They shared wild game with the early settlers. Chief Baw Beese was especially friendly, and when he delivered a gift of corn, quail, or turkey, he expected to stay for dinner. The native people helped the settlers survive the brutal winters.

Darlene and Jim often drove down Squawfield Road where the Potawatomi had camped long ago during the summer months. Sometimes they stopped and looked at the historical marker Ralph Lickley had built in 1938 to honor the tribe. There the chief and his tribe had made their last camp before the government had forced them to leave.

When the government troops rounded up the Potawatomi in 1840 and sent them to Iowa, the people at the Corners were sad to see them leave. They dismissed school for the day so the children could wave goodbye as Chief Baw Beese and his tribe left the home they loved, walking down the road the Potawatomi had made themselves centuries before.

Had the Potawatomi ever sat under "her" tree? Darlene wondered that often as she gazed out of the window when she was supposed to be writing. That tree often preached its own sermon to her, about how fast one life or even an era passes, and how only God is permanent. To the tree, Jim and Darlene's years at the Corners were only one leaf falling softly to the ground, one morning fog disappearing in the sun. And yet, to God, the years of the ancient tree were nothing, a single breath in the eons of eternity.

Darlene liked to imagine the tree smiled tolerantly in their study window, watching them as they tried, sometimes frantically, to complete the day's tasks. Did it say, "Slow down, little humans, here for only one morning. Does your Creator want you rushing around like you do? Consider what to do and what to leave undone. And make time to look at the sky, and at me, and at the God who made me."

# THE HAPPY AND THE WISE—CHRISTMAS 1995

"How much money did Della have to buy her Jim a Christmas present?" Darlene asked her family. "Was it one dollar and twenty-seven cents?"

Jim thought it was $1.33; Jimmy guessed $.49; April thought the amount was $1.67; Becky Joy remembered Della but not the amount, and Davey wasn't home, so Darlene couldn't ask him. They checked the book. They were all wrong.

O. Henry wrote Della had "$1.87. That's all. . . .and the next day was Christmas."

Every Christmas Jim read aloud to the family O. Henry's story, *The Gift of the Magi*. Sometimes the kids fell asleep during the reading, but Darlene loved the story of Della, the young wife who sold her long hair, her only treasure, to buy a watch chain for Jim—who sold his treasured watch to purchase combs for Della's long hair.

O. Henry wrote that Della and Jim "most unwisely sacrificed for each other the greatest treasures of their house. But in a last word to the wise of these days let it be said that of all who give gifts, these two were the wisest. . . .They are the magi."

Is there any art more beautiful than the art of giving? God often gives to His children through His other children, and He gave so much to Jim and Darlene the year of 1995. When they decked the halls with boughs of holly that year, they decked different and much larger halls.

Jim and Darlene often reminded each other when we accept a gift, we must remember the responsibility that goes along with it. They agreed completely with Phillips Brooks, composer of *O Little Town of Bethlehem*, who wrote, "We take God's gifts most completely for ourselves when we realize that He sends them to us for the benefit of other men who stand beyond us needing them."

No other art brings such joy as the self-forgetful art of giving. Why wouldn't God love a cheerful giver? He's the most cheerful, extravagant giver of them all. The Lord Jesus gave until He had no more to give, and He experienced not only the deepest sorrow but also the highest joy.

Jim and Darlene admired all the Dellas and Jims—in parables and in real life. They knew it's not only a story; it's true; givers are the wisest and most joyful ones among us. They had been given much, and they prayed God would help them always be cheerful givers.

## THE FIRST WEDDING

Davey had been first to get married. He'd tapped Darlene on the shoulder one Sunday in church and had handed her a scrap of paper with a Bible reference scrawled on it, Proverbs 18:22. Curious, she'd looked it up. "Whoso findeth a wife findeth a good thing, and obtaineth favor of the Lord."

She'd glanced back at Davey, who'd been smiling and sitting next to Beth, the beautiful girl he'd liked since fourth grade. Jim and Darlene loved Beth, her siblings, and her parents, Miles and JoAnn.

Not long after Davey's note, he and Beth had gotten engaged and then married. They'd had a beautiful wedding at Corners Church, and both sets of parents were delighted, and the Corners Church family was too. They hadn't planned it, but Darlene and JoAnn suddenly decided to stand in the entryway and greet people as they entered the church for the wedding.

Someone squeezed between them. "Is it okay if I stand here with you?" Jenna Roseheart asked. "I feel like I'm family too!"

They laughed and hugged her. She and Dale were more than good friends; they were family.

Chatter quieted; everyone found a seat and the wedding began. Jim officiated.

The ceremony had been unforgettable, especially the part when Jim had gotten his words twisted and had said to his son, "You may put the ringer on her finger."

Darlene tried to memorize every beautiful moment. Her eyes grew wet, thinking of the sorrows they were sure to face in years ahead. *God bless you two dear kids! May your love for God and each other grow stronger and sweeter and carry you through all of life's storms.* She prayed for them a George Matheson prayer she often prayed for herself, "Show me that my tears have made my rainbow."

Beth and Davey's reception was at Camp Michindoh where they both worked. People lingered a long time; no one wanted the day to end.

Then, as so often happens, sorrow invaded joy. It seems a pattern in life—weddings and funerals, birth and death, loss and gain.

While Davey and Beth were on their honeymoon, Deacon Pete died. Jim and Darlene mourned almost as deeply as the family. Gone was their friend and mentor, the dear man who had taught them so much. Would they even still be at Corners Church if they hadn't had Deacon Pete's help, encouragement, and gentle correction? They doubted it.

Davey and Beth returned early from their honeymoon to attend Deacon Pete's funeral. No one expected them to cut their honeymoon short. They came back because that was the kind of people they were, and as years passed, they became more and more caring.

Three more beautiful weddings would follow in Jim and Darlene's family. Each one became a wonderful memory Jim and Darlene held close in their hearts, and each gave her reason to pray and to keep praying for love to grow.

## 73
# KIDS GOTTA HAVE FUN

With a crash of shattering glass, a baseball sailed through the stained glass window. The people in the entryway stopped talking and looked at each other. Whose kid had done it; was it theirs?

A couple of tearful boys ran into church. "We're sorry, Pastor! We didn't mean to!"

"It's okay. The ball only broke one pane. I can repair it Just play farther from the church and hit the ball in the other direction, okay?"

Baseball wasn't the only game the kids played after church. When it was cold, snowy, or rainy, they brought board games and played inside after church. The little ones sometimes climbed under the communion table and played house.

One little girl walked and talked late. When she started walking her balance wasn't good, and she'd often tip sideways, smack her head into a hard pew, and cry. Darlene almost cried herself when she saw what the other kids were doing. They were taking turns walking with arms outstretched behind the little girl, ready to catch her before she could bang her head. As she toddled her way up and down the aisles, one child or another stayed with her every minute, leaving friends to make sure she didn't get hurt. And every child participated in the "let's keep her safe" effort.

*If there could be a painting to represent Corners Church that would be it,* Darlene thought. *That's what we do; we take turns walking behind each other with arms outstretched to keep each other from falling.*

With plenty of green grass and sunshine outside, the church kids invented many ways to have fun when the weather was nice. They had weekly races, and a small girl always won, beating much larger boys, to their disgust. She grew up to run track and cross country at college.

"Horse" was a favorite game in the early years. The girls grabbed each other's dress ties and yelled, "Giddyup!" They raced around the church using the ties as reins. Every week or two a dress tie ripped off, and an unhappy mom sewed it back on.

Darlene smiled whenever she looked out the church door and saw little shoes lined up on the steps. The smallest children left their shoes there and ran barefoot in the grass.

Any mud was an instant attraction, and parents sighed over inevitable grass stains, but Corners' kids grew up with forever memories of playing outside after church and climbing the pine tree with its low-hanging branches.

The kids were generally good, with a few exceptions. A few bigger boys terrorized Becky Joy by pulling the arms, legs, and head off Teddy and threatening to hurt her if she ever told who did it.

"Please fix Teddy, Mommy," she'd beg after church.

As Darlene sewed an arm or leg or head back on the beloved bear that went everywhere with Becky Joy, she'd ask what had happened.

"Oh, we were just playing."

Not until she was grown up did Becky Joy tell.

One Sunday, Samuel stuck his head in the church. "Can someone come out here and help us? A Frisbee got stuck on the church roof, and I tried to get it down with someone's flip flop and then a shoe, and. . . . Well, now there's quite a few things on the roof."

The entryway was full of people talking one Sunday. A child stuck her head in the door. "Tommy and Jake are peeing on the sidewalk."

Two horrified mothers with red faces hurried outside to confront two little boys.

"Tommy! Did you do that?" His mother pointed at a round wet spot on the pavement.

"Nope." He shook his head.

"Oh, good." She sighed with relief.

"Jake did that. Mine's that one over there." He pointed at another wet spot.

The church kids grew up; some stayed at Corners Church; some left and came back, and some left forever. Many continued to love God and church, but some turned away. Darlene and Jim held every one of them in their hearts, loved them, and hugged them with their prayers.

## THE ONLY ANSWER

Nine-year-old Becky Joy charmed everyone with her huge dark eyes, captivating smile, and long braids. She liked living on a dirt road on two acres, adored all the barn cats, and wanted to care for every wounded bird or insect she found. She loved her family and her friends.

Lenard Clark was a friendly thirteen-year-old African American boy who lived in the projects in Chicago. He loved sports and riding his bike. He was small for his age and looked much younger than thirteen.

Becky Joy and Lenard both loved life, and God loved both of them.

Lenard's life forever changed one early evening on March 21, 1997. He and two friends had been playing when they decided to ride their bikes a few blocks to check out Comiskey Park, the Chicago White Sox ballpark that was being prepared for opening day.

People give varying accounts of what happened that evening. All agree that the boys crossed the bridge from where they lived into the white neighborhood of Bridgeport. Some say they stopped to watch some white boys play basketball. Others say they were only riding their bikes through the area. All agree that at some point three young white men attacked the boys. Attempting to escape, the boys split up. The other two got away, but Lenard wasn't as lucky.

Shouting racial slurs, the white men, eighteen, nineteen, and twenty-one years old, pulled thirteen-year-old Lenard from his bike, beat and kicked him unconscious, and left him for dead in a pool of blood.

Lenard remained in a coma for a week and was left with permanent brain damage.

Police arrested the three white men two days later. The nineteen-year-old had his trial first. The judge gave him eight years in prison and said he was the one who'd instigated and finished the beating of the black child.

On October 19, 1998, the other two defendants, who had also participated in Lenard's savage beating, learned their fate would be just probation and community service. Chicago erupted into violence. The black community was justifiably outraged.

That's where the lives of Becky Joy and Lenard entwined. Jim and Darlene were taking Becky Joy from their Michigan farmhouse to visit the Museum of Science and Industry in Chicago.

Becky Joy objected when she couldn't sit in her usual seat. "I always sit behind Mom."

"I put the cooler there," Jim said. "Sit behind me this time."

Jim and Darlene were at a stoplight in Chicago when they heard what sounded like a gunshot. Becky Joy screamed, and Darlene turned to see what had happened. Horrified, she saw the passenger window behind her was shattered. A black man, his face distorted with hate, was running toward the car.

"You hurt my little girl!" Jim shouted at the man. Darlene

almost didn't recognize Jim's voice; she'd never heard him sound so angry.

The man grabbed the car window with his gloved hands.

"Go, honey, please, just go!" Darlene begged.

Jim gunned the car.

Darlene turned to look at Becky Joy. She was horrified to see her covered in glass; she grabbed her daughter's hand. "Are you okay?"

"My leg hurts."

Darlene's emotions were tumbling around inside her as she listened to her daughter's sobs. She wanted to comfort her daughter, and she was furious at the man who had hurt Becky Joy. *Couldn't Jim drive any faster!* They needed help.

Jim stopped at the closest gas station. As they opened the back door to get Becky Joy out of the car, they found a brick lying on the floor. A note attached to the brick with a rubber band said, "This is for Lenard Clark."

The black gas station attendants were horrified. They lovingly consoled Becky Joy, apologized for what had happened, and called the police. Jim and Darlene almost cried because the attendants were so kind. They were glad the people helping them were black, because they didn't want Becky Joy to associate violence with any color. Hate comes in all colors, but so does love.

Soon six police cars arrived, a white and a black officer in each car. They termed the incident a hate crime. They told Jim and Darlene the man who threw the brick probably waited on that corner for a car with a white child. They said that if Becky Joy had been sitting where she usually sat, her injuries would have been far more severe. Her only visible injury was a brick shaped bruise on her thigh and a small scratch on her hand. The emotional scars would become visible much later when she developed anxiety, panic attacks, and nightmares.

The police searched for the man who'd thrown the brick, but they never found him. Did he ever wonder what happened to the little victim of his hate?

"Daddy," Becky Joy whispered as the police filled out papers at the gas station, "will you bring my bag of candy from the car? And do we have any more of those tracts?"

With tears still drying on her cheeks and a beautiful smile on her face, Becky Joy gave a piece of candy, a hug, and a tract telling of God's love to every person in the gas station. Soon her eyes weren't the only ones wet. Thanks to a nine-year-old hate crime victim, everyone felt love and community that day in that place. Hopefully, they felt God's love too, because that's the only answer to all the violence in the world. God loves us all, and when we learn to love Him, we'll learn to love each other.

Finally, the paperwork was completed, and the three of them were in the car and heading home to the Corners. The broken window reminded them of how much worse it could have been. Darlene whispered a prayer of thanks and looked at Jim and Becky Joy. She'd never loved them more.

～

DARLENE FEELS Jim's hand tighten around her own. "Do you remember the trip to Chicago when Becky Joy got hurt?"

His face contorts with grief, and a tear rolls down his cheek.

"No time for tears," Darlene says. She scrambles to think of a memory that will make him smile. "Do you remember the testimony about the ass in the well?"

He nods, grins, and falls asleep.

## THE ASS IN THE WELL

It was Sunday night testimony time, and people started smiling as soon as Stan raised his hand. You never knew what he might say, but you knew it was going to be interesting.

"Those of you who were at Sunday school this morning heard Jack teach that sometimes working on a Sunday is necessary." Stan scratched his head. "Jack quoted Luke 14:5, 'And he said unto them, Which of you shall have an ass or an ox fallen into a well, and will not straightway draw him up on a Sabbath day?'"

"Well, folks, I got home from church this morning and noticed water bubbling from the ground right where my well is. That water had created quite a ditch. Still in my church clothes, I leaned over to look at it, and just like that, my feet slid out from under me. There I was, on the ground on my backside, and all I could think of was that verse about the ass that fell into the well. And that's my testimony tonight."

A few eyebrows rose. Had Stan used the word "ass" in church? Apparently, he had, and Jim rationalized it was a biblical word. The auditorium was quiet. It seemed no one else had a testimony that could compete with Stan's.

With the word *well* in his mind, and trying to keep the word *ass* out of his mind, Jim, in a hurry to fill the too quiet void, enthusiastically said, "And now, right before the sermon, we'll join together and sing, 'It Is Well with My Soul.'"

Stan sang loudly with a broad grin on his face.

## I THANK GOD FOR THEM

*When did I first start feeling older?* Darlene wonders. *I know I didn't feel old at fifty. That was the year I became a grandmother, and a whole new world of joy opened.*

～

As DARLENE's fiftieth birthday approached, so did two other events, becoming a grandmother for the first time and knee surgery. *Where,* she wondered, *is the wisdom that was supposed to come with age?*

Darlene didn't mind getting older, but it was happening faster than she'd expected. She and Jim agreed having a ten-year-old daughter made them feel younger than they were. Darlene wondered about the years to come when she would be old. What would she be like? She hoped to be like one of the older women she admired and thanked God for.

Three of the women on Darlene's gratitude list were past eighty: "Grandma" Roseheart,

Betty Fairchild, and Janet Sanders.

Darlene hoped she'd have Grandma Roseheart's passion for the Lord. Grandma Roseheart told neighbors about Jesus and worked in Vacation Bible School every night, listening to verses and doing chalk drawings. She helped in children's church too. She had an amazing amount of energy that lasted an astonishing number of years. She even finished a large quilt the night before her hundredth birthday party.

Darlene wished, when she got older, to have Betty Fairchild's faithfulness. Betty couldn't attend church any longer, because she had to stay home and care for Sam who'd lost his sense of balance but not his sense of humor.

"Guess where I fell this week?" Sam asked, laughing, when Jim and Darlene visited. "I fell right into Betty's laundry basket full of clothes!"

Betty never forgot Darlene's birthday, and well into her eighties, she made Jim and Darlene strawberry jam every summer.

"I think Betty would rather rob a bank than act selfishly, complain, or be unfaithful to a friend," Darlene told Jim. "I want to be like her."

"Better get a move on then." Jim teased.

Her eighties didn't slow down Janet Sanders much. Darlene admired her work ethic and her compassion. At Pete's graveside service, Janet comforted the rest of the family even though her own heart was broken. Even after Pete had died, Janet kept her garden, with help from her family. She still canned and froze food and offered to help Darlene with her canning. Janet sent in meals to church families when someone had a baby, or was sick, or had surgery, and in her eighties would still occasionally babysit for her toddler and baby great-grandchildren.

Younger than eighty but still past retirement age were

Debbie Kasey, Alice Marie Falks, and Daisy Reed. Debbie, a widow, had a contagious enthusiasm for life. The sudden death of her beloved husband, Mark, had stunned her and had broken her heart, but it hadn't slowed her down. She took lessons and painted two throw rugs for Jim and Darlene. Next, she started taking organ lessons and played the organ at Corners Church. Debbie had many reasons to complain but seldom did.

Alice Marie was an old-fashioned farmer's wife. She loved people, and she actually enjoyed hard work. Darlene decided if she ever decided to skip fall cleaning, she wouldn't tell Alice Marie, who was a stickler for cleanliness.

Alice Marie had called Annette one afternoon before Annette had died and said, "I see it's your turn to have the garden club meeting at your house. Do you want me to come over and help you clean?"

"No, I don't! I guess I'm not so old I can't clean my own house."

"Well, okay, but the last time we had a meeting at your house everyone sat there looking at a big cobweb hanging from your ceiling."

Darlene had tried not to laugh when Annette had indignantly repeated Alice Marie's remarks.

Alice Marie was a bit outspoken, but she had a good heart. Darlene could have papered a room with the notes and cards Alice Marie sent her over the years. When the old, stained glass windows at Corners Church needed putty, Alice Marie did it. She and Darlene painted the roof of the porch at the church and laughed at the white paint they managed to get in their hair.

"You know, our hair will be this color before we know it," Alice Marie said.

Darlene laughed in agreement.

Daisy was a beautiful woman with white hair and a soft

chuckle. She often drove tractor when her husband, Barry, was short on help. Her meals for the hired hands were legendary. Sometimes Jimmy and Davey worked for the Reeds. Reeds paid the boys for their work, but the boys told Darlene they'd work free just to get one of Daisy's meals.

Darlene thought Daisy Reed was a Proverbs 31 woman, and Barry would agree, most of the time. Barry was pretty upset with Daisy, though, the day he climbed on the roof and knocked over the ladder. He shouted for Daisy for hours, but she didn't hear him.

"I got so desperate I even told the dog to go get her," Barry said. "The dog didn't go."

~

DARLENE LAUGHS at the memories and stretches. Every muscle hurts. She looks longingly at the couch, but stretching out there would mean leaving Jim's side. There will be plenty of time to rest later, too much time.

Almost as though he senses her thoughts, Jim tightens his hold on her hand. "Come to bed soon. It's late. Don't be long."

"I'll be right behind you, honey." She keeps her voice light, but she's glad his eyes are closed so he doesn't ask why she has tears on her cheeks.

## REMEMBERING THE HOMEGOINGS

A few from Corners Church had died instantly. It had been terribly hard on their families, but perhaps not as difficult as it had been for the families who'd had to watch their loved ones linger in pain.

Beloved Deacon Pete who'd guided Jim and Darlene for twenty-three years had lingered much longer than he'd wished. Confined to his couch, he'd just wanted to go home to heaven.

Dale Roseheart had sung at Pete's funeral:

> *On that happy golden shore*
> *Where the faithful part no more,*
> *When the storms of life are o'er,*
> *Meet me there;*
> *When the night dissolves away*
> *Into pure and perfect day,*
> *I am going there to stay,*
> *Meet me there.*
>
> — Henrietta Blair

So many of the people from Corners Church were already in heaven. Some deaths had been so abrupt they'd left the family and church family reeling, and only God's grace had kept them going. Others had been so long, lingering, and heartbreaking the exhausted families had been numb when it'd ended.

Jim and Darlene didn't pretend to understand the way of God in death. They could only share with others the comfort God gives in His Word:

> *"Precious in the sight of the Lord is the death of his saints."*
>
> — Psalm 115:15

After Deacon Pete died, his wife, Janet, lived several more years, strong and independent at first, but then growing weaker, and spending her last years in assisted living. Several times her heart stopped beating. When it started again on its own, Janet sighed with disappointment. Each time she hoped her failing heart would let her go Home to her Lord and Pete, and one day, it finally did.

Sam, the cheerful member of Jim's first church board, and his wife, Betty, both lingered on earth, trapped in failing bodies long after their spirits wanted to be free. To the very end they loved their pastor and church family.

Darlene would never forget one of the last times she'd seen Sam. He couldn't come to church anymore, so Corners Church often went to him. Sam, a people person, loved those visits and laughed and joked with everyone. He always wanted the group to sing. On the last visit, Sam had been too weak to open his eyes. He'd lain in his hospital bed but had still moved his mouth with every word of the songs he loved so well.

Betty spent months in that same hospital bed when she got too old and weak to function. Darlene held her hand and often told her how much she loved her and how much her friendship had meant through the years.

Grape hyacinth grew along Betty's front porch. *They are your flower, gentle, beautiful but strong. I'll never see one without thinking of you,* Darlene thought. And she never did. Heaven had a sweeter fragrance when God called Betty home.

Debbie's Mark was active and lean, a retired prison guard. The two of them often took long walks.

On one walk, Mark said, "Debbie, I don't feel so good. Let's go home."

They went home, and Mark lay on the couch. "That feels even worse!" he said. He stood, dropped to the floor, and instantly went Home to heaven.

Years later, Darlene was in the shower when she heard frantic pounding on the door. It was Debbie's granddaughter. "Please, come with me right now," the granddaughter begged. "Grandma is on the kitchen floor. She was fine one minute, and then she was gone."

There had been so many deaths and so many tears. Jim couldn't forget standing with a young husband who had to make the decision to take his wife off life-support. There had been a baby's funeral and a funeral for a man who hadn't made room for God in his life. His family didn't know God, and bitter cries filled the room at the funeral home. As Jim preached, Darlene prayed the light of Christ would blaze through the darkness and show the grieving family the way Home.

Rick and Belle, gentle souls and sweet friends, became Christians late in life and started attending Corners Church. They often gave Jim and Darlene baskets of strawberries and bushels of squash.

"Can you use anymore bikini squash?" Rick loved to ask

Jim, just to see Belle get flustered as she corrected him.

"Zucchini! It's zucchini!" The word "bikini" embarrassed her.

Rick and Belle sat at their kitchen table every morning, held hands, read the Bible, and prayed for Corners Church.

Darlene cried after they left Rick's hospital room. "Why did God have to let his foot be amputated? Why does he have to suffer like this?"

"We don't know, honey. We never know. We have to trust. Remember? We choose to trust." Jim hugged her.

It seemed even more unfair when, after suffering for a few days, Rick died in that hospital. His faith hadn't wavered and neither had Belle's. She lived alone in the farmhouse for many years with her wonderful family coming by to do everything she needed. Thad and Caroline Nowling visited Belle so often they became part of the family.

When Belle couldn't get out to church anymore, Corners Church often took a service to her. All ages crowded into her living room to sing hymns and share hugs. Sometimes Thad played his harmonica. Jim always preached; although, Belle was so deaf by then she couldn't hear a word. It didn't matter; church had come, and she was happy.

Jim and Darlene sat in a hospital room fighting back tears. They loved Joy and Jesse, who'd become dear friends. The two of them had added so much caring to the Corners Church family. Now Jesse was dying.

Hours passed, and Jim and Darlene sat with Joy at Jesse's bedside. Jesse wasn't going to wake up; there would be no last goodbye. Then Jim and Darlene saw love in its most sacred form. As Jesse struggled to breathe, Joy laid her head on his chest. "It's okay, honey. You can stop fighting. You can go Home now. God will take care of me." As soon as she said that, Jesse went Home. In spite of her own sorrow, or maybe because of it, Joy became a steady light of comfort to all who were grieving. People instinctively know the authentic voice of someone who has suffered and is still suffering; someone who has been comforted and is still being comforted by God.

Nathan fought a long hard battle with cancer. He was determined to see that everything was done to make Cathy's life easier once he was gone. They'd been together for sixty years; what would she do without him?

"Nathan will be gone six years next Friday," Cathy said during a testimony time at Corners Church. "I've learned to depend on the Lord. I never really depended on Him before; I had Nathan. I've grown so close to the Lord these last six years, and He's never failed me."

∽

OUR WIDOWS, Darlene thought, *with their strong, sturdy faith—will I be able to be as strong as they are?* She knew they'd be there for her. More importantly, God would be there too. She continued thinking of the ones already at Home.

∽

JIM AND DARLENE had said goodbyes to everyone at church one Sunday and had locked the front door. They were heading for the side door to leave when they heard furious pounding on the front door.

"Jim! It's Lois! She's crying!"

They rushed to unlock the door. *What was wrong?* In all the years they'd known Lois and her husband, Mitch, they'd never seen Lois cry, not even when she'd had to spend extended time in the hospital before the twins had been born.

"Please come," Lois sobbed. "Dad's gone, and Mom doesn't

know yet."

As they hurried to Peggy's to be there for her when she heard the news that her husband was gone, Jim and Darlene were stunned. How could Jack be gone? Just that morning he'd talked to Jim on the phone. Jack had gotten sick on a business trip and was recovering in a hospital out of town and expecting to get discharged the next day.

After chatting, Jack had told Jim, "Look out for Peggy for me."

About the time Jim was closing the service in prayer, God called Jack home.

All the way to Peggy's they prayed and cried. What would Peggy do without Jack? What would Lois, Mitch, and the grandkids who adored him do? What would the church family do without Jack, their beloved deacon and Sunday school teacher, whose smile lit rooms and warmed hearts? He'd never been anything but kind and comforting.

But God was enough. He was enough for Peggy, for Lois and Mitch, for the three grandkids, and for Peggy and Jack's wonderful son, Trey, and his wife, Char. And when years later, God suddenly called Char home, God was enough for Trey. His smile, so like his dad's, said God was enough.

∼

THERE HAD BEEN MORE, so many more. In her mind, friends already in heaven are gathering around Jim, the way they had at the door of Corners Church, where for so many years they'd shared laughter and tears. Soon, they will have only laughter; the tears will be forever gone.

*I'm not ready yet. I don't want to leave my wonderful family and church family. But I don't want to stay without Jim. Couldn't we both stay awhile longer?*

## THE LAST ROSE

Sometimes a simple visit turned into a sweet friendship and that happened with Howie and Gwen.

Howie was Sam's brother. Sam often told Jim he wanted all his family to accept Jesus as Savior because he wanted to see them all in heaven. Sam was especially close to Howie and asked Jim and Darlene to go see him and his wife, Gwen.

Becky Joy was in high school by then, and whenever she heard her parents were going to see Howie and Gwen, she said, "Wait for me; I'm coming with you." She enjoyed hearing their funny stories and seeing the love the two older people shared for each other.

Howie was a lot like Sam. He shared Sam's love of life and laughter, and sadly came to share his older brother's balance problems.

"The guys won't let me go fishing with them anymore," he told Jim, Darlene, and Becky Joy. "First, I fell on the dock a few times. Then, the other day, I fell off the dock right into the boat. The guys think I should do my fishing from the shore now." He laughed. "I guess they're probably right, seeing as next time I might fall into the water. I can't swim, and the rest of those geezers are probably too old and weak to jump in and save me."

Time passed, and Howie and Gwen had to begin using Hoverounds. They still lived independently in their little cottage by the lake and still shared love and laughter. They grew especially close to Becky Joy and wanted to know all about what was happening in her life.

Gwen told Becky Joy, "Howie drove his Hoveround out back mushroom hunting. I thought he'd been gone a long time, so I took my Hoveround out looking for him. There he was, on his back, laughing, looking at the sky. 'Took you long enough,' he said. 'I wondered when you'd come find me. I reached over to get that big morel mushroom and fell right out of this thing. Give me a hand, will ya?' So, I leaned over to help pull him up, and he pulled me clean out of my chair, and there we both were on the ground.'"

By now Jim, Darlene, and Becky Joy were laughing too; although, they were wondering how much longer Gwen and Howie would be able to live alone.

"What happened next?" Becky Joy asked.

"Nothing much!" Gwen laughed again. "We stayed there until a neighbor spotted us and got us back into the house. It was a nice day, though; wasn't it, Howie? We were just glad it didn't start raining."

Often on their visits, especially after Sam died, Jim brought the conversation around to the Lord. "Don't forget how much Sam wanted to see you in heaven."

Howie and Gwen nodded and smiled. One or the other said, "Someday. We aren't ready yet."

Illness sent Gwen to the hospital, but she was recovering by the time Jim and Darlene went to visit her. She smiled her delightful smile.

"I don't know about Howie," she said as soon as she saw them before they even said hello, "but I'm ready now to ask Jesus to be my Savior."

"Well, I'm more than ready too," Howie said.

And just like that, the elderly couple became children in the kingdom of God.

When they could no longer live alone, Gwen and Howie shared a room at a nursing home. It was quite a distance from Jim and Darlene, but they visited often. By then, Becky Joy was in college. Gwen and Howie always asked for news about her. When they heard about her good grades or her drama or orchestra performances, they smiled at each other as proudly as if she had been their own.

Whenever Jim and Darlene visited, they noticed there was always a long stem rose somewhere in the house. In all the years of their long marriage, Howie had purchased a single red rose every Thursday for Gwen. When Gwen had a stroke and lingered unconscious for months with a feeding tube keeping her alive, Howie still arranged for that red rose to come every Thursday and sit on the table next to her bed in the nursing home in the room they shared. And then there was one last rose. It wilted as Howie went home to heaven. Gwen followed not long after.

## TWO SENTENCES TOO LATE

Corners Church had guest speakers when Jim got sick or went on vacation, and the congregation grew fond of some of the substitute preachers. They especially loved Pastor Percy, an older, quiet man. Unlike Pastor Todd Pritchard, he didn't shout or terrorize anyone by leaving the pulpit and roaming the aisles. He also let people out before noon, because his wife, a sweet lady with white curls, raised her arm and pointed at her watch at exactly 11:55 a.m.

"I have to do that," Betsy explained to some of the congregation. "He's a bit forgetful about time, and once he preached so long that a lady's roast burned and almost set her kitchen on fire."

"Too bad Pastor Todd's wife don't have a watch," Fred muttered. "Maybe we should send her one as a kind of love offering, don't you know."

Fred, who slept through most sermons, really liked Pastor Percy, because he seldom woke him during the service. Except that one time. That one, unforgettable time.

Even though he was now eighty and retired from his

church, Percy liked to keep learning and improving. He attended a rather expensive one-day pastor's conference in Toledo, Ohio.

"I learned something I want to try out this Sunday when I fill in for Jim at Corners Church," Percy told Betsy when he got home from the conference. "The speaker said to be sure to vary your rate of speech and your tone when you preach." Betsy looked puzzled. "You know, say some things fast, and some slow. Say some things quiet, and some things loud. What do you think?"

"I think the way you usually preach is just fine."

"No," Percy shook his head. "There's always room for improvement. When I get to heaven, I want to hear the Lord say about my sermons, 'Well done, Percy!' You listen closely Sunday, Betsy. I want to know what you think the Lord will say about my sermon."

The next Sunday Percy practiced what he'd learned at the pastor's conference. He preached on Psalm 6:6. Slowly, and with a dramatic pause, he said, "David wet his bed every night."

As he had learned at the conference, Percy looked left, right, and center before continuing. A bit louder, he repeated, "David wet his bed, *every night.*"

Again, there was a long dramatic pause as Pastor Percy, jerkily, kind of like a ventriloquist's dummy, turned his head left, right, and center. As loudly as he had ever in his life said anything, Pastor Percy yelled, "David wet his bed, *every night* with his tears."

Betsy heard a few snickers. She was glad Percy was deaf. On the way home, he said happily, "I think that sermon went well, Betsy. I enjoyed using the new things I learned at the conference. What do you think the Lord will say about that sermon?"

Quietly, Betsy said, "I think He will tell you the words 'with his tears' came two sentences too late."

"What's that, dear?"

Betsy looked at his smile, still boyish at eighty years old. She couldn't. She just couldn't. "I think He will say, 'Well done, Percy. Well done!'"

Percy's smile grew wider with satisfaction.

## ONE IN A HANDBAG

Missy arrived at church a bit late. Corners Church was accustomed to latecomers, but her arrival created unusual interest. Even Jim, who was usually oblivious to everything when he was preaching, noticed the whispers, giggles, and glances at Missy's pew. Missy sat, serenely focused, listening to the sermon, but people around her were paying more attention to her handbag than to the sermon Jim had spent twenty hours preparing.

At least half the congregation knew what the disturbance was. Missy had brought her little dog to church in her handbag. Now and then the dog poked his cute little head out, either to get a breath of air, or to see if he approved of the sermon.

The people in the front of the church had no idea what was happening. Jim, seldom disturbed by howls of babies or misbehaving toddlers, knew something in the back of the church had captured the attention of his congregation. Since the dog was tiny, and Missy's handbag was on the pew, he couldn't see the dog.

Partway through the sermon, Missy took the dog out of her

handbag to let him stretch his legs, and he promptly took a pee on the floor—apparently, he didn't approve of the sermon. That did it; laughter erupted.

Jim still had no idea a dog was part of the congregation, but a smart pastor knows when he's lost his audience and it's time to cut the sermon short. He called for the piano player and announced the closing hymn, "All God's Creatures Great and Small." Someone in the back snorted when he announced the hymn.

As a deacon closed in prayer, Jim and Darlene hurried to the door, as they did every Sunday, so they could shake hands with people as they left. As the deacon continued praying for the homeless, the missionaries, earthquake victims, and the disruptive teen who rode his noisy four-wheeler up and down the road during the sermon, Jim whispered to Darlene, "What was going on in the back of the church?"

"Missy brought her dog. In her handbag. She let him down, and he peed on the floor. And then you closed with 'All God's Creatures Great and Small.'"

Jim and Darlene laughed. By then the church had a sound system. It was unfortunate that Jim had forgotten to turn off his lapel mic.

"I heard you laughing about Peanuts," Missy said to Jim.

He managed not to smile. "Missy, I know you love Peanuts, but he really is too much of a distraction. Please leave him home when you come to church."

"Well! I never!" Missy responded. "Peanuts never made a peep. You should tell the South family to leave their squalling baby home when they come to church. And what about last spring when the Coles brought a whole box of peeping chicks and left them in the entryway during the service? That wasn't a distraction?"

Jim tried to explain the Coles had picked the chicks up

right before church, and the sudden cold snap had made it dangerous to leave them in the car, but Missy was having none of that.

"It's discrimination plain and simple," she snapped. "And I will thank you not to sing 'All God's Creatures' anymore. God may love them all, but it's obvious you favor chickens over dogs. Good day!" And Missy and Peanuts flounced out of the church and down the steps.

∽

DARLENE GLANCES at the hospital bed and is surprised to see Jim is wide awake. He chuckles when she reminds him of Peanuts.

"Do you remember the pastor from Second Baptist telling us about his dog adventures? My favorite one was the story about the Golden Retriever. The pastor took off his shoes when he went calling, like we all do so we won't track in mud. When he went to leave, the Golden had carried off his shoes. The family was still looking for the shoes a week later. I wonder if they ever found them."

## TO HANG OR NOT TO HANG

"**K**eep telling our story, babe"
Darlene kisses Jim's wrinkled cheek. "Do you remember when Jesus almost caused a riot?"

He looks puzzled.

"Oh you do, honey. It was the picture of Jesus knocking on the door of the heart, you know, the one Becky Joy called 'Aryan Jesus' because the artist painted him fair-skinned, blond, and obviously not Jewish.'"

He raises one eyebrow, remembering with her.

"That was the first thing the Kellogs didn't like," she says, "They wanted the picture gone from behind the pulpit, and they weren't going to back down. They felt like it was an idol hanging there."

∽

DARLENE HAD LIKED THAT PICTURE, and another one the church had, a reproduction of Sallman's *Head of Christ*. When

Jenna Roseheart had started attending, she'd kindly pointed out that the burgundy drapes that hung on either side of the gold tone ornate frame were inside out! How had no one else noticed that through all the years?

Jim tried to keep the peace, so even though he didn't want to do it, he moved the picture from behind the pulpit to a Sunday school room where a child scratched it with a pen. Some people were outraged at the damage. There were people who wanted Jesus back behind the pulpit and people who wanted Jesus permanently banned from all church property. To hang or not to hang, that was the question.

The congregation compromised by moving the picture to the fellowship hall, the old one-room schoolhouse they used for almost fifty years until the new fellowship hall was completed.

∽

"I DON'T THINK Jesus cared if His picture hung in the church or not," Darlene says. "He just wanted His people to stop fighting. And we did too!"

That tug of a smile at the corner of Jim's mouth and the raised eyebrow are a look she knows well.

∽

THE PICTURE DEBATE wasn't the last one; there were other things the Kellogs didn't like about Corners Church. Still, Jim and Darlene felt devastated the Sunday the Kellogs left for good. The couple had good hearts, along with their strong opinions. They were willing to do any job that needed to be done, and that's a rare treasure in a small church. Despite differing opinions on some things, Kellogs and Jim and Darlene had grown to be close friends.

On the Sunday their friends informed them they wouldn't be back to church, Darlene thought it was ironic the closing hymn had been, "The Fight Is On." They never sang it again.

## I QUIT!

When Jim and Darlene got home that Sunday the Kellogs left the church they both collapsed in tears. For the first time, both were discouraged at the same time. "Two are better than one" wasn't true this time. Always before, when one fell, the other lifted up. This time, Jim said he was going to resign, and Darlene said to go ahead! It had been a rough time at Corners Church. Others had left the church in the past few years too, people the pastor and wife had loved and poured their lives into.

Now their hard-working friends were leaving. You've heard of the proverbial straw that broke the camel's back? This was that straw.

"Look at your Christ, not your crisis." How many times had Jim preached that, and how many countless times had they practiced it? They were old hands at choosing to trust, but not this time.

Darlene again questioned whether she'd ever been called to be a pastor's wife. Jim thought it was time for Corners Church to get a new pastor. He was worn; he was weary, and he was heartsick. What had he really accomplished with all his years at Corners Church? He pushed away the truth that it's not what we do for God that counts, but what God does through us. A battle was raging, and the devil was winning.

"Professor Nick Machiavelli was right after all," Jim said to Darlene. "Nothing ever happens where two dirt roads meet. At least for me nothing ever happens. I'm tired of trying, and the church needs someone better."

The grown kids came home and tried to convince Jim not to resign, but he was determined. He was done with the ministry. He was going to get a job in a factory and let his heart heal.

The church was hurting, reeling from the loss of this couple and others who had left earlier. Jim worked on his resignation letter all week. He met with the board the next Sunday morning.

"I'm going to give this letter to the church tonight. I thought it was only fair to let you know first," Jim said.

"Oh no you don't, Pastor," Deacon Ken said. "We don't accept your resignation. You aren't leaving us when so many people are hurting. Stay with us until things get better, and if you still want to quit, we'll talk about it then."

Jim agreed to stay. He'd preached before that discouragement is the sharpest tool in the devil's toolbox, but when he preached it after that, he preached it from his heart. He knew firsthand how sharp that tool can be.

Darlene pushed away the thought that maybe God had never called her to be a pastor's wife. Once again, she quoted Emily Dickinson to herself, a poem that was one of her guiding lights: "They might not need me; but they might. I'll let my head be just in sight; a smile as small as mine might be precisely their necessity."

If Jim was in for the long haul, so was she.

The heartaches began to heal, and the church entered a time of God's blessing like they'd never seen before. New families came, and a fresh joy of the Holy Spirit filled the church. Jim never again wrote a letter of resignation.

When people asked how he'd stayed so long in the same church, Jim said, "I couldn't figure out a good time to leave, and the people couldn't figure out a good time to get rid of me."

Friends from a neighboring church, where pastors came and went with the seasons, chuckled at Jim's answer. "We don't seem to have that problem," they said.

It wasn't that Jim and Darlene didn't feel exhausted again, or struggle with the temptation to give up, but Jim reminded Darlene that they wanted to hear God say, "Well done!" not, "You quit too soon."

It seemed they were perpetually learning the lesson that the Lord had been blessed, broken, and given, and they must be too, and in that way, and no other, would they find real joy.

Darlene wrote a poem she titled "Blessed, Broken, Given."

> For the times I wanted to hibernate, and you showed me someone in need,
> > For the times I longed to read a book, but you showed me someone to feed,
> > And when you clapped your hand on my mouth when I had a thousand words to say,
> > And love and friendship remained unwounded and strong—at least for one more day,
> > For the times I wanted to cry and mourn for what I dearly wished was mine,
> > And you showed me the million uncounted blessings that quickly stopped my whine,
> > For the times you filled my heart with your love and taught me how to share,

And giving filled my cold heart with joy and left it no longer bare,

For all the times you shined your light through the broken cracks of me:

I thank you, Lord, with chastened grace, on my heart's bended knee.

~

"Jim, do you remember when you almost resigned?"

"That would be hard to forget."

"Remember that poem I used to quote to you? 'To live above with saints we love will certainly be glory. But to live below with saints we know—well that's another story.'"

Jim smiles. "That was one of your favorite quotes. I don't imagine we were too easy to live with ourselves. Do you know who wrote that?"

Darlene shrugs. "I looked it up. It has lots of different versions. I guess it was originally an old Irish rhyme. I suppose disgruntled saints have been quoting it for quite some time."

"We didn't want to be that did we? Disgruntled saints. And now life above is right around the next corner."

"For you, maybe, but don't be in a hurry."

"I'm not, but it will be wonderful."

He sleeps. She should tell him it's okay to go, but she can't. Not yet.

*Vaya con Dios*. How many times had she stood at the little kitchen window and whispered those words as she watched Jim or one of the kids or grandkids drive away? She hadn't told them. They would have laughed and reminded her she is Italian, not Spanish. But it had been the prayer of her heart for all of them, and it always will be, *Go with God*. She wasn't ready to whisper it to Jim for the final time.

# NEIGHBORHOOD WATCH

Some people called the Corners "the last best place." It did have more of a *Little House on the Prairie* flavor than most neighborhoods. Many people at the Corners still left their doors unlocked, but that was about to change.

Thefts started, petty things at first, but when shotguns started coming up missing, the neighborhood became alarmed. Someone even shot two holes in the old white frame building of Corners Church.

Connie decided to organize a neighborhood watch, and it met in the Corner's Church fellowship hall.

One of the first speakers was the county prosecutor. The Corners people were impressed he would come out to speak to them. He told them to lock their doors. They showed him the emergency phone list they'd compiled, and he was pleased to see neighbors knew who to call if they needed help.

Every name on the list was backed by an arsenal of shotguns, except the preacher's name. Everyone knew the only gun he had was a .22 that might or might not fire, and when pressed, he admitted he had no bullets. Among themselves, out of his hearing, the neighbors agreed that if there was trouble, no one would call the preacher unless someone was dying or dead. To fight off burglars they would depend on people who actually knew how to shoot and had real bullets. When he was seventy, the preacher got a gun, a real one with real bullets.

The neighborhood had many questions for the county prosecutor. "Are we allowed to shoot someone who's in our yard, on our property?" Ralph asked.

The prosecutor shook his head. "The law says you can only shoot an intruder after he's in your house and then only if you have no way to escape."

The group looked at each other in disgust. They would protect their homes and their families, law or no law, and the prosecutor knew it.

"I'll tell you what," the prosecutor said, "if an intruder's in your yard holler, and fire a warning shot over his head. If he keeps coming, shoot him. After he's dead, grab him by the ankles, and haul him inside. As long as I'm prosecutor, there will be no charges filed."

The prosecutor went out after his speech and easily found his vehicle. It sat among trucks and was the only clean vehicle, and the only car, in the parking lot. He felt a bit uneasy. He'd meant that "haul him in by his ankles" as a joke, but he wasn't sure it had been taken that way.

~

"WEREN'T the neighbors at the Corners wonderful?"

Jim nods and smiles. "You should write a book about them."

"Maybe I will someday."

"Hey, remember that renegade Amish man who had the forbidden cell phone? He didn't have any way to charge it, so he snuck up to the church at night and used our electricity. I don't think he ever knew we found out about it."

"What's a little electricity between good neighbors? Didn't cost that much to charge his cell phone. I hope his bishop never caught him."

## 84

## PROTECTING THEIR OWN

The rural county where Corners Church sat was country strong. They took care of their own, and justice usually prevailed. It did for Lisa.

Lisa had married too young, and her husband, Butch, was a mean brute when he was drinking, and that was most of the time. He tormented his coon dogs for fun. He used Lisa as a punching bag, but she made excuses for him to everyone.

"What happened to you?" a coworker asked, noticing bruises on her legs and around her left eye.

"Oh, I fell down the stairs." Lisa shrugged and attempted to laugh.

"Again?"

"Clumsy is my talent." Lisa smiled a sad smile.

She wasn't fooling anyone, least of all her dad. Lisa's dad, Ralph, was a good man, easy going, tending his farm with care, and gentle to all God's creatures. The only time his children had ever been afraid of him was the time he'd caught them pulling legs off flies.

"Can you make a fly?" he'd thundered at them. "I didn't

think so. Them's God's creatures you're tormenting. I never want to see you do nothing like that ever again. I can't abide cruelty, and I won't. Do you hear me?"

Some of the dads at the Corners would have taken off a belt at this point, but Lisa and her brothers knew their dad wouldn't do that. Still, he had a look in his eyes that day the five kids didn't forget. Never again did they hurt any of God's creatures.

Lisa had reason to remember that look in her dad's eyes when he showed up unannounced at the trailer where she and Butch lived. She'd seen her dad at Market Home that morning, and he'd frowned when he'd seen her new bruises.

"Don't give me none of that 'I fell down the steps' crap again, Lisa. Your coworkers might fall for that, but I know your trailer don't have no steps. I know what it does have, though. It has a mean son—"

"Dad!" Lisa interrupted. "Everything's okay, really."

"It's not okay, but it will be," Ralph said grimly. "It will be."

Around two that afternoon, Ralph pounded on the trailer door. Butch was drunk, lounging on the couch. Ralph brushed by his daughter and stood over his son-in-law.

"You touch my daughter again," he said in an icy calm voice, "and I'll kill you."

Butch yawned and almost laughed. He lazily unwound himself from the couch and stood to his full six feet, six inches, looking down at the older, much shorter man. The laugh stuck in his throat when he looked into Ralph's eyes. There was something there to be reckoned with.

"Leave, old man, while you still can," Butch said menacingly. "You ain't welcome here."

"I'm going," Ralph said in that same flat, icy calm voice, "but you remember what I said. And, Lisa? You ever need me, you call me."

It wasn't more than a month later when Ralph's phone

rang. "Daddy?" Lisa's voice was barely above a whisper. "Come quick. He's in the bathroom. This time I think he's going to kill me."

Ralph loaded his twelve gauge and threw it in the backseat of his rusty Ford. He floored the truck and spun out of the driveway. A cloud of dust followed him down the dirt roads as he sped the five miles to Lisa's house.

This time, Ralph didn't knock. He kicked open the trailer door. Lisa was huddled, bruised and bleeding on the couch. Butch stood over her, taunting her with a bloody knife.

Did Ralph warn Butch to put down the knife? There were varying stories about that. One thing the neighbors did agree on. That shotgun blast through the head made very sure Butch would never again hurt Lisa, or any of God's creatures.

The case didn't go to court. The prosecutor said it was justifiable homicide. When people asked Jim and Darlene what they thought about it, they said only God, Lisa, and Ralph knew the whole story, and they were content to leave it that way.

## THE CENTIPEDE AND THE TOAD

"Need to see Monica at Medical Care," Jim says, moving restlessly in the hospital bed. "Have to stop by Alice Marie's. Can you make her some soup? Too much to do. We can't keep up anymore, can we? Can't keep up."

"It's okay," Darlene says. "Jesus knows we can only do what we can do." She smiles ruefully. *Dying, and still thinking of his to-do list.* She is no better. They'd tried to practice back burner living, but it hadn't always worked.

"Look at Jesus," Jim says. "Just look at Jesus."

"That's right, honey." Darlene agrees. "We tried to do that, didn't we?"

~

WHEN SHE'D BEEN YOUNGER, Darlene had sometimes struggled with the many things she and Jim had to do. Ministry involved helping people out of ditches, but people seldom fell in ditches at convenient times. A God-centered life was a people-centered life; she knew it, and usually she loved it, but sometimes she got tired and a bit overwhelmed.

Jim listened compassionately when Darlene told him she was struggling, but he seldom allowed her to wallow in a puddle of self-pity, unless he had fallen into the same puddle.

"Are you looking at Jesus or looking at our many jobs?"

She sighed. "You're right, I know. You know what, though? It isn't all the things we have to do that bother me as much as the things we don't get done. The world is so. . .needy! Marriages are crumbling; people are hurting; the lonely are friendless; more people need meals than I can cook for—and there are only two of us!"

After that conversation, they decided to practice back burner living. They were going to quit worrying about everything that needed to be done. When they saw needs, they'd take them to the Lord who, unlike themselves, had limitless resources. Then they'd do the next thing that needed doing and leave the other jobs on the back burner. If a task persistently worked its way to the front burner, they'd stop what they were doing and attend to it.

Bill kept moving to the front burner. He was a member of another church but frequently visited Corners Church. Time passed, and poor health sent Bill and his wife Margaret to a nursing home.

One week, Darlene couldn't stop thinking about the sweet, lined faces of the elderly couple. *We need to visit Bill and Margaret.* The thought refused to be quiet, so even though the week was already busy enough for two weeks, Jim and Darlene went to the nursing home.

"How did you know how much we needed company today?" Bill asked.

The day after their visit, Bill fell and could no longer recognize anyone. They were glad they'd gone when they had.

Darlene memorized a poem by an unknown author to help her remember to focus on the job at hand instead of getting distracted by the million and one things waiting to be done.

∼

Jim used to quote the poem with her. Did he still remember it? She'd see.

She leans close to his ear and recites:

A centipede was happy, till, one day a toad in fun,
    Said, 'Pray, which leg goes after which?'
    Which strained his mind to such a pitch
    He lay distracted in a ditch...

Darlene pauses, waiting. She's disappointed when he doesn't open his eyes or appear to hear. She leans back in her chair and closes her eyes, when suddenly, quite clearly, Jim says the poem's last line, "Considering how to run."

Darlene doesn't know what she'll do when Jim is gone, how she'll pay the bills, where she'll live, but she's not going to listen to that ugly toad. Jim's here now; she's sitting next to him in his last hours, and God will show her the next step.

Darlene had insisted she didn't want to live with any of the kids. She smiles now, remembering the plan Beth, their sweet daughter-in-law, had jokingly offered for elder care, since her parents didn't want to live with their kids either. She'd buy a big boat, stock it with food, put Jim and Darlene and her parents on it, and set it adrift. Beth's parents, Miles and JoAnn, and Jim and Darlene were good friends, so the four of them had said Beth's imaginary plan sounded pretty good to them.

"I'll even give you one book and one movie!" Beth had said.

Darlene, the book lover, had protested. "Only one?"

"Sure! By then you'll be so forgetful the book and movie will be new every day! You and Mom and Dad will forget each other every night too, so you'll have new friends every morning."

New friends. God had sent many new friends to Corners Church over the years. Darlene thinks of the ones who'd joined them in the last decade or two. It was amazing how quickly they'd become like family. It hadn't taken long before it seemed they'd always been a part of Corners Church. They'd added not just love and laughter but wisdom and progress. Several of them were on the board now serving as trustees, a clerk, and a deacon. One taught the adult Sunday school class; another led Bible studies for the women.

Darlene whispers their names in grateful prayer and sees their dear faces as clearly as if they were here with her now. Surely, no pastor and wife had ever been more blessed than she and Jim.

## BRAIN TROUBLE

The trees in Hillsdale, Michigan were nearly at peak color that sunny October day as Jim drove Darlene to another visit with her neurologist. Darlene had been seeing a neurologist since she'd survived a stroke three years earlier. Her family doctor had sent her back this time because of some recent unusual symptoms.

Darlene felt happy, lost in the glorious autumn color, when she suddenly thought, *Today, my life will change forever.* She shrugged it off. *Where did that come from? Quit being so dramatic.*

The neurologist looked serious. "I have good news and bad news. The good news is you haven't had another stroke."

Darlene smiled, relieved.

"Now the not so good news, have you ever heard of a brain aneurysm?"

Before the visit ended, Darlene found out she'd be going for a consultation with a brain surgeon.

Darlene's amazing neurosurgeon was top in his field at the University of Michigan.

"Sometimes I recommend a wait-and-see approach," Dr. T. said, "but not this time. You need surgery, and, because of the wide neck of your aneurysm and its location, the surgery you need is clipping."

Dr. T. explained clipping an aneurysm deprives it of its blood supply and has advantages, risks, and side effects. Darlene agreed to the surgery, and the hospital scheduled an angiogram for early December and surgery a week before Christmas.

An angiogram is usually a simple procedure but not always. An accidental puncturing of an artery sent nurses running down the hall with Darlene on the cart, heading for an MRI. Blood filled Darlene's pelvis, and her blood pressure plummeted to 40/30. They rushed her to the ICU and inserted central lines and IV's. When they let Jim in the room, he was horrified to see a crowd of doctors and nurses around her bed, shouting orders.

At a support group meeting, one of Darlene's nurses later told her, "We thought we were going to lose you."

Instead of a planned trip to Maine to see Becky Joy graduate from a photojournalism program, Darlene spent the next few days in the ICU and the step-down unit.

As she recovered, doctors came to explain what had happened during the angiogram and to discuss upcoming brain surgery.

Darlene woke to hear the doctors talking to her roommate. "Your angiogram showed the aneurysm is larger than we thought," a doctor said.

"What?" the roommate exclaimed. "I had an angiogram?"

"You may not remember it," the doctor replied. "You lost a lot of blood."

"What!" the roommate said in a higher voice. "I lost a lot of blood?"

"You're fine now," the doctor replied soothingly, "but we need to talk to you about your brain surgery."

The roommate really panicked. "I need brain surgery?" she shouted.

Darlene had a hard time making her voice heard from the other side of the curtain. "Hey!" she hollered. "I think you guys want me!"

Later, Darlene and her roommate laughed about the incident. "They about gave me a heart attack!" the roommate said.

"Well, if you have to have one, I guess this is a good place to do it," Darlene replied.

Darlene's neurosurgeon postponed her surgery twice, waiting for her to recover from the hematoma caused by the angiogram and to get strong enough for surgery. At last, the day arrived, February 25, 2013.

On the day of surgery, Darlene's grown children, their spouses, and other family members came to support her. Her sisters came too, Jennifer from a few hours away in Michigan, and Lou all the way from New York. Even Eve, frail from fighting advanced ovarian cancer, came and all the brothers-in-law too. Everyone waited with Jim for many hours as the neurosurgeon and his team took apart Darlene's brain and put it back together.

The big words for what happened in surgery were "right-sided supraorbital craniotomy for aneurysm clipping." They immobilized Darlene's head, cut through skin and scalp, drilled through her skull, and opened the dura, the protective membrane that surrounds the brain. The doctors continued down until they got to the aneurysm on the anterior communicating artery at the bottom of the brain.

Later, Dr. T. explained the aneurysm had been so close to rupturing he'd done something he'd seldom had to do. He'd used temporary clips to deprive the aneurysm of blood flow so he could safely work on it. He'd then attached three permanent clips to the aneurysm.

When the surgical team finished, they backed their way out, using four-way flashers. Okay, kidding about the flashers. They replaced some torn dura with artificial material and closed the skin with temporary staples. Becky Joy counted forty-eight of them. Darlene later wished she'd saved them but hadn't thought to ask for them. They may have come in handy for deck repair.

The staples in Darlene's head looked like a zipper, making her a proud member of what brain surgery survivors call the Zipper Head Club. The surgery left thirteen pieces of permanent hardware in her head, three clips, three burr-hole covers, and seven screws.

The surgical team sent Darlene off to the ICU with instructions for frequent "neuro checks"; that's hospital code for pester the patient with questions day and night. After repeatedly answering the same questions, Darlene decided the serious team of the University of Michigan doctors and nurses needed a laugh.

When they asked for the umpteenth time if Darlene knew what hospital she was in, she answered she was at Ohio State, U of M's arch football rival. After a moment of shocked silence, the room exploded with laughter.

Dr. T. said, "I was going to tell you that you were one of my favorite patients, but not now!"

Darlene loved the competent, compassionate U of M neuro nurses, especially the sweet, short one with the Scottish accent. She challenged Darlene to do what she needed to do to get out of the hospital and sent her home with a hug and a kiss.

When Darlene arrived home, flowers, meals, calls, cards, gifts, and visits from family and church family surrounded her like a blanket of love.

Healing was a challenge. Darlene couldn't tolerate strong pain meds, so she could only take Tylenol. She tried to sleep off the pain as much as possible, but nightmares made that tough. She dreamt Jim had replaced the old family van with a rhinoceros. Darlene felt sorry for it because it didn't have room to turn around in the garage.

∼

Darlene chuckles, remembering the nightmare that made her angry with Jim.

"Do you remember when I got upset with you after brain surgery?"

He grins and squeezes her hand.

∼

While recovering from surgery, Darlene woke in the night and needed to use the bathroom. The problem was the alligator in the toilet. Jim had warned her about the alligator, but she couldn't remember which bathroom it was in. She woke him from a sound sleep.

"Honey, will you get the alligator out of the toilet? I need to use the bathroom."

The poor guy was exhausted. "You had a bad dream. There's no alligator in the toilet." He rolled over and went back to sleep.

Darlene woke him again. "Well, if you won't get up and get the alligator out of the toilet, will you at least tell me what one it's in?"

Jim spoke slowly, the way you talk to a difficult child. "Go use either bathroom. There's no alligator in the toilet. You had a bad dream."

Darlene was furious. One end of her was already closed with forty-eight staples, and apparently Jim didn't care if her other end needed staples too.

"You have your theology wrong," Darlene later informed Jim when the horrific pain eased, the nightmares stopped, and she could think semi-clearly again. "There is too a purgatory. I spent weeks there."

It took a long time for Darlene to separate dreams from reality. A few months after surgery she began having epileptic seizures because the nerves in her brain didn't heal correctly.

Darlene once experienced twelve hours of global amnesia. She didn't recognize the house or Jim. When he convinced her they were married, she asked if they had any babies.

"We had four babies, honey, but they're all grown up now."

Darlene sobbed, and Jim held her close. "What's wrong? Why are you crying?"

"Because we don't have any babies!"

For quite a while, Darlene's brain filter was out of kilter. At a church service in a shut-in's home, a man was getting ready to play his harmonica. "Are you going to play 'Ninety-nine Bottles of Beer on the Wall?'" Darlene asked. There was a stunned silence. No one was more surprised by the words than Darlene herself.

Corners Church family, ever-loving and tolerant, broke the silence with laughter. They were patient with their pastor's wife as she struggled to come to terms with her new normal.

She later told Jim, "Honestly, those words never went through my brain. They just came out of my mouth!"

Things that were simple before surgery confused Darlene. She couldn't smell well; that came in handy because of the mountain of manure in the neighbor's barnyard behind their house. Nothing tasted the way it had before, but it didn't stop her from eating. She struggled with balance, and her short-term memory problems could have given three comedians enough material for full-time work.

Still, Darlene felt grateful to God, her surgeon and nurses, and to Jim and her kids who did so much when she could do so little. She'd never forget Becky Joy sitting on the floor next to her couch and coaxing her to eat tiny bites of food from pretty, small dishes. It hadn't taken Becky Joy long to realize that looking at a normal size serving would result in her mom flatly refusing to eat anything.

Darlene knew she was blessed. She couldn't have asked for a more caring family or for more love than she got from the wonderful family at Corners Church.

Most of all, Darlene was happy to be alive. She determined to celebrate love and laughter every day. She felt her aneurysm was a gift that reminded her that life is too short for anything but love.

## HE LIVED BY LOVE

Before her aneurysm surgery, Darlene had been like the energizer bunny and hadn't needed Jim's help for much. Even her stroke hadn't slowed her down for long. After surgery, though, circumstances swiftly redefined their marriage. Darlene often experienced the care she'd seen Jim freely give anyone who needed anything.

~

DARLENE SHAKES HER HEAD, remembering the times Jim had dug cars out of snowbanks for people, changed tires, helped chase stray cows, or lain on a floor between piles of dog poop to fix a leaky kitchen pipe.

~

"SHE COULD HAVE at least cleaned up the dog poop before she asked you to come over!" Darlene exclaimed indignantly when Jim returned home from doing requested plumbing work.

Jim did many things some of his pastor friends wouldn't do. Did a church toilet need cleaning? He scrubbed it. Did the church basement flood? He did his best to fix the pump. Did a church lawn need mowing? He mowed it, until the church hired someone to do that. Did the sidewalks need shoveling? He shoveled, in the dead of winter, even after his cardiologist warned him not to.

"You have trustees," Darlene reminded him when a church toilet overflowed.

"Honey, they live so far away. Do you really want me to call them to come fix something I can fix myself?"

No, she really didn't want him to call one of those men who already had too much to do themselves, and she admired Jim for being willing to do whatever needed to be done.

*I wonder what Professor Nick Machiavelli would say about Jim lying between piles of dog poop to fix a leaky pipe or repairing an overflowing toilet at church?*

Jim never told his professor or anyone else. He didn't even tell the trustees about the small jobs he did around the church. He was a silent partner trustee himself. *His sermons are good, better than good,* Darlene thought, *but what makes him a wonderful pastor is his servant's heart.*

In one sermon, Jim quoted Sam Earle Owen:

> True compassion means to recognize
>> Anyone in need;
>> It also means to organize
>> Your feelings into deed.

Darlene knew better than anyone that Jim practiced what he preached. The words Jill Morgan wrote about her father, the famous G. Campbell Morgan, could have been said of Jim: "It was not his way to express sympathy by word alone if it were possible for him in any way to alleviate the hurt by deeds."

∼

THERE MUST BE *a special reward in heaven for preachers like Jim,* Darlene thinks as she watches him restlessly sleep.

## CHRISTMAS 2014—THE CHRISTMAS OF THE BELLS

The kids did a wonderful job with the program that year. They remembered their lines for the play. Mary and Joseph looked sweet holding baby Jesus, even if they did laugh when they dropped the Jesus doll under the communion table, and the shepherds' head coverings stayed on. The angels' halos looked a little straighter than usual. The children closed their part of the program by seriously ringing their plastic bells and singing, "Christmas Bells." Then one little boy rang the Corners Church bell. He even remembered to open the door so people could hear it.

Jim said:

> Our church bell you just heard first rang out over farms and fields one hundred and seventy years ago. This building was built from native timber in 1844 by men from the Congregational Church of South Jefferson. A man from that church said, "We raised nothing much but weeds in our fields that summer, but we had our church." The building

first stood on Lake Pleasant Road. For many years, the bell rang on Christmas Day.

This bell was not the first to ring out from the Corners on Christmas Day. The first church on this spot was a Methodist church. Sadly, on April 7, 1942, lightning struck the steeple. The Waldron fire department extinguished the fire, but a second fire began later and destroyed the building.

The Methodist congregation was left without a building, and the Congregational Church of South Jefferson came to the rescue. Their building on Lake Pleasant Road had been empty for fifteen years and had become home to honeybees, goats, and rabbits. For fifteen years, no bell rang out over fields and farms. The Methodist congregation at the Corners would make that empty building into their new church home.

The building had to be moved from Lake Pleasant Road to the Corners. That happened on September 19, 1944. The process was delayed for several hours on Squawfield Road because the steeple was too tall to pass under the wires. Two men from the congregation removed the steeple so the building could continue its journey.

People lined the roads to watch. The men called to each other, "Hats off! The church is passing by."

Darlene got distracted for a few minutes, thinking of that beautiful sight. How she would have loved to have been there, hearing the men shout, "Hats off! The church is passing by!" She swallowed the lump in her throat and blinked the tears from her eyes. What was Jim saying? Something about bee's wax.

The congregation removed bee's wax, replaced broken windows, and worked hard to get the building ready to use.

They dedicated their building on July 15, 1945. Historical reports don't tell us, but maybe a bell rang joyfully again over farms and fields.

The Methodist congregation dwindled in size until sadly, on the last Sunday in September, 1969, the Methodist congregation left the building. Their membership automatically transferred to the Methodist church in Osseo. Once again, the building sat empty. No pastor preached the Bible from the pulpit. No choirs sang. No children went to Sunday school. The bell was silent.

Another group used the building for a short time; then once again, an empty church building sat at the Corners.

On December 13, 1972 the congregation of Corners Church bought the building. They scraped and painted walls and ceilings, repaired the furnace, and converted it to LP gas. They cleaned floors and woodwork and worked hard to get the building ready for church services. In late May of 1974, the congregation began using the building, and they dedicated it on June 10, 1974. Once again, the church bell rang joyfully out over farms and fields.

Church bells have long been used to signal significant events. I recently read this, "For centuries, church bells rang out news of every kind. Whether calling parishioners to service, announcing joyous news, signaling the passing of a community member, or simply tolling the hour, bells let everyone in the city and surrounding villages know what was going on."

Many newer churches no longer have bells. Sadly, some churches no longer tell people how to get to heaven. I pray Corners Church will share the good news until Jesus comes again. Will you stand and quote the good news with me?

The congregation stood and recited a verse they loved, John

3:16. Even the little children knew it. "For God so loved the world, that he gave his only begotten Son, that whosoever believeth in him should not perish, but have everlasting life."

The service ended, but the congregation lingered, talking, laughing, wishing one another Merry Christmas. Darlene and Jim stood at the door, cherishing every handshake, smile, and hug. It had been another wonderful Christmas at the Corners, the Christmas of the bells.

## A CHRISTMAS LETTER

Jim smiles up at Darlene, and she thinks about how much she'll miss that smile, his laugh, his crazy puns, his comfort and encouragement—even the things about him that bothered her like his perpetually messy desk. "I love you, honey," she whispers. It seems like yesterday to her that she had written this Christmas letter to Jim:

> If I had Shakespeare's pen, I couldn't find enough beautiful words to tell you how much I love and admire you and how wonderful you are. I'm so happy to celebrate this forty-sixth Christmas together. I know we can't have forty-six more, but I wish we could. You grow dearer to me every year. I don't think our marriage has ever been as close and sweet as it is now, and maybe that's because of the recent trials we've faced together.
>
> We share so many memories of laughter and tears, and they have all made our lives together beautiful. This Christmas Eve I'm remembering. I'll never forget our first Christmas in that little house on Eynon Street in Scranton. I

can still see our first tree standing in the corner. We were so young and so much in love.

The years passed so quickly—years with new babies, little money, and lots of love and laughter. April was five months old her first Christmas. Davey was six months old when he celebrated his first. Weren't they adorable babies? Jimmy missed Christmas by two days and came home from the hospital in that big red stocking. Christmas 1988 was a special one as we waited for our February beautiful baby girl. We chose a perfect middle name for her because look at the joy she gives us now.

I remember curling up together around the kerosene heater, trying to get warm, and listening to you read *Little House on the Prairie* and *The Gift of the Magi*. I recall a rough, homemade barn and a little girl's doll cradle with a hand stitched blanket. Those years when we cut Cedar trees and brought them in for Christmas and put mostly homemade gifts under them were the best.

How many times have we driven up Lickley Road to our country church at Christmas time? There too we've had our share of laughter, and yes, of tears, but God has blessed and used us, and that's all that matters.

And now we are grandparents to our wonderful grandchildren, and we get to see the love and joy in their eyes as we celebrate another Christmas together. Our grown kids love the Lord—what more could we want?

You really are all I want for Christmas, this year and every Christmas of my life. Your love and laughter warm my heart, and your arms are my shelter from the cold winds of the world. Curling up next to you at night and seeing your smile in the morning are gifts money can't buy.

No package under a tree could compare with what I have in you—your crazy jokes, your deep wisdom, your wanting to fix everything and make life easier for me, our walks and talks, your love for me and others, everything we do together!

For all these years we've held hands and reached out with our free hands to help others, and I wouldn't want to have lived life any other way. When we have God, each other, our wonderful family, and our dear friends, we have everything even when we have little else.

Just you. That's all I want this Christmas. That's all I want every day for the rest of my life. Please take care of yourself and be as healthy as you can because I need you. You make life wonderful.

In case you can't tell, I love you, Dear Jim; I love you with all my heart.

*Please, God, give us many more Christmas days together.*

But they won't have another Christmas together; she knows it. She thinks of what Bruce, her brother-in-law had told them, "Make memories, because someday that's all you'll have." She's so glad for their memories. They might not look like much to anyone else. There are no trips to Hawaii, no cruises, no cross-country trips in her memory box. But the box is full of homespun love and laughter; it's so full the lid won't close.

## SPARE TIME

In their early years at Corners Church, Jim and Darlene had more time to spend with family and friends than they did in later years. They sometimes invited friends to supper three or more times a week.

But it seemed the longer they were in the ministry, the less time they had. Jim added a Monday evening jail ministry to his already overcrowded schedule. Jim thoroughly enjoyed being able to share the gospel with the men and women in the jail. It took more time than just Mondays, because often inmates would ask him to come back to the jail for counseling on another day.

Even though the jail ministry swallowed what had been his day off, Jim seemed refreshed by it. It gave new life to his sermons, and though it too was a ministry, like the church was, it was something different. Jim found it invigorating.

Darlene had a favorite spare time activity herself. She agreed with Annie Dillard who wrote there are people who "if you told them the world would end in ten minutes, would try to decide—quickly—what to read."

Reading was Darlene's favorite activity and writing was next. She never seemed to run out of words to write. Jim called her his Henrietta Wordsworth Shortfellow.

Darlene used to keep in her wallet every library card she'd ever owned, but Jim's teasing and his habit of using her as a sermon illustration finally cured her of that. She moved the cards from her wallet to a box in the attic, reasoning a person who keeps a collection of library cards in the attic isn't quite as eccentric as one who carries them in her wallet.

Sometimes Darlene thought about writing a book for young preachers' wives. She'd say that if the preacher had an incurable sense of humor his wife needed to be prepared for public humiliation. Make a few honest mistakes—get lost while driving the mile home from church, call a wrestling hold a half-Arnold instead of a half-Nelson, spell the word disciple wrong a hundred times in a curriculum assignment, and it was sure to come out in a sermon. Sometime, when you least expect it, the entire congregation will turn, look at you, and howl.

Jim teased Darlene about her love of books. She readily admitted that some of her best friends lived on a dusty shelf between two hard covers and wore jackets on even the hottest summer days.

When Jim and Darlene had been married twenty-three years they decided to go away overnight for the first time ever without the children. Jim told Darlene to pick any place within a few hours of home for their outing. She chose Grand Rapids, Michigan, the Mecca of book lovers.

"Used bookstores, how romantic," Jim teased. He loved books too, though not with the passion she did, and they had a wonderful time browsing.

Darlene enjoyed reading about people, who like herself, loved good books. She discovered that for more than twenty years F.W. Boreham bought and read a book a week. She wished she could do that, but Jim pointed out he and the kids did like to eat once a day or so, and the only way to get book money was to rob the slender grocery fund.

Thomas Edison sometimes read until 2:00 a.m., even when he was eighty years old and had to be awake and dressed the next morning before 7:00 a.m.

W. Robertson Nicoll read every biography he could find. He had 25,000 books in his library, and 5,000 were biographies. He read all the biographies. He was able to read 20,000 words in thirty minutes.

When she was a young mother, Darlene picked up a book at a library book sale and settled down to read it after the kids were asleep. In beautiful cursive writing someone had written on the flyleaf, "To my mother whose faith sings."

Tears filled Darlene's eyes. She wanted her children to see that her faith sang. She prayed often, "Lord, help me turn all my thoughts to prayers." She knew that was the only way her faith would sing.

After brain aneurysm surgery, Darlene was devastated to find she no longer enjoyed reading. She'd read a paragraph and forget what it said by the time she got to the next paragraph. She read much slower too, but she persevered. It took a few years, but Darlene was able to read and enjoy a book again, even though she couldn't lose herself in books the way she had before.

Though it was more work, reading remained a favorite spare time activity, and some of her best friends sat between hard covers on dusty shelves next to her desk where she wrote.

## TRUCK AND JAIL

Jim had wanted a pickup for years. "Thou shalt not covet thy neighbor's truck," he'd remind himself as he looked out over the church parking lot, seeing many trucks. True, the others needed their trucks. They hauled seed, fertilizer, and wood, but he didn't really need a truck. That didn't stop him from wanting one.

When Jim heard his brother-in-law had a twenty-year-old truck for sale, he couldn't resist. He bought it, and it was worth every penny to him to step high into that old Ford and run through the five gears of the floor shift. When the clutch and shift operated perfectly, it reminded him of music. It gave him the same feeling he got when the choir came together in perfect harmony at the Christmas service after many disastrous practices.

Jim drove his truck to his jail ministry on Monday nights. He felt it gave the men in the jail common ground with him when he could talk about his truck.

Truck or no truck, the prisoners seemed to like him, and

usually, but not always, sat quietly through his sermons. After noticing he'd gone over time one night, he apologized.

"That's okay, preacher," someone called out. "It's not like we have anywhere to go. We're a captive audience!"

Two men played the guitar before the Bible study at the jail service. The inmates' favorite song was, "I'll Fly Away." They belted out the part, "When the prison bars are broken, I'll fly away!" Jim often wondered if they comprehended the spiritual meaning of the song, but it broke the ice before the Bible study every time.

Jim was past retirement age when God opened the door for the jail ministry. Darlene told him they could claim Psalm 92:14 together, "He shall still bear fruit in old age; he shall be fat and flourishing."

"You can do the bear fruit part," Darlene told him laughing. "I'll be fat and flourishing."

Pastor Cliff Waters was Jim's inspiration. Well into his eighties, despite his declining health, he pastored his church, had a radio program, went calling, and preached many funerals. But one bad health episode put Cliff in the hospital, and Jim went to visit him.

"Can I do anything for you?" Jim asked the older pastor. Jim thought maybe Cliff would ask him to pour him a drink of water or move the call button closer.

"Sure, you can," Cliff replied. "Will you take over preaching at the jail on Monday nights for me?"

Cliff continued going to the jail, but Jim did the preaching. The inmates loved Cliff and would sometimes shove each other to sit closer to him.

After the jail service, Jim, Cliff, and the two guitar players went out for ice cream. Darlene called it "boys' night out." As they relaxed, Cliff sometimes told stories.

"Back in the day," Cliff said, "a man could sign his name on a line at the local hardware store and get dynamite to blow out tree stumps."

Cliff got a man to help him take out some tree stumps surrounded by stones. They decided they needed a bit more dynamite than what they had put there, so they added more.

"What we really needed," Cliff said, as he told the story, "was a longer fuse."

Cliff lit the too short fuse, and both men took off running. They felt the ground shake and heard stones hitting branches above them as they ran through woods.

Chuckling, Cliff said, "We had enough toothpicks for the whole county for the next ten years."

"Once," Cliff said, "a bunch of us went fishing. We sat for hours at the creek, and no one caught anything. Some of us had bait; others had fancy lures. Then a kid put WD-40 on his hook and caught five fish in a few minutes."

The other men laughed.

"Well, you know what they say," Cliff said. "Anyone worth his salt can fix anything with a coat hanger, baling twine, and a can of WD-40!"

Sometimes Jim asked Cliff for advice about the ministry. Cliff dispensed it with his characteristic brand of humor. He gave unsolicited advice too.

"It's important for a preacher to be honest, right?" he asked Jim.

Jim nodded.

"So, what do you say when you make a hospital visit and the proud mama shows you the ugliest baby you've ever seen, a red, wrinkled, squirming prune of a thing?"

"Well..." Jim hesitated.

"It's not a hard question. You say, 'Well my, my, my, that sure is a baby, now; isn't it?'"

One night, Jim said to Cliff, "I hear you're going to retire from your church. You're not old enough to do that are you?"

Cliff laughed. "If I'd known I'd get this old, I would've taken better care of myself."

Even after Cliff retired from his church, he stayed busy filling pulpits, helping with the jail ministry, and preaching funeral services. It seemed half the county knew and loved him, and when a loved one died, they turned to him.

Cliff said to Jim, "When I die, everyone in the county is going to come to my funeral. You know why?"

Before Jim could answer what he was thinking, *because you're the best loved man in the county*, Cliff said, "They'll all come because they'll want to see for themselves if I'm really dead!"

Years passed as years do. It was a sad day for the ministry team and for the prisoners when Cliff could no longer attend the jail services. Then God called one of the guitar players home to heaven. The team of four became two, but those two became close friends. The one guitar player left probably didn't know how much comfort and encouragement he was to Jim.

## THE CHRISTMAS DARLA CAME HOME TO THE CORNERS

What's true? You can't go home again, or the greatest adventure of your life is finding your way back home?

One of Darlene's favorite holiday memories was the Christmas Darla came home. Two Sundays before Christmas she'd asked Darla's parents if she'd be home for the holidays.

"No," Darla's dad had said.

Darla's mom said nothing, but she looked more frail than usual, and tears filled her eyes. Darlene could have kicked herself for asking, but much to everyone's surprise, Darla did come home.

Darla later told the whole story to Darlene.

∼

DARLENE WISHES Jim was awake to hear the story in Darla's words. She'll have to enjoy the memory herself. Jim is smiling in his sleep. Perhaps he's dreaming of something even better than Darla's homecoming. Is it his own Homegoing? Her mind drifts back to Darla.

∽

ONE HOUR AND FIFTY-NINE MINUTES. That's how long it took to fly from Boston to Detroit. "Under two hours to fly to a different planet," Darla muttered, "and wouldn't you know, Mom and Dad would be late picking me up."

Holiday music filled the crowded airport terminal. Travelers rushed to get to their destinations this Christmas Eve morning.

The old song crooned, "I'll be home for Christmas." Darla wished she had earplugs. Detroit was only the beginning of what was sure to be an almost unendurable week. The ride to the family home south of Jackson, Michigan, would take thirty minutes longer than the flight from Boston to Detroit had. From experience, Darla knew the trip would be filled with Mom's irritating, optimistic chatter. And the questions! Mom asked so many questions, but the question Darla dreaded most was the one she knew Dad would ask.

Who was it who said, "You can't go home again?" Maybe they should have said, "Only a fool tries to go home again."

Darla retrieved her bags, found a seat, and sighed. This wasn't where she'd wanted to spend the holidays. She and her friends had planned to party through Christmas and then go to Times Square in New York to celebrate New Year's Eve.

Darla almost wished she'd refused when Mom had called asking her to come home for Christmas and to stay for Grandma's memorial service on December 31.

Grandma. In spite of her black mood Darla smiled, visualizing her short, white-haired, grandmother. Darla could almost smell the almond flavoring in Grandma's Christmas cookies.

Every Christmas of Darla's childhood had been spent at Grandma's house and at Corners Church.

Finally. There were the parents, hurrying toward her. People smiled at the contrast between her and her mother. Mom said Darla, at five-eleven, looked like Beauty in *Beauty and the Beast*, and that she looked like Mrs. Potts—the little talking tea pot.

As a little girl, Darla used to sing, "Mommy's a little tea pot, short and stout," until Dad made her stop. He'd feared she'd hurt Mom's feelings. Darla still referred to Mom as "The Tea Pot" when she talked about her to her Boston friends.

As always, Darla felt half-amused and half-embarrassed by Mom's looks. The way Mom dressed did nothing to enhance her five-foot frame. Even on tip toe she couldn't quite reach Darla's cheek.

Darla bent to let Mom kiss her. Then she felt Dad's arms around her. They didn't feel as strong as she remembered. She was surprised at the amount of gray in Dad's hair and at the many wrinkles that lined Mom's face. She glanced at Mom's cheeks. The pink cheeks she remembered were gone. Mom's face looked pale and fragile.

The ride home was emotionally exhausting. Darla bit her lip more than once to stop from snapping.

"No, Mom, Devon and I have no plans to get married."

"Yes, Mom, I know *The Boston Globe* is New England's largest newspaper. I've worked for them for two years."

"Yes, Mother, I keep my doors locked."

"No, Mom, I don't eat three healthy meals a day. You have no idea how demanding my schedule is."

Blessed quietness. Mom slept, her head leaned against the window. Darla noticed how the sunlight made Mom's hair look even grayer than it had at the airport.

Dad cleared his throat. Oh no, here it came. "The Question." Might as well get it over with.

"I'm retiring the first of the year."

"What?" Darla bolted up in her seat. "You told Mom not to talk to you about retiring until you were seventy-five! Dad, why retire? You love your job!"

"Guess this is as good a time as any to tell you. Mom needs too much help now. I'm retiring to spend what time she has left with her."

"What do you mean 'what time she has left?' Does anyone in this family ever tell me anything?"

Dad's voice was quiet. "I wanted to wait and tell you in person. Mom has lymphoma. Stage four."

The size of the lump in Darla's throat surprised her. She hadn't felt close to her parents for years. She seldom thought of them except when she skimmed their long weekly letters. Darla hadn't been home for five years, and Mom and Dad had never visited Boston. Darla was glad they hadn't come. The parents meeting her friends?

Darla didn't know what to say to Dad. The car was silent except for Mom's soft snores. Darla texted Devon the news of the lymphoma.

"So, The Tea Pot's going to whistle her last tune?" He texted back. It was exactly the kind of sarcastic, dark humor that had drawn Darla to Devon, but now it made her inexplicably angry. She turned off her cell phone and shoved it into her jacket pocket.

The trip seemed to take an eternity. Ann Arbor. Chelsea. Jackson. Spring Arbor. As Darla well remembered from college days, there were still thirty minutes of travel left.

Dad slowed as they passed the college. It looked even smaller and quainter than Darla remembered. She'd tried to forget her years there. If anyone asked where she had gotten her education, she said NYU, where she'd done her graduate work in journalism.

"Do you want me to stop at your old Alma Mater?" Dad asked.

"Don't bother." Darla sighed. "Let's get home and get this week over with."

Dad glanced at her in the rearview mirror. His eyes looked sad. That was another thing Darla hated about coming home. It felt like she always said or did something to hurt Mom and Dad.

Dad reached back over the seat and handed Darla an ad ripped from the paper. "I thought you might want to see this, for what it's worth."

Darla laughingly read out loud: "Wanted. Experienced journalist for the *Hudson Daily News*. Salary based on experience. Benefits." She remembered as a kid snickering at a story the paper had carried on its front page, "Calamity Cow Causes Car Crash."

The "Daily Blues," as some called it, wanted to hire a reporter? Darla was surprised the paper hadn't gone belly up years ago. When even *Newsweek* couldn't survive the upheaval in print journalism, how had that little newspaper survived?

Hudson was only about ten miles from her parents' home. Did Dad really think she'd return to this hick town and work for that nothing newspaper? It was ludicrous. She crumpled the ad and shoved it in her jacket pocket. Her fingers touched her phone. Should she text Devon so they could mock her dad's idea together? For some reason, she didn't feel like it.

Darla carried one suitcase into the house, and Dad carried the other. Mom clung to his free arm. Darla knew she should say something to Mom about the cancer, but what? They hadn't communicated well, not even when Darla had been a child. Mom was all the things Darla secretly despised, a stay-at-home mom, with no higher education, and church as her only social life.

Darla felt like she'd walked back in time when she stepped into the house. The tree was in the same corner. As usual, the top was crooked, and the tree topper had the same crack she remembered. The scent of pine filled the air, and Darla sneezed. She'd forgotten about her pine allergy.

Looking around, Darla sighed. Every nook was filled with something red and green. Her eyes widened at the array of home baked goods that filled the kitchen counter. She hoped her parents didn't expect her to eat all that. It took strict discipline to stay in her size six clothes. Dad saw Darla's glance and smiled proudly.

"You think that's something? Wait until you taste the turkey, the ham, and the pork roast Mom has in the fridge."

"I'm a vegan!" Darla hadn't meant to sound so angry.

"What's a vegan?"

How could anyone not know the definition of vegan? Darla tried to be patient. "I don't eat anything that causes an animal to suffer. I don't eat meat, eggs, or dairy."

"What do you eat?" Mom sounded stupefied.

"Veggies. Lots of veggies. And no baked goods."

Mom took a long look at the counter. Tears filled her blue eyes. "I think I'm going to go take a nap," she said softly.

Dad helped Mom into the bedroom and returned to Darla. "Sit, young lady!" he thundered. Darla almost laughed, but she sat. "Your Mom has been cooking for days for your visit. She has so little energy, and she used every bit of it to prepare for you to come home for the holidays."

"Okay, well I'm sorry." Darla almost winced at the weak sound of her own voice. She spoke louder: "I'm a vegan by conviction, and I'm not going to change just because Mom cooked!"

Dad's face reddened. "By conviction!" He thundered. "Since when do you have convictions about anything? You don't even bother attending church. And do you think Mom and I are stupid? We know you and Devon are living together. And that last article you wrote on abortion? That made Mom cry. We prayed none of our friends would see it."

Darla could feel her heart pounding in her head; one of her migraines was starting. "This isn't going to work," she said. "Home for Christmas? What a joke! This place isn't home. I shouldn't have come. We live in two different worlds, and there's nowhere left for us to meet. I'm flying back to Boston."

"Perhaps that would be best." Dad sighed. "We'll take you back to the airport in the morning. Maybe you'll stop thinking of yourself long enough to go to the Christmas Eve program at church with us tonight?"

*Selfish? Dad thought she was selfish?* She almost told him how much she'd donated to Planned Parenthood last year but realized in time Dad wouldn't consider that a point in her favor.

"Speaking of church—" Dad began.

"I'm going to do like Mom and take a little nap if I have to go to church tonight," Darla interrupted hastily. She already regretted her bitter words and didn't want to argue anymore with Dad.

Lying on the twin bed in her old room, Darla looked around. Everything in the room looked like cotton candy. *Why did I ever love pink gingham?* Pink was now her least favorite color. She tried to sleep despite the pounding headache.

Darla could hear Christmas music playing downstairs, and Mom and Dad were talking softly. Her angry words with Dad must have prevented Mom's nap. *Is Mom crying?* Darla buried her head under a pillow. She would get through church. She would spend the night. She would fly back to her world in the morning and bury this one in the past where it belonged. Home for the holidays was an outdated phrase that had nothing to do with her.

Surprised she'd slept so long, Darla woke. Downstairs Mom and Dad were waiting supper for her. No meats or treats were in sight. Two large trays of veggies and fruits waited.

"Are fruits okay?" Mom sounded timid.

"Oh, Mom!" Darla reached down, hugged her, and realized Mom's clothes no longer covered a plump frame. Mom was so tiny Darla could feel her bones. Darla pulled away, shocked.

"You didn't tell me you had cancer."

"I didn't know what to say."

Darla nodded. She understood that, the not knowing what to say.

After supper, the three of them walked together through the snowy parking lot and into Corners Church. This part of Michigan enjoyed a white Christmas only fifty percent of the time. For some illogical reason, Darla was glad it was snowing this year. She liked hearing the snow crunch under her feet.

The white frame church was even smaller than Darla remembered. Just like every year of her childhood, there was candlelight, laughter, and music. The children in the play forgot their lines like they always did. Grandpas dozed, and Grandmas looked proud. Babies fussed and were comforted. The same wreaths hung in the same windows. The same ridiculous Charlie Brown Christmas tree stood in the same corner. Its only ornaments were construction paper handprints. Must be the children were still tracing their hands to make Christmas ornaments.

Could it be? Darla leaned forward and peered at the tree. There it was—the ornament she'd made so long ago. It was the only one with a big yellow smiley face on it. At age seven, Darla had decorated everything with that silly smiley face.

Mom leaned close and whispered, "Do you remember the

year you had to be Joseph in the Christmas play because there were no boys? You hated that. You wanted to be Mary so bad."

From somewhere deep inside laughter bubbled. Mom started chuckling too.

"Shhh," Dad whispered, but he was grinning broadly.

A little boy stumbled over the words in the old King James Bible. "And she brought forth her first born son, and wrapped him in swaddling clothes, and laid him in a manger; because there was no room for them in the inn."

*I still believe those words,* Darla thought, as a little girl placed a blanketed doll in a crude manger. *That's one thing Mom and Dad and I have in common.*

Suddenly, she no longer felt angry. Darla knew she couldn't leave before Grandma's memorial service. She leaned over and whispered to Dad, "I'm going to stay through the holidays."

Dad poked Mom, winked, and grinned. Had he known all along she wouldn't leave?

*I'll answer Dad's unasked question before I go to bed. It will make him happy.* "Yes, Dad, I'll look for a church when I get back to Boston. It's not going to be anything like Corners Church, but I'll start going back to church."

She knew what her Dad would say. "Well, that's a beginning."

She wasn't going to argue with him or Mom again, not about church, or politics, or anything. She was going to enjoy being home, home for the holidays, perhaps for the last time.

Or . . . perhaps not for the last time. Darla reached into her jacket pocket and fished out the crumpled ad. It wouldn't hurt to stop at the paper and talk to them. *Did Dad wink at Mom again?* She watched him a minute, but he and Mom were staring straight ahead, holding hands, and smiling at the little angels with crooked tinsel halos who were singing quite off key,

"Glory to God in the highest, and on earth, peace, good will toward men."

~

DARLENE CHUCKLES, remembering the rest of the story. Darla had stayed and taken the job at the Hudson paper. She'd stayed until her mom had died, and then she'd stayed several more years until her dad had gone to heaven too. Darla had attended a larger church in town during those years, but she'd come sometimes with her dad to Corners Church when they'd had special events.

Had Darla ever returned to the traditional views her parents had raised her with? Well, Darlene thinks as she watches Jim sleep, *whatever Darla's views, she'd realized you can come home again.*

## LOVE AT CHRISTMAS TIME

It was another Christmas service at the old country church. Jim helped Darlene climb the church steps slowly, one at a time. They smiled at each other as they remembered almost running up those steps their first Christmas service, forty-three years before. The author, O. Henry, said "Life is made up of sobs, sniffles, and smiles, with sniffles predominating." They had experienced their share of sobs and sniffles during those forty-three years, but they disagreed with O. Henry. They thought smiles, not sniffles, prevailed.

They'd raised four children in that church, or maybe the four children had raised them! Their children had taught them humility, that's for sure.

The babies had grown into long-legged grade schoolers. They'd stopped acting up in church. They'd listened carefully and had taken notes on the sermon. Usually. They'd all wanted to sit next to mom. Darlene had often reached over in a sermon and touched the shoulder of the child whose turn it had been to sit away from her. Those had been good years. Church no longer felt like a wrestling match the way it had when they'd been babies.

Those four children were grown and married now. Davey and Becky Joy, along with their spouses, still attended Corners Church. Davey and Beth's four beautiful children attended too. When Jim and Darlene counted their blessings, having family who wanted to attend Corners Church with them was at the top of the list.

Now Darlene often sits in the back pew with her four grandchildren who seem to be much better behaved than her own children had been. Or could it be she's grown more tolerant? This Sunday, their four grandchildren are already in that back pew. Their oldest, a high school senior with her baby sister in her arms, smiles at Darlene and moves over to make room for her. *Where did you get those blue eyes? An angel must have kissed your face as you came from heaven to earth,* Darlene thinks, not for the first time. What Darlene really treasures is her granddaughter's love for the Lord. Her beautiful younger sister, famous for her love and hugs, sits next to her on one side. On the other side sits her mischievous brother with golden curls. He does anything he can at church to help his grandpa. The baby stirs in her granddaughter's arms. The resemblance between the two is startling. Except for eye color and dimples in opposite cheeks, the two could have been twins, seventeen-years apart. Their parents are already up front, Beth at the piano, Davey getting ready to lead the singing.

Darlene thinks with love of her other grandchildren at their own churches. She's glad they are all in church. How she loves children. Jim and Darlene had seen two generations of children grow up in Corners Church. In summer, little shoes often lined the outside steps as beautiful children ran and played barefoot in the grass. Every church should be so blessed.

Darlene smiles at the blonde young woman coming into

church behind them. She'd once been one of those barefoot children. When she'd been two years old, she'd often slipped into the aisle during prayer and had knelt with her forehead touching the floor. From the time she'd been little, she'd loved standing on the church porch, watching the sunset with Darlene. *Please use her life; please use every one of their sweet lives.*

Where had all the years gone? Jim and Darlene wipe their feet on the carpet in the entryway and hang their coats. The auditorium is filling with faces they love. The love of this church family is as real as a warm blanket; they can almost reach out and touch it. For forty-three years they'd loved and had been loved.

So many beloved faces are gone now, spending Christmas in heaven. Life is short. They'd always known it, but now they felt it. They were learning, with the passing of the years, to keep the main thing the main thing. Love is the first thing, the last thing, and everything in between.

In his Christmas sermon, Jim asked, "The walls in the original part of this church are one hundred and seventy years old; how many sermons and prayers have they heard? How many weddings, funerals, and baby dedications have they seen? How many times have they seen Christians hug each other or stand in prayer? We feel so permanent, but we're only one of many congregations to meet inside these walls.

"If the walls could talk, what would they say about us? If they described us in one word, what would it be? I hope it would be love. I pray we'll always be known for loving God and each other, and for reaching out with love to those beyond these old walls."

Darlene noticed snow was falling. She loved when snow fell during the Christmas sermon.

Jim continued, "John was the apostle of love. When he

visited churches in his older years they hung unto every word of his sermons, and those sermons were often about love. John grew so old and feeble he had to be carried into church on a stretcher. He grew weaker; his sermons grew shorter, and then they became one sentence, 'Brothers and sisters, love one another, for love is of God.' At the end of his life he was so weak he had only enough strength to preach one word, 'Love.'"

Jim looked tenderly at his people. Only a few had been part of the original congregation. Most of them had come later. They were all family to him, all dearly loved. "We're really blessed to have each other; let's keep loving each other and walking each other Home.

"Love. That's what Christmas is. God gave until He had nothing left to give because He loved. Merry Christmas, dear friends."

Jim and Darlene's grandson rang the church bell. The snow covering the fields didn't muffle the sound. Even neighbors who didn't attend church heard the bell and knew the real Christmas story was once again being told at Corners Church.

## 94

## MORE HEALTH SCARES

If Darlene thought a stroke and a brain aneurysm had filled her quota of health problems and would give her a "get out of the hospital free" card, she was wrong. The next few years brought a bleeding small intestine AVM that needed repaired and then a diagnosis of Myasthenia gravis that required infusions at a hospital every few weeks.

Jim began having serious health problems of his own, kidney and heart disease. Once an ambulance came to Corners Church and took him away before he even started his sermon.

Was it time to retire? They thought and prayed about it often. Corners Church deserved someone who could give everything and then some, but they didn't feel peace about leaving yet. They determined to give all they could and trust God to use it. They also decided not to bore people with a long list of their problems and medications. When asked how they were feeling, if they could get away with it, they said, "Fine! How are you?"

It wasn't a lie. They were fine, fine in the Lord and fine

with His choices for their lives. They often reminded each other to choose to trust.

∼

WHEN THEY HAD FIRST COME to Corners Church, Darlene had found a prayer she loved by A.W. Tozer and had started praying it.

She prays it now at Jim's bedside, hoping she remembers all the words:

> O God, be Thou exalted over my possessions.
>> Nothing of earth's treasures shall seem dear unto me
>> if only Thou art glorified in my life.
>> Be Thou exalted over my friendships.
>> I am determined that Thou shalt be above all,
>> though I must stand deserted and alone in the midst of
> the earth.
>> Be Thou exalted above my comforts.
>> Though it mean the loss of bodily comforts and the
> carrying of heavy crosses
>> I shall keep my vow made this day before Thee.
>> Be Thou exalted over my reputation.
>> Make me ambitious to please Thee
>> even if as a result I must sink into obscurity and my
> name be forgotten as a dream.
>> Rise, O Lord, into Thy proper place of honor,
>> above my ambitions,
>> above my likes and dislikes,
>> above my family,
>> my health and even my life itself.
>> Let me decrease that Thou mayest increase,
>> let me sink that Thou mayest rise above.

As she watches Jim struggling to breathe, she knows saying goodbye to Jim is going to be part of that prayer.

## GOODBYE, ALICE MARIE

The sun was turning the snow-packed gravel roads to diamonds on that frosty November morning. After the funeral, people carefully maneuvered the diamond roads to lay Alice Marie to rest in the Corners Cemetery.

The next stop was Corners Church, where two dirt roads meet. Neighbors and family sat around tables in the old one-room school where Alice Marie had been in the last graduating class back in 1948. She'd also been part of the community club that had met in the schoolhouse for many years and had been one of the first to welcome Darlene. Sadly, of the twenty-four members there had been when Darlene had joined community club, Shirley and Darlene were the only two still living.

Darlene thought of those wonderful ladies as she helped serve the funeral dinner in the old schoolhouse the community club had sold the church to use as a fellowship hall. Alice Marie had joined Corners Church shortly after Jim had become pastor. Dementia had kept her from attending for several years, so some of the newer members hadn't known her well, but they'd all joined in to help make a wonderful meal.

Two women had offered to make turkey, stuffing, mashed potatoes, gravy, and corn. The rest filled in with things like salads, rolls, meatballs, calico beans, and a long table full of desserts. There was plenty of hot coffee to warm frigid hands and laughter to warm hurting hearts. Fixing food for others is one of the things Corners Church does best. It's one way they show their love and the love of Jesus.

"How do so few people make so much food?" someone asked Darlene.

The question surprised her. *We just do; doesn't everyone? I suppose they don't, but sharing food, love, and support is still a way of life at our Corners, and I hope the same is true in many places. Little House on the Prairie knew the value of community. People are lost, isolated, stranded without each other. You don't have to be back roads country like Corners Church to cultivate community. It can happen anywhere. It just takes one person to realize we all need each other and to do something about it.*

Darlene gave herself a mental shake. Time to stop philosophizing and see if forks, spoons, or coffee were running low. No, everything had been taken care of. Things had changed so much from the days when Darlene had to do most everything herself. She did very little now; others taught Sunday school, helped in children's church, planned Vacation Bible School, and served on hospitality committees. She could probably get a job at Market Home now, if they would hire an old lady, and no one at church would complain.

Darlene smiled. Just last week Becky Joy had asked her, "Mom, if you had it to do all over again, and you could be and do anything you wanted, what would you choose?"

Darlene hadn't hesitated. "I'd be exactly the same thing, a

wife, mother, grandmother, and a pastor's wife right here at our wonderful Corners Church."

*Does that mean I was called to be a pastor's wife after all? I'm tired of trying to answer that question. I'm called to let Jesus be Jesus in me, no matter what it is I'm doing.*

When the last person had left the funeral dinner, Jim locked the door to the old schoolhouse. It still locked with a simple skeleton key. Its roof was sagging; paint was peeling from its sides, and a new fellowship hall was going up next to it. The new building would have many conveniences this one didn't, running water and bathrooms, but Darlene would never forget the wonderful times they'd had here.

Darlene glanced at the blue November sky; Alice Marie was enjoying streets of gold now, but Darlene thought maybe she still had a soft spot in her heart for where she'd spent so many years at school and at church, the place where two dirt roads meet.

"Goodbye, Alice Marie," she said. "I'll see you soon."

"Oh no you won't," Jim said. "You aren't going anywhere without me. You know perfectly well you'd get lost. Don't think I've forgotten the time you got lost driving the mile home from church and ended up in Ohio."

Darlene looked at him and laughed. She would get lost without him, in every way.

## REFLECTIONS ON GETTING OLDER

In later years, the church gave Jim and Darlene four weeks of vacation. As much as they missed their church family, they loved every minute of the time away. On one vacation, Jim and Darlene walked hand in hand along the narrow Lake Michigan channel pathway, admiring the boats, when yesterday passed them. They moved over to let a young couple pass by. Her ponytail swung side to side, and the couple's pace tripled Jim and Darlene's. *When did we slow down so much?* Darlene wondered. She tried to walk faster, but her body ignored her commands. Boats forgotten she wistfully watched the carefree young couple ahead of them. She felt a little sad.

Then Jim and Darlene passed tomorrow. A white-haired, very elderly couple sat in chairs watching the boats. Their channel walking days were over. Tomorrow smiled at them, and they smiled back.

Yesterday was so far gone Darlene could barely see the ponytail in the distance. She stopped feeling sad; it was a gorgeous day; Jim held her hand, and the boats were beautiful. What's better than today?

It's not easy to grow old gracefully. "I hate being old," Darlene's eighty-seven-year-old mother-in-law said to her. Darlene wrote:

> Why? Why do we mourn the passing of our youth,
> > The prune-ing, raisin-ing,
> > Sagging
> > Bagging
> > Freckling
> > Veining
> > Of our skin when graying happens to us all?
> > Our spirits sigh protest.
> > Dreams of ocean breeze and morning dew and worship
> of a newborn's skin all whisper
> > The same truth.
> > We were not born to age—
> > To creak
> > To stoop
> > To slow
> > To stop.
> > Eden birthed us to eternal youth.
> > When young eyes hungered for poison fruit,
> > Sin and Satan stole the breathless freshness of our
> treasure.
> > A cloud hid the shamed face of the sun,
> > And earth wept and grew her first gray hair.
> > The lost will be found.
> > Our earth—
> > And we, her children, will yet be young again.
> > Gloriously
> > Goldenly

> Sweetly
> Young again
> In the newborn kingdom of our God.

Being in the last years of life, Darlene thought, was like being a baby in the womb about to be born. If the baby only knew the freedom, joy, and light waiting, he or she might not mind so much the pain of birth. The Bible tells us enough about the freedom, joy, and light of heaven to make us want to go there. Jim and Darlene looked forward to heaven, but they knew the getting born part might not be too easy. It seldom was.

Their old friend, Landon, often said, "Death is a defeated enemy, but make no mistake; it's still the enemy."

∼

JIM SIGHS. Darlene prays his pain won't get too bad. She hopes he'll go home peacefully, in his sleep. Soon he'll see not only Jesus, but also his parents and so many loved ones.

Darlene loves what J.I. Packer wrote about heaven: "It will be like the day when the sick child is at last able to leave the hospital, and finds father and the whole family waiting outside to greet him—a family occasion, if ever there was one."

∼

THE YEAR they'd turned seventy, Jim's health problems worsened, and their own mortality started to feel real. Darlene wrote:

### Forever Young

It's sin that makes us old.

My Lord is ever young;
The battle over age and death He has already won!
The dew of His sweet youth reflects in every rising sun.
In Him our glorious eternity has already begun!
Praise to the eternal Father, to the Spirit, and the Son!
I've been a carefree child
In His yard all lifelong!
My soft spring days, sweet summer nights, and autumn all but gone.
As winter's chill touches my soul and life is close to done,
I feel His joyous call to me that life has just begun!
What will it be, home in His Home,
Where beauty and order rule the days,
Where all is love and light and song and we hear only praise?
I fear not my creeping age, with Him I'm forever young!
Praise to the eternal Father, to the Spirit and the Son!
In Him our golden eternity has already begun!

~

OUR GOLDEN ETERNITY, she thinks. *This night feels like an eternity, but it sure doesn't feel golden.* As exhausted as she is, as much as her back hurts from sitting in the chair next to Jim's bed, she wishes the hours weren't inching toward dawn. Not yet.

## A GOLDEN DAY

"I wish Becky Joy would let us help her! She's exhausted. She's been working nonstop on this party for weeks, all year really."

"I just walked over there, and she has it under control. She said she has enough people helping her right now. Come sit down."

"What does it look like, Jennifer?"

"It's beautiful. Now don't ask any more questions because I'm not telling you anything else. She wants you to be surprised."

Darlene and Jennifer walked out to the backyard of the rented house next to the venue where the party was going to be held. Jim sat in a swing with his sister, Lonnie, who had come with her daughters all the way from Georgia for this grand event, Jim and Darlene's fiftieth wedding anniversary party.

"Look at the two of them! I wish they could be together more often."

"They sure are having fun," Jennifer said.

Darlene took a mental snapshot she wanted to keep forever.

Jim was leaning toward Lonnie, laughing with his head thrown back. Lonnie was laughing as hard as he was. If ever a brother and sister loved each other, it was those two.

Finally, it was time to go to the party. Jim and Darlene felt like they'd walked into heaven's entryway. Darlene looked at the tables—white tablecloths topped with blush pink runners and beautifully decorated with fresh flowers, candles, swags, and lanterns. Flowers spilled out of vases and peeked out of gold geometric terrariums. Flowers topped the cake too, a chocolate cake with raspberry, salted caramel, and peanut butter fudge fillings.

Holding hands, Jim and Darlene walked over to the cake table. Pictures from their wedding smiled back at them from gold frames. A dress form displayed Darlene's wedding dress, the one Mom Peters had made fifty years before. Trays of heart-shaped cookies and macarons in many flavors looked tempting.

"Look!" Jim poked Darlene. Brookies were there too, his favorite.

"Did you see that?" She pointed at the popcorn stand, chosen just for him, with three kinds of popcorn—movie theater, white cheddar, and caramel.

Darlene hugged Becky Joy and started crying.

"I had some help, Mom," Becky Joy said. "Did you see the fruit?"

The huge tiered fruit trays looked divine.

"I picked one of your favorite foods for the main part of the meal. It's Tiki Sam's wood fired pizza. His food truck is right outside."

Darlene's eyes widened at the array of nine kinds of pizza, stuffed mushroom caps, caprese skewers, garden salad, and meatball sliders.

Drinks were glass bottled pop, lemonade, and iced tea: raspberry Earl Grey, oolong peach, and blue confetti. Homemade sugar cubes sat in a glass jar for people who wanted sweet tea.

Becky Joy hadn't forgotten the children, either. They had fun packs with crafts and coloring pages for inside and games to play outside.

Jim and Darlene couldn't keep admiring the food and decorations, though; the room was filling with familiar, beloved faces. Family, church family, and friends had come to celebrate with them.

Jim and Darlene wanted to spend hours talking to their guests, but there was barely time to greet each one. All their children and grandchildren were there, and many sisters, brothers-in-law, nephews, and nieces. Almost everyone from Corners Church came with smiles and hugs. Many of their pastor and wife friends came too. Andrea travelled all the way from Tennessee; Pastor Michael had gone to heaven a few years earlier. Katrina and Pastor Landon came with their loving smiles; they had celebrated their fiftieth anniversary just a month before. Darlene's eyes filled with tears when she looked at them. They had been dear friends for so many years.

Jim and Darlene repeated their vows; Jim had to help Darlene remember the words. Vows made fifty years into a marriage mean even more than vows made at the beginning; by then a couple knows how much they need God's grace. Their college pastor prayed for them, and Darlene cried again. Would the tears never stop? But she didn't mind. They were golden tears.

Darlene tried to memorize every minute. She knew this was as close to heaven as she was ever going to get on earth. How could there be so much love and so much beauty in one room?

All too soon the party ended. Darlene's heart ached as she

said goodbyes; some faces she knew she'd never see again this side of heaven.

Family worked together cleaning up, and soon all evidence of the celebration disappeared. But Jim and Darlene would treasure the precious memory of that golden Saturday afternoon when a room was filled with beauty, love, and laugher, and even heaven smiled.

Tears came one more time late that evening when Jim and Darlene were alone.

"We can't have fifty more years," Darlene said.

"No, we can't, babe, so let's make the best of the years we have."

## STATE CONVENTION

Jim didn't always attend the state convention. In his early years, when he listened to the glowing reports from pastors of larger churches about huge numbers of people saved and baptized, he remembered Professor Nick Machiavelli's advice to always climb ladders from smaller churches to larger ones. Where was he on the ladder? Truth be told, he was at the bottom of it.

The conventions made Jim feel a bit inferior. It wasn't that no one had been saved or baptized; several had, and Jim loved Corners Church. He just wasn't sure how long he'd stay there.

As years passed, Jim didn't attend the state convention very often, and when he did, he no longer felt inferior. He'd learned that doing the will of God from the heart was all that mattered. He was seventy when he attended his last state convention. When pastors began reporting the huge financial and attendance increases their churches had experienced, Jim sat contentedly, thinking of the open fields surrounding his church and how well the corn was growing. The beans had done well last year. His thoughts were interrupted by a question.

"Does the pastor from the southernmost church in the state have any progress to report?" the moderator asked.

Jim smiled. "I don't believe I do. We aren't much for counting nickels and noses."

He heard someone whisper, "That church is on the corner of two dirt roads. Everyone knows nothing ever happens where two dirt roads meet."

Jim almost laughed out loud. How many times had he heard that? It wasn't true.

Jim thought of Wayne, mentally slow, socially awkward, and terrified of people. Wayne had come to feel so much at home at church that he no longer threw up at the potlucks. He went around offering smiles and hugs that were gladly accepted and returned. Wayne had understood enough to accept Jesus as his Savior from sin. That was a happy day at Corners Church.

Then there was Justin, who hadn't talked much at family gatherings or at other churches but now hung out laughing and conversing with all the men at the back of Corners Church after services. That might seem like a small thing to pastors of megachurches, but it was a big thing to Jim and Justin's family.

Jim thought fondly of Joe who was fighting alcoholism but trusting the Lord and still courageously fighting.

*Nothing ever happens where two dirt roads meet?* Jim knew better; a lot had happened. *Important things happen there,* Jim thought. *Jesus is with us. We feed His sheep. And every time we meet, we listen for the soft sound of sandaled feet.* He'd read that somewhere and loved the thought.

So, what if he hadn't climbed Professor Nick Machiavelli's ladder? Everyone has a different ladder to climb, and success doesn't look the same for all people. Success is nothing more or less than doing God's will. Jim knew now that Corners Church was his home. He'd made the right decision to stay.

～

Darlene gently touches Jim's elbow. "I'm thinking, honey. Do you think there will be some great pastor's convention in heaven?"

He grunts. "If there is, I'm not going."

Darlene smiles. "Oh yes you will, and you'll love it too. I don't think there will be any nickel and nose bragging there. Maybe the one at the bottom of the ladder will be honored, the way the Bible says; the last shall be first."

Jim's sleeping, but Darlene's heart fills with love remembering his fifty years in a tiny country church, loving on the broken and the hurt.

*Surely you will honor him for that, won't you, Lord?* But she knows Jim wouldn't want any honor. The only thing he'd want to do with his crowns is put them at the feet of Jesus.

Darlene quotes Psalm 115:1, one of their favorite verses: "Not unto us, O LORD, not unto us, but unto thy name give glory, for thy mercy, and for thy truth's sake."

## RETIREMENT

To retire or not to retire, that was the question that kept returning. Darlene had one opinion; Jim had another.

"You act like retire is a four-letter word," Darlene often said.

"Well, it is."

"You don't know how to spell."

"Hey!" Jim laughed. "That was our first argument when we were kids, remember? You said I didn't know how to spell my name. So maybe this can be our last argument."

They seldom argued. When a granddaughter asked why, they told her it was because they were too old and tired. The real reason was experience had taught them that life is short, and goodbyes come far too soon. They didn't want to stop holding hands to point fingers at each other.

Darlene wanted to retire and enjoy a few good years together.

Jim protested, "I want to die with my cowboy boots on, behind the pulpit, preaching a sermon."

"Wouldn't that be traumatic for the congregation?"

"Okay then, I'll wait until they've all gone home, and then I'll die at church with just you and me."

Darlene sighed. "You know, a preacher has only a few good years between when a congregation thinks he's too young and inexperienced and too old and forgetful. We're both getting forgetful."

"I'm not forgetful." Jim insisted. But he was. His repeated heart episodes had disrupted the blood flow to his brain one too many times.

"Vern Crawford." Darlene reminded him.

They both laughed. "Well, there was that," Jim agreed. He'd called on Vern Crawford to close in prayer, and the congregation had looked at each other, alarmed. Vern Crawford had died ten years before.

"I made some bloopers through the years, didn't I?" Jim asked, looking rather pleased with himself. "What was your favorite?"

"The Mother's Day one, for sure."

Jim had been giving the invitation one Mother's Day and had wanted to encourage the people to become Christians if they had not already accepted Christ. With great sincerity he'd said, "And if any of you here are not mothers, I encourage you to become one before you leave this place."

Darlene had made the mistake of glancing at Mary Beth who'd been sitting next to her. The two of them shook the pew with silent laughter.

"I don't think anyone ever forgot that time when you substituted the word 'mother' for 'Christian,'" Darlene said.

Jim looked into her eyes.

"What?" Darlene asked, half-alarmed at his serious expression.

"Well, you know how Paul mentioned to the Colossians he was filling up the sufferings of Christ?"

Darlene shook her head. Sometimes she called him her Bible concordance; he could remember so many verses and references.

"It's in Colossians 1:24. Look it up sometime. I think it means being willing to suffer anything to minister the love of Jesus to others. I want to do that, right until the end. Do you understand?"

She saw a rare thing, a tear in Jim's eye. She hugged him. "It's okay. You can die with your boots on. I'll be right there next to you."

She did plan to be right there next to him until the end, but she felt uneasy about his health and declining memory. She prayed, and then she called her sisters, Lou and Jennifer. They both said the same thing.

"You know you can trust God with this, Darlene. You've trusted Him all these years. God will tell Jim when it's time to quit."

Darlene stopped trying to persuade Jim to retire. Jim and her sisters were right; God would tell him when it was time.

When God told Jim it was time, it wasn't easy hearing it. First, he forgot a word or two, then a point or two in his sermon. Then came the turning point Sunday. Even with his notes right in front of him, he forgot what he was preaching. About ten minutes into his sermon, he abruptly left the pulpit, sat in the front pew, and cried. His people cried with him. They knew what it meant.

The church had already planned a celebration of Jim's fifty years in ministry. It didn't take many adjustments to make it a retirement party, and a wonderful party it was. The tributes would have made a less humble man proud.

As Darlene sat next to Jim, watching him listen to the comments, she remembered that Proverbs 27:21 says a man is tested by his praise. She could see into Jim's heart, and what she saw was an orchestra conductor who steps aside during a standing ovation and with a sweep of his hand bows to the orchestra. After every quiet "thank you" Jim was bowing low in his heart and with a sweep of his hand he was honoring his Lord.

Todd Pritchard, the man with all the degrees thrice over was there. He had ridden with Professor Nick Machiavelli, and the expensive Camaro looked as out of place in the parking lot as Todd and Professor Machiavelli's designer suits looked among the casual dress of the country congregation. The two of them were telling anyone who would listen that even at their age they were still in great demand at home and abroad as church growth consultants.

Darlene noticed the flashy diamond on his finger when Professor Nick Machiavelli patted Jim on the shoulder. "My boy, if only you'd listened to me all those years ago and done a little ladder climbing, you might be traveling to Europe with us next week. We're flying first class all the way!"

Jim smiled. "If my health holds out, I'd like to visit the Philippines. Over there, some church pastors and their families have to live on their church platforms with just curtains for privacy. Then, I'd like to go shake hands with some pastors from Cuba. Most of them walk everywhere. The lucky ones have a bicycle or a burro."

The professor smiled smoothly. "I guess we took different roads, my boy."

As Jim turned to talk to someone else waiting for him, Darlene heard Todd say, "Yeah, Nick, Jim took the dirt road."

*So did Jesus,* Darlene thought, but she didn't say it.

The two men laughed. They left soon after. The country air closed peacefully into the space where they'd been, and no one missed them. Jim didn't even notice they were gone.

After the service ended, the church family enjoyed a potluck in the wonderful new fellowship hall addition. Jim looked around with damp eyes at the building he'd thought he'd never live long enough to see completed. That wasn't his legacy, though; his legacy was the people. He knew a new, younger preacher would do a better job than he'd been able to do in recent years, but no one could love the people better than he had.

The church would be fine without him; he knew it. His congregation had God and each other. He looked around at his people with a full heart.

His church board sat a table in the corner, eight men and two women. Jim grinned as he heard them laugh, and his eyes filled with tears when he saw them bow their heads for a quick prayer. He'd counted on their common sense and spiritual wisdom in these last few years more than ever before. *Best board in the world,* he thinks.

This wasn't an official board meeting. He knew they wouldn't stay at that table long; they'd be mingling soon, spreading love, hugs, and laughter.

Darlene slipped her hand in his. "Thanking God?" she asked, following his gaze.

He nodded. They stood trying to memorize the moments. How they loved these people, from the youngest to the oldest. They hated to leave them, but it was for the best. It was time.

Darlene feels contented. She knows she hadn't been pastor's wife like Mrs. Kole, but she'd asked God to love through her, and that was the best she could do. She thinks maybe, just maybe her best had been enough. Perhaps God really had chosen her to be a pastor's wife, and she's certain she and Jim made the right choice to stay at Corners Church.

One by one, after handshakes, hugs, and well-wishes, the people drifted off. Jim and Darlene stayed to lock Corners Church for the last time.

Suddenly, the door opened, and their grandson popped back in. "I have to hurry; Mom and Dad are waiting for me. But I thought maybe you'd want to hear the bell ring."

He propped the door open so they could hear the bell ringing out over farms and fields as it had many Sundays of their fifty years.

"Bye Grandma and Grandpa," their grandson said, hugging them.

They watched him run down the steps. "Wouldn't it be something if God calls him to be the pastor here someday?" Jim asked.

Darlene smiled. "Do you really want him to be a pastor?"

"No. All I want is our grandkids to be whatever God made them to be."

Theirs was the last car in the parking lot, as it always had been. Jim and Darlene hobbled down the church steps one at a time. Darlene looked at him. She couldn't hold back the tears.

"Well done, honey." She choked on the words. "Well done."

"Hey!" He smiled at her tenderly. "This is no time for tears. Now we'll have all that time together you've wanted. We have lots of good years ahead."

∽

DARLENE LOOKS at Jim in the hospital bed and smiles sadly. They'd had a few years, but they hadn't been the good years he'd promised. His heart and kidneys had failed too quickly.

Well, he wasn't much of a prophet, but he sure had been a terrific pastor. He'd learned from the wise people at the Corners; he'd asked God to live and speak through him, and God had done it. Wonderful things had happened where two dirt roads meet.

## 100

## THE BEGINNING

Darlene looks tenderly at Jim and stretches her cramped legs. A sharp pain makes her catch her breath. Jim hears her stifled gasp, opens his eyes, and looks at her questioningly.

"It's okay. I'm fine," she assures him. "It's only a little headache."

She hears his soft mumble. "You're tired. Come to bed soon. Don't be long."

"I promise, babe, I won't be long."

He's sleeping now, and she wonders if he can hear her, but she recites a poem he loves she'd written long ago:

For You

> Shot from the cannon of life,
>     Ten-thousand times the speed of light
>     Hands at my sides stiff tin-soldier style
>     Eyes on the round patch of blue opening in the clouds
>     And I'm through.

Past the memory of your tears
I twirl; I twist;
I dance; I laugh.
So this is what it is to be free at last
From all that stops the dance.
And yet, I mourn your glance.
That vision of you that held my heart by years
Is fading. What are tears?
I used to know.
Before I forget your smile,
I linger on the thought of you awhile.
Hush dear; don't mourn;
I'll wait for you in our forever Home.

How she hates seeing him suffer. He moans twice.

"I thought it would be darker than this," Jim says in a clear voice. "It gets lighter and brighter! I see a ladder with angels on it."

She nods. Struggling to keep the tears from overflowing, she says, "You're finally moving up that ladder your professor was so fond of mentioning."

His voice is weak again. "I like it here just fine. I wouldn't mind spending a little more time here with you. And I don't think my work is quite done. The nurse. . . ." She can barely hear his voice; it's so soft. "Do you think she knows Jesus?"

"We'll ask her in the morning," she promises.

*I'll have to keep that promise alone; you won't be here in the morning. I hope the kids aren't going to be furious with me, but I wouldn't trade these last, precious minutes alone together for anything.*

He whispers something else.

"What?" She leans in closer.

"I am resolved to the very end."

"Psalm 119:112?"

He nods. "Read, please."

She picks up her Bible and reads, "I am resolved to obey your statues to the very end." He loves Psalm 119 and has preached many sermons from it. Hoping to comfort him, she reads on and on from Psalm 119. She starts at verse one and reads until close to sunrise. He's sleeping so soundly he doesn't notice when she quits.

*I'm so tired,* Darlene thinks. She's still the keeper of their story, but she's too exhausted now to say any more words.

Still, she thinks of the Corners people. *I love every one of them, the ones who loved us and stood by us, the ones who moved away, and the ones who left us because they were upset or because they wanted something bigger and better. They're all part of Corners Church family in my heart.*

"God bless them, everyone. And God bless you most of all." She leans over the side rail of the hospital bed and kisses Jim's hand. She wishes she could crawl in and sleep next to him, but she doesn't want to disturb him when he's finally sleeping so soundly.

"It's okay, my dearest love," she whispers. "*Vaya con Dios.*"

∼

TRUE TO HER WORD, the hospice nurse returns at 7:00 a.m. She rings the doorbell, but no one comes. She tries the door, and it's unlocked. Had she forgotten to lock it the night before? She takes off her coat, drops it on a chair in the red gingham kitchen, and tiptoes into the living room. Startled, the nurse hurries to the hospital bed. Darlene looks asleep, with her head resting on her husband's bed rail, but one glance tells the nurse she's gone. Her Bible, a pen, and the scrap of paper with the phone number she'd pressed into Darlene's hand the night before are on the floor. The nurse stoops and picks them up.

Under the nurse's phone number, the old lady had written, "Thank you." She'd died the way she lived, with gratitude. Just yesterday, when Jim had been suffering and Darlene crying, the nurse had heard her whispering a thank you prayer.

Seeing the nurse's shocked expression, Darlene had said, "I think gratitude is the crack in our hearts that lets the light shine in very dark places."

*I might try that myself,* the nurse thinks. *I'm in a very dark place right now.*

Was he gone too? That would be wonderful, but that only happens in fairy tales. The nurse takes his pulse, and he rouses a bit. Looking at Darlene he asks, "Is she coming to bed soon?"

"She is," the nurse says. "She is."

∽

*"And now abideth faith, hope, love, these three;
but the greatest of these is love."*

— I Corinthians 13:13


The Beginning

"O Lord, we bring Thee him for whom we pray
Be Thou his strength, his courage, and his stay,
And should his faith flag as he runs the race,
Show him again the vision of Thy face."

— Amy Carmichael

# EPILOGUE

Jim lingered, day after day, mystifying doctors and hospice nurses. He never asked for Darlene; perhaps he knew she was gone, perhaps not. Either way, he seemed at peace.

When Jim went Home, there would be a memorial service at Corners Church. The sweet sound of the bells that first drew Darlene's heart to the church would sound out again over farms and fields as the family, church family, and neighbors drove down the dirt roads to say goodbye to Jim and Darlene. Goodbye, for now.

# NOTES

## Dedication

1. Some of the family spells the name "Lickly" and some spell it "Lickley."

# ABOUT THE AUTHOR

Donna knew she'd flunked another of Mr. Joseph Tedeschi's history tests, so, to fill the rest of the class period, she flipped the test over and wrote on the back. She did flunk, and her heart sank when she saw "See me" scrawled at the top of the paper.

"I read what you wrote," Mr. Tedeschi said. "You're going to be a writer, but don't try to write any historical fiction!"

Donna sold her first short story to Regular Baptist Press in 1973. She began writing for Union Gospel Press in 1976. A Michigan magazine, *Baptist Testimony*, carried her column, "Rainbows and Dustmops," from February 1978 through 1980.

In 1981, an editor from *The Baptist Bulletin* asked Donna to write a column, and she did that for twenty-three years. Some of the stories from that column found their way into this book.

Like Jim in *Corners Church*, Donna did a poor job of counting nickels and noses, so she doesn't know exactly how many articles and stories she has published. She estimates the total is over 3,000. This is her first fiction book.

Donna is a member of American Christian Fiction Writers. When she isn't writing, Donna loves spending time with her family, church family, and friends. She enjoys camping, a crackling campfire, and a good book. She's a wife, mother, grandmother, and has been a country church pastor's wife for more than forty-five years. Donna is a brain aneurysm survivor and is currently battling cancer.

Made in the USA
Monee, IL
14 August 2020